To Cath

GUTS & GLORY: MERCY

In the Shadows Security, Book 1

JEANNE ST. JAMES

Happy Reading!

Jeanne St James
xoxo

Photographer: FuriousFotog

Cover Artist: Golden Czermak at FuriousFotog

Cover Model: Zeke Samples

Editor: Proofreading by the Page

Warning: This book contains sexually explicit scenes and adult language and may be considered offensive to some readers. This book is for sale to adults ONLY, as defined by the laws of the country in which you made your purchase. Please store your files wisely, where they cannot be accessed by under-aged readers.

Keep an eye on her website at http://www.jeannestjames.com/ or sign up for her newsletter to learn about her upcoming releases: http://www.jeannestjames.com/newslettersignup

"Justice is for those who deserve it; mercy is for those who don't." ~ Woodrow Kroll

"It is mercy, not justice or courage or even heroism, that alone can defeat evil." ~ Peter Kreeft

Chapter One

You must fall before you can rise.

With his fingers curled around her delicate skin and the fragile frame of her neck, he increased the pressure.

"Harder! Do it harder," she hissed at him.

Mercy had a feeling she wasn't talking about fucking her. Fuck no, she was one of "those."

His grip twitched but he didn't do as she demanded, instead he pretended to misunderstand her demand and slammed his dick deeper. His pounding rhythm became mindless. Because that's what she was, just another mindless fuck.

One that had a freaky side.

He seemed to attract those types of bitches.

Random snatch he picked up at the bar. A woman who saw him as a freak and had someone like him on her fuck-it bucket list.

Or one who thought they could bring the life back to his eyes. They saw him as a challenge.

That last kind he tried to avoid since they became the

challenge. Especially when it came to scraping them off at the end of the night.

But nights like this were typical for him. Him doing the using, and him being used.

Just busting a nut into some, what the DAMC brothers called "strange."

No numbers exchanged.

No after-fuck cuddling.

No deep conversation.

Hell, he didn't even bother to ask their names.

And if they asked him, he just told them his name was John.

It didn't matter if he was John, Joe or Jack. They just wanted to fuck a cold-hearted, dead-eyed, scarred freak. They got off on that shit. And he let them for the moments it took for him to get off.

Then it was over.

A few nights later, it would happen again. New night, new woman.

Rinse. Repeat.

But the one he was sliding his dick into now?

Fuck. Total fucking freak.

He realized she was still talking. Why didn't she shut the fuck up?

"C'mon. Show me what you got! Don't be a pussy. You look like you'd like it rough. Squeeze harder."

Mercy adjusted his grip on her neck, his fingers curling tighter into her flesh, and he pumped his hips faster and harder.

She was just a "her" to him because if she had told him her name at the bar earlier, he hadn't paid attention. Or even fucking cared.

"Pretend I'm the enemy, soldier, and your life's on the line."

Yeah, bitch, if you were, you wouldn't be breathing or flapping those gums.

"That's it, fucker. Give it to me like you mean it."

He did his best not to sigh out loud.

"Fuck me hard while you tell me how you got those nasty scars. I want to hear every detail."

Since she could still talk, he apparently wasn't squeezing hard enough.

But choking her out or telling her about his past was never going to happen. Just like he was never going to end up in this bitch's bed again.

Suddenly, out of nowhere, she just out and out sucker punched him right in the face. His head jerked back from the impact, and his body went solid. His hips stilled, and his eyes met hers.

Her brown eyes surrounded in thick mascara widened, and her red lipsticked mouth became slack. He dropped his gaze to his fingers and realized he'd finally done what she asked for. Only now he could see the fear in her expression.

Total fucking panic.

When a gurgle bubbled up, he willed his fingers to release her and, luckily for her, his brain was still connected to his digits. He pulled out, rolled away from her, yanked off the condom and threw it on her now heaving stomach. He sat on the edge of the bed, a chill sweeping through him at how close she came to dying.

He could have killed her without a second thought.

Her voice was raspy when she demanded, "What are you doing? We didn't finish!"

Mercy scrubbed a hand over his short hair.

"I'm not done, you... you monster!"

"You're done," he growled without looking at her.

"No, I'm not."

He pushed to his feet, found his pile of clothes and methodically pulled them on, making sure his knife was still in the back pocket of his jeans and his .38 still tucked in his boot. The only weapons he usually carried into a bar since they were easily concealable.

He strapped on the ankle holster after yanking his cargo pants up over his hips.

Mercy ignored her sitting up in bed, glaring at him.

"Are you seriously leaving?"

He ignored that, too.

"Why are you taking what I said personal?"

He concentrated on lacing up his combat boots.

"Hey! I can have any guy I want!" she screamed as he straightened and focused on the door to his freedom. "Asshole! You ugly-ass freak! It was only a pity fuck!"

A few strides later, he was out of her apartment door and jogging down the steps. At the bottom, he hooked a right and saw his true love waiting for him under the halogen light.

His Harley. A Jag Jamison custom he paid a fortune for. But his sled was more steadfast and loyal than any female.

The only thing he appreciated more than his bike was his Terradyne Gurkha RPV. Every time he drove that sweet bitch, he got a hard-on.

As did other men simply by looking at it.

He had needed to relieve some tension tonight. And also to forget another female he'd had on the brain lately. One who would never be his.

Normally, there'd be two ways to relieve his pent-up frustration.

A round with the punching bag or an anonymous fuck. Tonight, the fucking didn't work since his balls were still heavy and in need of some relief. Which meant he now had only one other option.

His fists.

With a grunt, he struck the well-used, patched-up heavy bag that hung in a dark corner of the warehouse with as much power behind it as he could. The impact jarred his bones and teeth. Not that he cared.

He adjusted his stance and put his weight behind the next strike as well. Sweat dripped off his brow, soaked his sleeveless tee both front and back, and mottled the concrete floor beneath him.

The exertion was just what he needed to get that bitch's face, and words, out of his head. He needed to stop picking up females in bars and start looking elsewhere.

He just didn't know where.

He thought of Jazz, and how he would've stopped his midnight trolling for her. But Crow had claimed her before he could, and the biker wasn't giving her up without a fight.

Not that Mercy blamed him.

If he had that in his bed, he wouldn't give her up without a fight, either. Fuck the fight, there would be total devastation before Mercy would let anyone else have what was his.

But Crow won her. Crow deserved her. Crow was right for her.

He saw that clearly now.

Still didn't mean that Mercy liked the outcome.

But Jazz needed someone who could be softer with her than he could. Someone who could love her, which he wasn't sure if he could love anyone anymore. It was a concept foreign to him. He might not even recognize it if it bit him in the ass.

And, truthfully, Jazz deserved to be treated like the treasure she was, which was how that pussy-assed Crow treated her.

Fucking motherfucker.

His upper lip curled, and with a grunt, he pounded the

bag with a quick jab right, quickly followed by a left uppercut.

One of the overhead halogens lit up and Mercy squinted from the sudden brightness until his eyes adjusted. Once they did, he saw his boss lumbering in his direction. And like normal, he wasn't alone.

His youngest daughter, Indigo, was tucked within his arms. That man didn't go anywhere without at least one of his two baby girls glued to him. He took their safety to the extreme.

He pitied any guy wanting to date them when they got old enough.

"Brother," D's deep grumble was low, probably so he wouldn't wake up a sleeping Indie. His dark brown eyes slid to the bag, then to Mercy's hands.

Mercy glanced down at his clenched fists. He hadn't bothered to wrap them, and now his knuckles were raw and bloody. Even a bit swollen.

He glanced over his shoulder. The bag had blood smears on it, too.

"I'll clean it up, boss," he muttered.

"Ain't out here to talk about that." Diesel adjusted Indie in his arms. "Got a job for you."

Thank fuck. "Need to stay busy, D. This down time's getting me torqued."

"Know it. Know why. Got it."

"Right. So, what is it?" When Diesel hesitated, Mercy frowned. "Don't tell me it's another douchebag football player. I'm not a fucking babysitter."

"No."

"An entitled celeb who shits out gold turds and has an assistant who cleans his ass with handwoven silk wipes?"

"No."

Mercy's buzz of getting an assignment quickly turned to shit. "I'm not liking this."

"Got a package for you to move."

Mercy lifted a brow. "From where?"

"Vegas."

He grimaced. He fucking hated Vegas. A city of greed and overindulgence. Too many damn people, the press of bodies, the lights, the noise, the non-stop action. A good place to blend in. A bad place for his head.

"Delivered to where?"

"Safe house."

His brows shot up. "We don't have a safe house."

"Not ours."

"Whose?'

"Rich fucker. Gettin' one set up. Get the package, deliver her to the fuckin' house, an' then go from there."

"Her?" *Oh fuck no.* "Send Steel."

D shook his head. "Sendin' you."

"He's up for the next babysitting job."

"It's yours."

Mercy asked through clenched jaws, "This have to do with the shit that went down with Jazz?"

D cocked a brow at him.

Fuck. It was. "Is she the rich fucker's piece?"

"Don't know. Don't fuckin' care. Payin' big. Just gotta keep her safe 'til he handles the threat."

He handles the threat? "Wait, we don't even get a fucking piece of the fun?"

"Ain't gettin' paid for that. They wanna pay for that, you get a fuckin' piece of it."

"What's the threat?"

"Soon as I get that shit, gonna email the deets to you."

Mercy snorted and cocked a brow at D.

Diesel scowled. "Jewelee's gonna email it to you."

That was more like it.

But even so, he wasn't liking this at all. Walking into a job without all the details prior? "When?"

"Soon as she gets it."

"No, when do I have to fly out?"

"Tomorrow, first thing. Gonna set you up at one of his casinos for the night 'til we get the details an' further instructions. Got me?"

He was liking the sound of this job less and less. "Fucker owns casinos?"

"Fucker owns a lot of shit. Sure a lot of his businesses ain't legit."

"So, this job is a possible dirty side piece?"

"Or main piece. Who fuckin' knows. Who fuckin' cares? Keep 'er ass safe. Bonus in it for you at the end if you keep 'er in one piece. You don't, we still get paid. But the bonus might be worth you keepin' her breathin'."

"I can do whatever needed to protect her, right?"

D smirked. "Fuck yeah."

Mercy grinned, too. Maybe this job wouldn't be so bad after all. How hard was it to watch one female and deliver her breathing at the end of the job?

Diesel's nostrils suddenly flared and his face twisted. "Fuck," he muttered, staring down at his daughter.

A second later, Mercy caught a whiff of what he was smelling. "Fuck," he agreed.

"Gotta find Jewelee."

Mercy pinned his lips together as he watched D, his biker boss and the Sergeant at Arms for the Dirty Angels MC, lumber back toward where he came from.

Then he realized he never asked how long this job was going to take.

Fuck.

Chapter Two

"WHAT DO YOU MEAN, Michael? Why would I go away with some..."

Her baby blues landed on Mercy, who sat in a corner where he could keep everyone in front of him. He could see and hear everything.

"Stranger," she finished, frowning at Mercy.

Even wearing a fucking frown, she was downright smoking hot.

But then, that was to be expected for some high-class, high-maintenance pussy.

"Just until things settle down here, Parris, then you can come home."

Parris.

Highfalutin name, too.

He wondered if she was French. Or liked to French.

Probably not. She was most likely a frigid bitch who loved money more than dick. Only dealt with dick to get money.

Her hair, her makeup, her clothes, her manicure. All required a boatload of fucking cash.

So, fuck yeah, she was hot, had curves that wouldn't quit, but she was also too much trouble.

However, he only had to deal with her for a short amount of time.

For what this "Michael" was paying, he could suck it up.

Her expression was curious as her gaze ran slowly over his face. No fear. No disgust. But he could see the questions. The wondering.

Her eyes eventually continued on, taking in his jacket, which he was wearing in this fiery hell-hole of a city on meth. She didn't ask why he was wearing it. Most likely because she already knew. If she was getting boned on the regular by Michael Paranzino, then she was used to his own men wearing shit to keep their weapons concealed.

She paused briefly on his lap. Her expression remaining the same, but she was checking him closely. Most likely because she was a side-piece who kept her own side-piece. Or pieces. The ones she didn't dick for money. Or maybe ones she dicked for even more money.

The corner of Mercy's lip curled as she continued with her visual journey, noticing how he sat low in the chair, his thighs wide, his booted feet outstretched but planted solid, his hands tucked close to his hidden weapons.

He wasn't surprised when she raised her gaze, and this time made it obvious that her eyes were tracing his scar. From the right corner of his hairline, down over his eye, his nose, his cheek, to where it ended, pulling up the corner of the left side of his lip just slightly.

Again, no disgust. Just curiosity.

She took a visible breath, which lifted her huge knockers from the snug deep V-neck dress she wore that hugged every one of her generous curves. Including those enormous tits.

He noticed something he normally didn't give a shit about. Her blue dress emphasized the color of her eyes.

"He pass inspection, sweetheart?" While the tone should

have been full of jealousy, it wasn't. The man sounded amused.

She blinked, then turned back to her man. *Michael.*

"I don't understand any of this."

"You know why this has to happen."

Mercy wished he knew why. He was still waiting for a better explanation. He figured Paranzino would give him more details now that he was in Vegas ready to take this package with him.

And she certainly was a package.

Her long, light brown hair brushed past her shoulders, curling into big waves at the ends. A section of it had fallen over one eye, which, of course, earlier he noticed were as blue as the sky on a clear day. Her deep red lips were full, her mouth tempting, perfect for wrapping around a man's dick.

She probably hated it but would most likely do it for some diamonds.

Mercy wondered what she'd had to do to get the huge rock—which looked at least four carats—that hung on a gold chain nestled in the crease between those heavy knockers. Possibly anal. Maybe even double penetration.

If that was true, then she probably did it often, since she had some big-ass diamonds hanging from her ears, too.

Sometimes it paid to be a female.

Not that he wanted diamonds. Or a dick up his ass.

"How long is this going to be for, Michael?"

Mercy wanted that answer, too.

"As long as it takes, sweetheart."

Well, that just fucking blew. The man had no idea how long this job was going to last?

Mercy cleared his throat, and both sets of eyes came to him. He pulled himself up in the chair. "You got men assigned to handle the reason why I'm taking care of your package?"

Parris's lips parted, and she breathed, "Package?"

Fuck. She even made that one-word question sound hot as fuck.

"He means you, sweetheart," Paranzino said with more amusement, evident by his bright white, obviously bleached smile.

Mercy was glad the man was entertained. However, it seemed to be pissing off his piece. Might be a while before the man got any of that again if he wasn't careful.

Paranzino's eyes came to him. "Yes, that's being handled."

Why didn't that answer ease his discomfort? "They good?"

"They're good."

Right. Except... "They couldn't watch her?"

"I want her out of town, away from all of this until things settle. Right now, it's all hands on deck, and I can't spare anyone. Plus, I need someone good. Skilled. A professional. Not afraid to do what he needs to. Your boss's 'security business' came highly recommended."

"Couldn't find anyone closer just as 'professional?'"

"I don't want to keep her close. She needs to get out of Nevada. No one will look for her in Pittsburgh."

"Pittsburgh?" Parris squeaked. It was sort of cute. Sort of. "Pittsburgh, Michael? Really?"

"Nothing wrong with Pittsburgh," Mercy muttered.

"Yes, if you like steel, football and a lot of hills," she answered with annoyance, hands planted on her round, grab-worthy hips.

"Sounds like you've been there before."

"Sweetheart, I set up a house there for you. With all the comforts of home. It's just temporary." Paranzino flipped a hand in the direction where Mercy was sitting. "I'm sure Mr. Mercer—"

"Mercy."

Both sets of eyes landed on him again.

"I'm sure *Mercy* will be glad to show you all the best spots in the city."

Like he was a fucking tour guide. And that's not what you did when you had a package to protect. You didn't go sight-seeing and gallivanting all around a fucking city.

Asshole.

Paranzino came around his desk and slid an arm over her bare shoulders, leaning in to press his lips to her cheek.

"But, Michael, I have a busy work schedule."

"Don't worry about any of that."

"Will I be able to take my laptop?"

"No."

"No?" she squeaked once more. Again, borderline cute. But could quickly become annoying if she did it too often.

"You're leaving your cell phone, tablet and laptop here. My communication with you will be through... Mercy here. I'll keep him updated through his boss, Mr. Dougherty."

Mercy's gaze slid to the floor as he tried not to choke.

Mr. Dougherty.

There was no "mister" about Diesel.

Diesel was just that. Diesel, D or Boss. Hell, even "Beast," which his woman called him. But then, Jewel was the only one that got away with that and lived to call him that another day.

"What can I take with me?"

"Clothes, magazines, books, shit like that. Anything that can't be pinged or tied to you," Mercy answered.

"This is serious," she whispered.

"Sweetheart, you know it is. We've discussed this. It'll be over soon enough, then you can come home and get back to work."

"If I can't work, I'm going to climb the walls."

Paranzino smiled and gave her shoulders a familiar squeeze. "I know." He released her and turned to Mercy, his expression now business-like. The man might be soft and sweet to his piece, but when it came down to business, Mercy just bet he was ruthless. "I have a private jet—not mine—fueled and on stand-by. I had a third party rent it, so won't come back to me. You'll be taking that back east. I sent someone to pack up her clothes. Her bags were handed off to another person, who will be delivering them to the airport. This way there'll be no connection to her if the house was being watched."

Mercy gave the man a nod and pushed to his feet. He was tall and he should tower over her, but she wasn't any petite female, either. She'd probably be five inches shorter than his six-foot-three if she wasn't wearing those three-inch heels. "She got a disguise to get her out of the building undetected?"

"Yes, we have a very high-profile patron being comped in the Presidential Suite. He's from the UAE. The women with him—family, I'm assuming—wear niqabs. One of my men has obtained one. Parris will be covered from head to foot, except for her eyes." His voice softened again. "Please, Parris, just be careful. Wear your sunglasses or keep your eyes downcast until you're safely inside the limo, yes? A blue-eyed Arab woman may catch some attention." His tone became cold and serious once more. "Mr. Mercer... I'm sorry, *Mercy*... you will take a taxi. Parris will go in the limo with the Sheikh and his wife. Or wives." He flipped a hand in the air. "Or whoever they are."

"Does this Sheikh know why Rissa is being disguised?"

Once again two sets of eyes landed on him. One very plush, lipsticked mouth hung open. She better shut it before she choked on a suicidal fly.

"Rissa?" Paranzino asked. He blinked, then visibly gathered himself. "Uh, I simply explained to him that she was escaping an abusive husband."

"Why would a Sheikh care about that?"

"He wouldn't. What he cares about is how he'll benefit greatly from providing his assistance."

Mercy studied Paranzino. The man's dark hair was turning grey at the temples, he wore a very expensive suit, his fingernails were clean and perfectly groomed. The man oozed money. And a lot of it.

Mercy had to assume Rissa wasn't his only side-piece. He probably had them scattered across the globe.

When Paranzino had raised his hand earlier, Mercy couldn't miss the expensive Pierre Arpels watch on his wrist and also his wedding ring, which was a wide gold band embedded with a center circle of diamonds. His eyes dropped to Rissa's left hand which was pressed to her chest right above her very large tits.

No wedding band or even a tell-tale diamond on her ring finger.

Yeah. Side-piece.

"That'll be the perfect cover," Mercy finally muttered.

Paranzino smiled, then returned to stand behind his desk. A fancy desk in an opulent office in a fifty-story-high casino on the Strip. He reached for his desk phone, pressed a button and put the receiver to his ear, only saying, "It's time," before hanging up the phone.

It's time.

That simple.

Before the man could even make it around the desk again, there was a single knock at the office door before it opened and a huge, bald man lumbered through. Hired muscle.

That was quick. He had to have been stationed outside the door.

"Sweetheart, Manny will escort you back to your room to get changed, then take you to meet the Sheikh."

"Michael," she whispered, taking in Manny's bulk.

Paranzino came back around to her, grabbed her bare

shoulders in his hands and gave her a kiss on one cheek, then the other. "You'll be fine and in good hands."

Sending your woman off with a Sheikh and no body-guards was not placing her in "good hands," but Mercy bit his tongue. Until she was solely under his protection, he wasn't in charge.

He knew when to keep his mouth shut.

Paranzino pressed his lips lightly to hers. He didn't linger, it wasn't passionate, and Mercy found that curious. "Now go. I'll be in touch." He nodded to Manny. "You know what to do."

The goon nodded back and swept a hand in the direction of the door. With an annoyed look, Rissa moved toward it.

The room remained silent until the door closed behind her.

Then the real talk began.

"Need to know the shit I'm up against. Need to know I can do whatever's necessary to keep her safe. Need to know everything you know. No bullshit. No lies. Nothing. You want me to keep her safe, then I need full disclosure."

Paranzino nodded his head, leaned against the front of his wide desk and began to tell Mercy what he wanted him to know.

But Mercy knew it wasn't everything.

The man was charming and genuinely concerned with his woman's safety. But just like Mercy thought, the man was ruthless.

It made him wonder if Rissa knew just how ruthless her lover was.

PARRIS STARED up the steps to the Cessna Citation jet. A tall, dark figure stood just within the door.

What the hell happened to her life?

She glanced over her shoulder at the retreating limo. She had just exited a vehicle that had included a freaking Sheikh and three women, who she had no idea what they looked like because she could only see their dark brown eyes due to their niqabs.

She didn't envy them wearing what they did every day. She felt like she was suffocating.

"Gonna just stand there or bring that ass of yours up the steps?"

The low rumble of his voice skittered through her. Those steps would take her from the frying pan right into the fiery depths of hell.

"Are my bags on board?" she asked this *Mercy*. Could he even hear her through the stifling fabric covering her mouth?

Apparently that answer was yes, since he replied, "Loaded. Just waiting on your ass."

Parris pinned her lips together.

Her life had flipped upside down since witnessing what she did a few days ago. Since then, she'd been holed up in Michael's casino, had bodyguards stationed outside her suite and now she was headed to Pennsylvania.

Pittsburgh to be exact. And from what she remembered—from the one and only time she was there as a child to visit a distant family member—it was home to pierogis and Pirates baseball.

Steelers and steel mills.

The Duquesne Incline and Point State Park.

Just. Freaking. Great.

Before her cell phone had been confiscated, Parris had called her assistant, instructing her to cancel all her appointments for the next two weeks. And now that she had no phone, her patients had no way to contact her in case of emergency.

Although, those cases were rare. And weren't life or death. For the most part.

"What the fuck, woman? You're standing out on the tarmac exposed. If you don't get your ass up those steps double-time, this job may be over before it even fucking begins."

Good, since she didn't like being a "job." Or a "package."

Or even getting into an expensive private jet with a stranger who seemed to be a real dick.

She gritted her teeth as she grabbed the handrail—which was so hot from the searing Vegas sun, it burned her hand—and carefully hoofed it up the metal steps in her Christian Louboutin pumps with three-inch heels. At least once she was inside, she could take off the black polyester "outfit" that was making her sweat like a glass of iced tea sitting out in the desert heat.

She didn't know how women wore this crap.

Or why.

However, it wasn't up for her to judge somebody else's idea of modesty.

A curse slipped from her lips as she stumbled on the top step. A long arm snaked out of the doorway, snagged her and, with a violent jerk, pulled her into the cooler interior of the plane.

"Shut the door. Let's get this bus in the air," he ordered the flight crew.

The man sounded like he was used to giving orders. He probably was. He seemed bossy as hell.

He was probably just as bossy in the bedroom. *"On the bed. On your back. Spread your legs. Say my name. Now, come."*

Parris stifled a snort.

As a sex therapist for the past fifteen-plus years, she'd dealt with men like him as patients. Some women wanted and needed those direct instructions. Most did not.

The ones who didn't, and ended up with someone like this Mercy, also ended up in her office as patients.

Asking how to change their man.

Unfortunately, they couldn't.

Unless he wanted to.

Which he normally didn't.

Because usually they were selfish pricks.

Regrettably, those couples generally ended up in a divorce attorney's office in the end.

Most men like that didn't want to change, even to save their marriage or relationship. They'd just move on to the next woman, until that one got sick of their demanding bull-shit, too.

Her eyes slid to the tall man still holding onto her. His long fingers dug into her arm covered in black unbreathable polyester.

He was probably one of those for sure.

With a tug, he "encouraged" her to move deeper into the small plane. When he got far enough to be out of the crew's way, who were busy preparing for take-off, his firm grip released and he fell into a nearby seat.

Then he slouched, stretched out his obscenely long legs and put his boots on the seat across from him before crossing his ankles.

Like he owned the joint.

He jerked his chin up at her.

What did that mean?

"You get off the fucking plane in the Burgh wearing that shit, you're gonna attract more attention than we want. Take it off."

Gladly. She wanted it off, but not because he ordered her to remove it.

With a loud sigh, that she made sure he heard, she yanked the niqab off her head and threw it on an empty seat to her left. She smoothed a hand over her hair since she was sure it was standing on end from static created by the shittiest fabric man ever made.

She glanced down at the rest of the outfit. The nondescript black garment that covered her from neck to ankles. Did he just expect her to pull that off, too? Right there while he watched?

"Ma'am, you need to sit down and buckle up, please. We're about to taxi to the runway."

Fine, then. She'd just yank it off right there.

Parris glanced at the petite uniformed woman, who shot a patient smile at her before returning to the front of the jet. But not before running curious eyes over Mercy's face and giving him a little suggestive smile. *Hmm.*

Gathering the fabric in her fingers, she turned away from the silver-gray eyes that were pinned on her and slowly pulled it up, careful not to take her dress along with it and give this Mercy a show.

Maybe it wasn't a show he'd want to watch anyway. As she tugged the fabric higher until it was gathered at her waist, she took a quick glance over her shoulder.

Oh yes. He was still watching.

He was now sitting up straight and buckled in. Though, he no longer wore that jacket which was ridiculous to wear in the Vegas heat.

Parris now knew why he wore it.

He had a worn leather shoulder holster strapped on his torso, which of course, held a gun—not a very small one, either—secured to his left side.

And on his right hip was a sheathed knife. From what it looked like, that was pretty big, too.

She also wondered if he had a grenade tucked into the front of his jeans. Because if not, then...

Phew.

That was one weapon she wouldn't be seeing anytime soon, thankfully.

Hmm. Maybe regretfully.

Now she was sweating and couldn't blame it on the outfit. She finished tugging the fabric over her head and then tossed that onto the empty seat, too.

Good riddance.

She glanced down and noticed her boobs were stuck lopsided in her bra from that maneuver. Bending over, she shook them into place, then pushed both of them together to get them settled just right.

As she straightened, she sighed with relief. Now she could feel the air conditioning that was blowing through the vents.

"Sit your ass down and buckle up so we can take off."

Parris rolled her eyes at the grumble. But she couldn't tell if he was amused or annoyed.

Or maybe both.

"Rissa." Funny how that sounded like an impatient warning.

"What's with the 'Rissa?'" she hissed.

"You think I'm gonna call you Parris for the next *who-knows-how-many* days?"

She narrowed her eyes on him. "Yes, since that's my name."

"How 'bout no? And, for fuck's sake, you're keeping a low profile. Even in the Burgh. So I'm not calling you the name of a French city which is way too unique as a woman's name and could catch someone's attention."

"It's Parris with two R's," she corrected him.

"And now you're Rissa with two S's. Sit the fuck down and buckle up."

She turned and plopped her ass down in the seat across from him. Which unfortunately, faced him directly. There had to be a way to adjust it. She leaned over and checked to see if it had buttons or levers, anything to pivot it. Of course not. She was stuck facing him.

Well, he wasn't too bad to look at, even with that nasty scar. And she could always close her eyes and take a nap. Especially since she'd hardly slept a wink since witnessing what she did.

Which, unfortunately, was why she was in this very plane with this very man across from her at that very moment.

She sat back and grabbed the two sections of the seatbelt.

"Got great fucking tits."

Her fingers fumbled with the seatbelt and before she could latch it, it fell to her lap. She raised her gaze to his. "Sorry?"

"Nothing to be sorry about."

"I meant, sorry, I don't think I heard you clearly."

"You heard me."

"I swore you said that I have great fucking tits. But I must have misheard you since I have a hard time believing that a man like yourself, who's been hired to do a job, and I'm sure is being paid very handsomely, would say something so crude to a woman who has no choice but to be in your presence."

"I said it. You heard it. Let's move on."

She grabbed the seatbelt again and latched it. "I do have nice tits, though."

"Yeah," he muttered, hit the button to recline his seat, then closed his eyes.

That was it?

"Great tits," now I'm going to take a nap?

Oh no, that wasn't happening. She studied his face, which was the most relaxed she'd seen it since meeting him only a couple hours ago. "Want to tell me about the scar?"

"Nope."

She let her gaze roam over the long, narrow ridge, dying to know how he got it, then let her eyes travel farther south to where his fingers were laced over his broad chest. "Why not?"

"Because that story will haunt your dreams."

She adjusted her invisible therapist hat. Her fingers itched for a pad and pen. Or her tablet. "Like it does yours?"

"I don't dream."

"No, you probably never sleep. It's one way of avoiding nightmares."

"You're quickly becoming one of those nightmares. Now shut the fuck up, otherwise this is going to be a longer trip than I'd like. And I'm not a big fan of flying as it is."

"Why?"

He lifted his head up enough to open one eye and use it to glare at her with that icy gray stare.

Whatever.

With a huff, she hit the button on the side of the seat and let it recline until it couldn't go any further. As the seat back had slid lower, the front kicked out to support her legs, almost like a bed.

Now all she needed was a pillow and blanket and maybe she could catch up on some well-needed Zzz's.

"Ma'am, would you like a pillow and a blanket?"

Well, look at that, her silent prayer had been answered. Now someone just needed to wake her up when this whole nightmare was over.

Chapter Three

"HOLY CRAP," came the whisper next to him.

He didn't slow his roll to figure out why she was shocked.

He knew.

As soon as he reached the passenger-side door of his RPV, he dropped their bags and pulled open the door, ordering, "Get in."

"Uh..."

He glanced over his shoulder and saw her gaze lift from her stiletto-heeled pumps to his Terradyne. "Take them off and get in. Got no time to waste. This ain't a fashion show. No one cares what the fuck you look like. This is only about keeping you breathing. Get. The. Fuck. In."

He swore he heard a little growl before she bent over—once again giving him an unobstructed view of her amazing tits—yanked off her probably eight-hundred-dollar pair of shoes and then threw them into the RPV before stepping forward.

He heard her deep inhale of breath as she tried to figure out what to grab to haul her ass into his vehicle.

His growl was louder than hers when he grabbed her waist and helped her into the seat.

"I could've done it myself," she griped as she turned to him.

As her mouth opened once more, he slammed the door shut before she could say anything else.

He yanked open the rear passenger side door, threw his overnight bag and her one-too-many bags onto the back seat and slammed that door, too, ignoring whatever bullshit was spewing from her mouth.

He might have heard: rude, fuck, bastard, and some other accurate words.

His lips actually curled at the ends as he rounded the back of the oversized, testosterone-heavy vehicle and yanked open the driver's side door. He slid into the interior and was surprised to find it quiet.

Thank fuck.

He slipped the key into the ignition and, with a turn of his wrist, heard—and felt—the 6.7 L V8 turbo diesel roar to life. The only thing that sounded better was the rumble of his Harley. Or a woman having rapid, multiple orgasms.

Not the fake kind.

He twisted his head to see if Rissa was pouting, or fuming, but became distracted by her tits again.

Jesus. The woman needed to wear turtlenecks and an ugly sweater vest. Or a goddamn burqa. Didn't she know that no tight dress with a deep V would contain those puppies?

Maybe she did. Maybe that's how she snagged filthy-rich fuckers to buy her diamonds the size of Heinz Field and shoes that could feed the homeless for a month.

He yanked his cell phone out of his jacket pocket and texted D that "the package has landed and is out for delivery," before pulling up his boss's text string that included the address to this so-called "safe house."

Luckily, it turned out that D had a say in the location, so it wasn't in the city. Again, the press of bodies, the crowds, the traffic and the noise were not his scene. He hated it all. Instead, it was a house that had just finished being built inside the Dirty Angels MC compound.

Mercy was told it was supposed to be one of the brothers, he had no idea whose, but whatever this Paranzino paid them was enough to delay their moving in without complaint. The club's compound was not only secure with a high concrete wall surrounding the neighborhood, but it had an electric remote-operated gate and a bunch of badass bikers living in it, as well as a cop, who was the MC's president's brother.

So, for the most part, the location would be safe. There'd also be plenty of extra eyes. Including his boss's, who could thump anyone into the ground with a gentle tap of his fist.

Better yet, it was close enough to the warehouse, which was the base for In the Shadows Security, so if he needed back-up, he'd have it.

After hearing the grisly details Paranzino spewed, he might just need it. Diesel was now caught up on those specifics, too. Mercy thought his boss might now be regretting setting up the safe house in the same neighborhood as his family after learning everything they did.

Mercy didn't blame him.

But until something changed, that's where he pointed his RPV as he drove off the Pittsburgh International Airport short-term lot and headed toward the highway.

D said Paranzino had even paid to furnish the house and stock it with necessities, so whoever was moving into it after this mission was over, was getting a nice windfall. Especially since the shit didn't come from a Rent-A-Center. It all came from Three Rivers Furniture Emporium, which was upscale, expensive as fuck and not the typical place a biker would shop.

Kiki and Brooke, yes. Their ol' men, no. Hawk or Dex

would be perfectly satisfied kicking their feet up on an empty beer keg or reclining in an old, well-used Lazy-Boy.

The only problem Mercy saw moving into the compound, even just temporarily, was he might see Crow and Jazz. Here his boss sent him to Vegas to get him out of town and away from Jazz, but he ended up right back in their backyard.

Well, it wasn't like he was planning on taking leisurely evening strolls around the fucking neighborhood or visiting the neighbors to borrow a cup of sugar. Once they were in the house, they were hunkering down. He just needed to keep his package breathing until her wealthy lover took care of the "problem."

Once that was done, he was sticking her ass back on a plane—he didn't care if it was a fancy jet or a fucking hang glider—and shipping her back home to Vegas.

Out of sight, out of mind, with a big wad of scratch in his pocket left behind. And the bonus, if she remained alive, would be all his. He wouldn't have to give a cut of that bonus to Diesel.

Even so, most likely this assignment was going to be boring as fuck. Days of eating bon-bons and watching Nicholas Sparks movies. Nothing like hunting down the nomad motherfuckers of the Shadow Warriors MC. Now, *that* assignment had been the shit. D had let the whole team loose on that one.

Unfortunately, between him and the rest of D's crew—Hunter, Walker, Brick, Steel and Ryder—they'd pretty much wiped out all of the members of that outlaw MC. If any stragglers remained, they were laying so low they'd gone underground.

Normally he couldn't give a fuck about carnival games, but playing Whack-A-Mole with the Shadow Warriors was one of his favorites. As long as it was he, or one of D's team, doing the whacking. Taking out those Warriors had become personal not only for Diesel, but for his Shadows.

A half hour later, which remained silent, *thank fuck*, he pulled into a parking lot not far from their destination. "You hungry?"

"No," came the quiet answer.

"I am." He steered his beautiful beast through the drive-through of Bangin' Burgers, the best fucking burgers he'd ever had in his life. He'd eaten a lot of ground meat in a lot of different countries and nothing compared.

When he pulled up to the speaker, he placed his order, a few minutes later paid for it at the next window, then he continued south. The vehicle smelled damned delicious between whatever scent Rissa wore and the piping hot food in the bag. Ten minutes later, they were driving through the DAMC compound's gate and Mercy kept an eye on his rearview mirror to make sure no one slipped in behind him before it closed securely.

Two minutes later, he was pulling into a newly paved driveway in an undeveloped part of the neighborhood where D was sitting on his sled, waiting.

Knowing him, probably impatiently.

He shoved the shifter into park, set the e-brake, and turned to Rissa. "Stay in the vehicle."

"Why?" she asked without bothering to even look at him. She was too busy staring at Diesel through the windshield.

A muscle ticked in his jaw. "Just do as I say."

He climbed out so he could grab the house keys and the garage door remote from his boss.

"Boss," Mercy grunted in greeting.

D jerked his chin up and grunted back. "Fucker stocked the whole house. When Nash moves in, gonna be set for a fuckin' year. 'Specially if this job only lasts a couple days."

"Doubt it's going to last a couple days after hearing what

I heard. Paranzino sounds like a ruthless fuck and so do the people he's had to deal with."

"She fuckin' cryin' an' fussin' 'bout what she witnessed?"

"No, surprisingly. Maybe it hasn't hit her yet."

D grunted again. "Keep 'er breathin' an'..." His dark brown eyes lifted to something over Mercy's shoulder. "Shouldn't hafta say it, but keep your dick outta her, too. Got me?"

Mercy's jaw clenched. He knew what—or *who*—D was looking at. He didn't even have to turn around because he heard the tell-tale slam of the RPV's door. "Told her to stay in the fucking vehicle."

D's gaze met his and his lips twitched just slightly, but enough for Mercy to catch it. "Since when do women fuckin' listen?" He lowered his voice. "For fuck's sake, keep your dick outta her. Don't need to be makin' an enemy outta someone who can afford to launch a fuckin' missile an' take out Shadow Valley 'cause he's pissed you went there. Don't fuckin' go there no matter how temptin' that snatch is. Got me?"

Mercy sensed her presence and caught her scent before he even bothered to look. His eyes dropped to the hand she extended.

To Diesel.

Mercy didn't know whether to laugh or curse.

"Hello, I'm—"

"Know who you fuckin' are. Did you not fuckin' listen?" Of course, D ignored her hand, which, with a frown, she dropped.

Her "Sorry?" sounded surprised but held an edge.

Diesel shook his head, a scowl wrinkling his forehead. "No lip, woman. Gotta fuckin' listen." Without waiting for a response, he mounted his bike and hit the starter.

As D twisted the throttle and headed down the street, Mercy let his gaze land on Rissa.

She was still watching D ride away. "Well, isn't he rude?"

"He's not rude, he's Diesel."

Her light blue eyes slid to him. "Whatever that means."

"Let me clear something up about my boss, 'cause you might have to deal with him again in the near future. One, he's a biker. Two, he's the Sergeant at Arms of a club he was born into, which means he's their enforcer and does their heavy work. Which means he can be a target for the club's enemies. Three, he's particular about people, especially women, paying attention. He'd never forgive himself if anything happened to his girls. When I say girls, I not only mean his babies, but his woman. And believe me, he could never find another woman to deal with his ass like Jewel can. She deserves a medal, a brass plaque, the key to Shadow Valley from the mayor, and a statue in the town square in her honor. She might be petite, but that woman has tamed that beast. Just don't tell him I fucking said that."

Her gaping mouth snapped shut. "He has kids?"

"Two. Now, let's get inside so we can have a little discussion I didn't think we needed to have."

"About what?"

"If you're asking that, we definitely need to get a couple things clear."

"I need my bags," she murmured, turning to head back toward the RPV.

Mercy snagged her arm and yanked her to a stop. "Going to get you in the house first. Going to pull my vehicle into the garage where it isn't sitting out there like a fucking beacon. Then we're going to discuss the rules."

"Rules," she repeated with narrowed baby blues.

"Rules," he confirmed, ignoring her glare.

Without releasing her arm, he tugged her up the steps of the porch and to the front door. He unlocked and opened it, shoved her inside, went to the alarm keypad to punch in the code D texted to him earlier, then pointed at her. "Stay inside. That's not only an order, it's a requirement. Your life isn't your own right now. I own it as long as you're in my protection. That means you listen to everything I say. No exceptions. When this is all over, you can have your life back, but not until then. Until then, your ass is mine."

"I—"

Mercy turned and went out the door, slamming it shut.

Women.

IF HE THOUGHT he could scare her, he couldn't.

Okay, maybe he could. But she refused to let him.

None of the rules Mercy was so rudely listing right now could rattle her like what she had witnessed back in Vegas.

Nothing.

And because she had witnessed what she had, she was now a target. The same people she saw doing godawful things could be hunting her down right at that very moment, even though she had simply been at the wrong place at the wrong time.

She'd known Michael was insanely rich, but she always assumed all of his businesses were legit. She'd learned in the last week that they weren't. Since she was far from stupid, she should've known.

But she loved Michael. She trusted him. They'd been close for *years*. Michael had always taken care of her, even when she didn't want or need it.

She really didn't need it. Even though her practice was successful, he enjoyed spoiling her anyway.

At first, she'd fought it. Then she realized it made him happy, he wasn't going to be put off, and it was easier to just let him do it. However, the more he did it, the more she felt obligated to be there for him.

So she was.

Since she had no family besides her younger sister, Londyn, who lived on the east coast, Michael was it.

And now here she was on the same side of the country, and she couldn't even speak to or visit her sister.

That was one of his "rules."

"...your lover."

What?

What did he just say?

Maybe she should be paying closer attention to his rules. But the list was way too long and her attention had wandered. "My what?"

"Your lover. Paranzino."

She blinked. "My lover?" she repeated.

"Did you forget him already?"

Michael was a man who was hard to forget. So no.

"I haven't forgotten Michael, no."

"Any messages you have for him, you'll give to me. I'll make sure he gets them. Just make sure they don't include hearts and kissy faces or any intimate details."

She pressed her lips together to keep from laughing at a man like him saying things like that. "That rule won't be difficult to follow."

He gave a sharp nod. "Good."

Parris let her gaze wander once again over the man who towered over her now that she'd kicked off her heels. She was not a short woman. She was not petite in any way, shape or form. She'd always been considered a "big girl" by society's standards. Tall and thick. Not obese, but "luscious" as one of her former boyfriends called her. She had a "booty" and big boobs, two things that drew men's eyes.

However, at five-foot-eight, she could intimidate some shorter men. This Mercy was like... a freaking giant, though. Maybe an inch shorter than that Diesel, and that man had been *big*. Which made Mercy possibly six-three. Not freakish basketball player tall, but still... tall enough that she was forced to look up.

Plus, he was freaking solid. His snug T-shirt clung to every ripped muscle of his chest, abs, and veiny arms. The black cotton might as well have been spray-painted on. He had removed his shoulder holster, but kept it nearby. Now that she had a clear view of his expansive chest, she noticed he wore a chain around his neck. Not fancy, not gold, definitely not expensive. But metal and whatever was at the bottom of the chain ended between his well-developed pecs under that tight tee.

From the shape of it, most likely dog tags.

Which meant he was former military. Or perhaps current. Reserves, maybe.

She pursed her lips, then parted them to take a breath since she hadn't taken one the whole time she perused his torso.

The military background would explain his dark brown, almost black, hair being trimmed super tight, and the intensity of his gray eyes and direct-and-to-the-point words.

Also, his no-nonsense list of ridiculous "rules."

He would run this "mission" like a well-oiled machine, damn it. And Parris was expected to "fall in line" and simply take orders.

He wasn't aware of it... *yet*... but she didn't take orders from anyone. Even Michael. And Michael was well-versed in giving orders to people in his employ.

However, this Mercy was mistaken if he thought Michael was her lover. Current or otherwise.

Should she correct him?

Nah.

She lifted her gaze once more to his face to find his lips still moving. Now what the hell was he saying?

Honestly, she only needed one rule: don't get killed.

Simple.

"What's your real name?" slipped from her before she could stop it. Did she really care? She mentally shrugged. At least it got his lips to stop flapping.

"One of my rules is, you're on a need-to-know basis. Call me Mercy."

"You're saying when you came out of your mother's vagina, she took one look at her sweet baby boy and named you Mercy?"

His eyes narrowed and hardened even more.

"Is Mercy a nickname? Michael called you Mr. Mercer."

"Mercy's the only name you need to know. Let's get something straight..."

He sure liked to get things "straight."

"We're not here to make friends. We're not going to become pen pals. We're not going to meet for fucking coffee. We're not going to be Skyping or texting each other like best girlfriends after this. You're a job."

Parris shrugged. "I find the name fascinating. There has to be a story behind it."

"There are plenty of other stories much more *fascinating* on Netflix. Or on the e-reader you dragged along in the three bags of luggage you did not need."

She lifted a brow. "You went through my luggage?"

His nostrils flared and so did his eyes. Well, that was the first time she saw those silver shards of ice be anything other than cold.

His reaction could only mean one thing. "I take it they not only packed my e-reader but my vibrator as well." Probably because it had been tucked in her underwear drawer and they'd just thrown it in along with her panties, most likely thinking that it would be funny, and she'd be embarrassed. Which she wasn't, because using a vibrator was a normal behavior as she informed her patients all the time (and highly suggested it).

That one was one of her favorites, though not her *very*

favorite, which she conveniently kept in her nightstand. They didn't have a reason to dig into that drawer, thankfully, because it held a plethora of sex toys. Some of them a little more shocking than others.

"Impressive," he grumbled.

That it was. "Yes, it does a good job since it finds my clit better than most men."

Parris watched his face carefully. He steeled his response and his face remained unreadable. He might be a fun challenge since she was sure this time in Pittsburgh, or wherever they were, would be boring. Especially since she had no access to any of her electronics and couldn't leave the house. At least according to rule number five thousand, three hundred and fifteen.

Her eyes traced the long, ragged scar that diagonally divided his face. It was on the tip of her tongue to ask him about it once more. But it would be a waste of her breath, since he wouldn't even tell her his real name.

Ah. Another challenge. Finding out not only his real name but the reason his face had been sliced practically in half like a baked potato.

He probably had a very interesting life. She was sure he kept most of that life deeply buried.

Well, she was good at her job and could crack most nuts.

Maybe the time isolated in this house wouldn't be so boring after all. This could actually be entertaining, if men weren't trying to kill her.

But then, she was doing her best not to think about that. Because when she started to, her memories took her right back to that night. The scene she could still picture very clearly in her head.

If she hadn't stumbled in her damn Jimmy Choo's and gasped loudly as she barely caught her balance, they might never had known she was even there.

Unfortunately, she did witness the execution-style killings, simple shots to the back of those men's heads.

Pop. Pop. Pop.

Those three shots had made her ears ring, her heart thump wildly and her mind try to make sense of what she just saw.

Also what she had seen *after* those three well-placed bullets hit their destinations. She had actually had to fight the bile back down her throat at what remained of those men's faces, which looked like nothing but shredded meat, exploded skin and exposed bone, all dripping with blood.

And lots of it.

A rustle of paper pulled her from her thoughts.

Mercy was digging into the bag that had the Bangin' Burgers logo emblazoned on it. He offered her one and her stomach turned.

She'd pass on a burger made of ground meat, thank you very much.

He shrugged, unwrapped one and took a bite so huge that he made the thick burger look like a slider. Next, he pulled two containers of fries out of the bag.

He placed them both on the counter in the spacious, brand-new kitchen where they had had that little "discussion" he had so generously promised her. Though it wasn't an actual discussion. Because actual discussions usually involved at least two people. Instead, he had rattled off his long list of freaking rules.

Now, she watched as the muscles of his strong jaw worked to chew the mouthful of burger and, before he swallowed, he managed to shove about five fries in there, too.

"If you're hungry, this shit's the best," he managed around his mouthful of half-chewed food.

She wrinkled her nose. So much for manners.

"Don't tell me you're one of those."

Those? Someone who appreciated a man with manners? "One of what?"

"A vegetarian. Or vegan. Or whatever."

"I'm not. I like meat." Normally. Just not after remembering those blown off faces.

"Thank fuck. Because when you cook our meals, I like shit like bacon and sausage and lots of beef," he said around another large bite of burger with a chaser of more fries.

"I'm sorry?" Her eyes followed his hand as the back of it wiped across his mouth.

"House didn't come with a personal chef. Someone's gonna need to make sure we don't die from starvation."

Hold on. Pull back on those reins, cowboy. "You're probably pretty resilient. I'm sure you cook."

"Don't think you'll be happy with boxed mac and cheese mixed with sliced hot dogs. And I doubt your Michael stocked the kitchen with shit like that."

Your Michael.

She moved closer to the counter, grabbed a fry and popped it into her mouth. Surprisingly, they were good. She reached into the bag and pulled out the wad of napkins he forgot to remove.

She offered him one. Mercy stared at it for a moment, then lifted his gaze to her before taking it. After he wiped his mouth, one corner, the side with the scar, seemed to remain lifted.

Maybe it was just her imagination.

He was very handsome once you looked past that scar. For most people, it was probably all they saw, besides the icy exterior and the heavy bulk of muscle. He probably used all of that as a shield to keep people out.

To keep his secrets hidden.

Normally when someone smiled, you automatically smiled back. Smiles should be infectious. She had a feeling when Mercy smiled, the receiver of that gesture shit their pants.

She shook herself from her thoughts once again. "So you think because I'm a woman I know how to cook." It wasn't a question, but an astonished statement. Because she sure as hell was not living in the fifties. In fact, she hadn't even been *born* in the fifties. Or sixties. Not even in the seventies.

"Most women know how to cook," came the answering grumble.

Her eyebrows lifted. "In whose reality?

He also lifted a brow, the one with the scar separating it like a river cutting through a forest. "You don't know how to cook?"

With a resigned sigh, she admitted, "I do." *Damn it.*

"Then, there you go. I was right."

She rolled her eyes, and snagged two more fries before moving deeper into the kitchen. If she was assigned KP duty during this "covert operation," then she needed to see what supplies she had to work with.

"You probably think you're right a lot of the time," she declared to the interior of the fridge. For goodness' sake, Michael made sure to stock the refrigerator and most likely the freezer with only the best stuff. Including her favorite bottle of white wine. Hopefully he thought to get more than one. She had a strong feeling she'd need it.

She shut the door and moved around the kitchen opening the overhead cabinets, before checking the lower ones. *Ah, yes.* There were six more bottles, two red, two more white, two blush. As well as two six-packs of Molson. She didn't drink beer, so she knew they weren't for her.

She eyed Mercy, who still stood with his broad back to her, now working on the second burger that had been meant for her. He could have it. She was ready for a different type of meal. A liquid one.

Her quick study of the man made her conclude that he didn't look like the Molson type. He seemed to be more of a surly whiskey drinker.

Get a glass of liquor, sit in a dark corner and brood.

Yes, that seemed to be more his speed.

He didn't seem to be the *crack-open-a-Molson, invite-your-best buds-over-and-throw-a steak-on-the-grill-before-the-game* type of guy.

She couldn't imagine he'd be a barrel of fun at a party. She wondered if he even knew any jokes.

What's green and round and when you pull the pin, it explodes?

A grenade. Ha ha.

She snorted, went back to the fridge and pulled out that bottle of wine that had her name written all over it.

She placed it on the counter and began her hunt for a corkscrew. Of course there was one in the drawer to the right of the stove. Michael was the best. Or his employees were the best. She should give credit where credit was due. They knew what Michael required, so they probably stocked this house like the messiah himself was coming for a visit.

She went back to the cabinet which held glassware and snagged one of the stemless wine glasses she'd noticed during her kitchen exploration. A large one that probably held sixteen ounces.

That would be a good start. The only thing better would be drinking straight from the bottle.

Tempting. Very tempting.

She twisted her head to see Mercy now leaning back against the center island, the second burger demolished, and about a half dozen fries halfway to his lips. He'd been watching her.

Oh joy.

She lifted the bottle in a silent question.

Before shoving the fries into his yapper, he grunted, "No."

"There's beer in the bottom cabinet, too. But it's Molson, which is Canadian, and you seem to be a good ol' American boy who probably doesn't drink anything other than Miller or Bud. Being a staunch patriot and all that."

"My RPV was made in Canada."

Parris raised her brows in question. "RPV?"

"The vehicle that delivered your ass here."

"Ah, that." She concentrated on removing the cork from the bottle without breaking it. As she struggled with it, she suddenly felt a searing heat near her back. She glanced back... and *up*... as his thick arms came around her, one of his big hands holding the bottle just above hers, the other covering her fingers as he helped pry the cork loose. It released with a pop.

It wasn't until he freed her hands and stepped back did she breathe once again.

Damn. Something about that whole thing had made her clench, and the clenching wasn't her jaws, either.

She willed her fingers to stop shaking as she splashed some wine into the glass, then splashed a whole lot more. She waited for her heartbeat to slow down from one hundred miles an hour to ninety-nine before turning around.

"So, no wine or beer." She forced herself to take a sip instead of the gulp she really wanted, letting the beautifully layered chardonnay tickle her taste buds. Michael knew the vineyard's owners and had taken her along with him a couple years ago to Napa Valley to meet them. "You don't drink?"

"I drink."

"Then?"

"I drink alone."

Yes, in a dark corner, brooding. Just what she thought. Probably while plotting to take down some leader in a foreign country to make the world "a better place." At least on the surface, when in reality it made that country an even bigger shit show. But as long as the American government came out looking like the hero...

She sighed. She was going off track. "Isn't that a song by George Thorogood?"

"An M.O., too."

"M.O.? Really? You can't make an exception this time?"

"No."

"You're not a real flexible person." She tilted her head as she studied him again. No better time than the present to pull up her shirt sleeves and dig in. "Let me see... You're probably a routine type of guy. Set your alarm for the same time every morning, even on your days off. You have a daily exercise routine you follow strictly. Eat two egg whites, one slice of dry multi-grain toast, and drink black coffee for breakfast. Everything has a specific place in your house. It's most likely sparse and compartmentalized, just like your life. You only keep the necessities. If it doesn't have a place or a use, you get rid of it without a second thought. Not just things, but people, too. Nothing has sentimental value. No fluff. No muss. Cold, direct and calculating." All the time she had been talking, she watched the shutters lower over his already lifeless eyes. He didn't like anyone looking too closely or pointing out his weaknesses.

"You done?"

If he was angry with her assessment, one wouldn't know it besides the growl behind his question. He was very, very good at hiding emotions, even when pushed. But everyone had a breaking point.

"Am I right? I bet you let no one in. Your brain is a steel trap but your emotions are imprisoned there, too. Do you use that scar as a shield? Do most people leave you alone because of it? You probably like that, being emotionally unavailable."

"Got a question for you."

His frosty gray eyes bore straight through her and she fought the shiver it invoked. "What?"

"Do you ever shut the fuck up?"

"You only want me to shut up because I've pegged you perfectly."

"Not into pegging."

She blinked at that unexpected response, then snorted. "You've tried it, then?"

Mercy, with hands on his hips, dropped his head, shaking it. Probably in an effort not to strangle her. But even from where she stood, she could see his jaw tight, the muscles working. *Ah*, maybe he wasn't so cold and detached after all.

And maybe his breaking point wasn't as high as she originally thought.

Interesting.

He was beginning to fascinate her.

She took another sip of her wine before grabbing the bottle in her other hand and lifting it. "Well, if you're not joining me, I'm getting drunk as fuck since I have a guard dog."

"You need to eat."

She stepped up to him and snagged the last four fries from the container he held in his big paw. She smiled as she shoved them into her mouth.

She had to admit, those were damn good fries and paired well with her one-hundred-and-fifty-dollar bottle of chardonnay.

Chapter Four

MERCY TILTED his head and listened carefully. Silence. Lots of peaceful fucking silence. After Rissa had taken her wine into the living room, he had hauled their bags upstairs. He remained up there, catching up on emails, the news and anything else that kept his mind off strangling her.

He didn't appreciate her analyzing him like she was some sort of therapist.

Fuck that shit.

She could have her wine and get totally fucking smashed. As long as she didn't leave the house and left him alone, he was fine with it.

Two of the three bedrooms were fully furnished. He snagged the master bedroom since it had its own bathroom and he gave her the bedroom at the opposite end of the hall.

Luckily, the second furnished bedroom was as far away from him as possible. Which wasn't far enough. Because he didn't want to just strangle her until she was quiet, he wanted to fuck her until she had no energy left to think, let alone talk.

The first one was more likely to happen than the second.

Especially after running her information and finding out what she did for a living.

Which was not fucking rich guys. Though that might be a hobby of hers, who fucking knew. But instead, her job was taking rich guys' money because they couldn't fuck. Or some such shit like that.

She was a damn *sex* therapist.

A sex therapist.

It wasn't the first part that bothered him as much as the second. Though he wondered what kind of man needed a sex therapist.

Not him.

No fucking way.

He had no problem getting it up and getting the job done.

Her website, professionally done, listed all the issues she dealt with in her one-woman practice.

Parris Gregory

Board Certified Counselor, Sex & Relationship Therapist

Specializing in, but not limited to: relationship and sexual issues, life transitions, and LGBTQ therapy for both individuals and couples.

Her contact page included a very sexy profile picture of her. Her long light brown hair was pulled up at the top of her head, but a few strands remained loose, framing her face, and she wore glasses. He wondered if she really needed them or only wore them for the picture, so she looked more professional.

Professional or not, that picture made him want to do a little sexual therapy of his own by jacking off to it.

He didn't. But might consider it later. Because now, as he entered the living room, he was finding things weren't so quiet and it wasn't because Rissa was talking.

Fuck no.

She reclined on the couch, her head hanging over the arm, her loose hair almost reaching the carpet. She was either sleeping or passed out. Looking at the empty wine bottle on the side table, he would guess it could go either way.

He moved closer to the source of the noise. Rissa's mouth was hanging open and she was snoring. Not very feminine-like, either. No, like a seventy-year-old truck driver who just drank a case of beer.

He squatted next to the couch and pried the empty wine glass from her fingers, putting it on the side table.

The dark circles under her eyes were telling, as was the lipstick that had been gnawed off her bottom lip. She was more afraid of the circumstances that landed her in this house in Shadow Valley than she let on. He would just bet that it was eating her from the inside out.

But he was impressed at how well she'd kept it hidden. She could have been freaking out, crying and wailing. Instead, she had handled what she saw and what it meant for her like a pro.

It was easy to see now, though, it had taken an effort. And drinking a whole bottle of wine proved reality was beginning to set in. However, he appreciated her keeping the dramatics at nil since he couldn't deal with hysterical women.

No matter how hot they were.

While she could rest assured she would be safe while he was on the job, she probably didn't like the fact her life wasn't currently in her control. And she seemed the type who didn't like to rely on anyone else.

Except for Paranzino.

He reached out and carefully lifted the large diamond solitaire from between her tits, which were rising and falling softly with each cut of the log she was sawing.

His thumb brushed over the large stone. He hated that people bought into the bullshit that diamonds were needed to prove someone's love.

They weren't.

People only believed that bullshit due to effective marketing. Commercial brainwashing. There were so many better ways to prove or show love or loyalty. An expensive chunk of carbon wasn't it.

He set the diamond back in place, sat back on his heels and assessed the situation. He could leave her on the couch for the rest of the night, but she'd probably wake up with a crick in her neck, drool dried to her chin, and have sore muscles come morning. Or he could put her to bed, let her sleep off the bottle of wine on a mattress that probably cost more than a used car.

Either Paranzino loved her enough that he wanted to make sure she was pampered during her time in protective custody or he just didn't have a good grasp on reality. His woman didn't need to live the life of luxury for a short stint.

If she couldn't sleep on a three-hundred-dollar mattress set for a couple days, then...

A muscle in his jaw popped, and with a growl, he shoved his arms under her shoulders and knees. He squat-pressed her until he was standing with her in his arms.

Yep. Fucking passed out. Neither one of her eyelids lifted as he'd picked her up.

His nostrils flared in annoyance, but he immediately realized his mistake. He not only smelled the fruity scent of wine on her breath but that perfume or whatever she wore.

"Goddamn it," he grumbled under his breath. He steeled himself against the lure of the scent he was beginning to recognize as hers, the bounce of her tits practically in his face, and the fact that his fingers found not one bony spot on her body as he carried her up the steps.

He hated bony. Instead, he liked what he was touching. He liked it a lot.

Womanly curves he could grip. Flesh he could suck. Tits and ass he could lose himself in.

"Christ," he growled through gritted teeth as he hauled her up the steps and forced himself to hook a right instead of a left. By the time he nudged the door open with his foot, his dick was urging him to turn around and head back to his room with her.

But she was not only a job, which made him responsible for her and her safety, she was smashed.

And that wasn't going to happen.

Ever.

He flipped the light switch with his elbow and stalked to the bed. With a groan—because she wasn't petite and willowy like Jazz was when she first came back to Shadow Valley—he placed her on the bed. Okay, truth was, he let her drop. But not from his arms, maybe from just a few inches from the mattress. Just to make sure she wasn't faking it.

She wasn't.

Her shoes had been removed hours before and she didn't wear stockings, *thank fuck*. But the dress she was wearing...

No. Fuck no. She could sleep in it. She could afford a new one if it got ruined.

He unfastened the chain holding the diamond from around her neck, removed the matching diamond earrings and tossed them on the nightstand. Then he stared down at her. At least she had stopped that horrible snoring.

With a moan, she shifted and nuzzled deeper into the comforter. Should he cover her up?

No. He wasn't a nursemaid. He wasn't a butler. He was a fucking former Sergeant Major and Delta Force operator, goddamn it. He didn't bust his ass to stay alive and in one piece all those years to be a babysitter to a drunk, rich woman.

He bit off a curse and, carefully rolling her to her left, then to her right, he yanked the comforter free and covered her. On second thought, made sure her pillow was positioned properly.

Goddamn it!

He strode away from the bed, turned off the light and slammed the door shut.

He hesitated just outside the entrance to the kitchen, mentally bracing himself. As he stepped through the entryway, the early morning sun beaming through the glass sliders to the right of the kitchen lit up the room.

Two things hit him at once.

The first was the smell of fresh brewed coffee. And fuck if that didn't smell good.

The second was Rissa standing at the stove with her back to him as she was doing something. Most likely making breakfast.

She was wearing pink-striped pajama bottoms that hugged her ass in a way that should be illegal.

He adjusted himself in his tracksuit pants to hide his reaction before he cleared his throat.

She turned with a spatula in her hand.

He blinked, then forced himself to take a breath.

She had zero makeup on her face, her hair was gathered messily on the top of her head with loose tendrils falling about her face and neck, and she looked freshly showered.

Even better, she wore glasses.

Which meant she needed them, she probably just wore contacts normally.

He unstuck his feet and headed over to the fridge to grab a cold bottle of water. Cracking the top, he guzzled about a third of it down before lowering it. He also considered grabbing some ice cubes out of the ice maker and shoving them down his pants.

Because not only did those pajama bottoms turn him the fuck on, her camisole top hardly contained her tits and looked like it was going to explode at any second like one of those Pillsbury biscuit cans.

It might be a good morning for sausage and biscuits.

Jesus fuck. "Got a sweater or something you can put on?"

"Why? I'm not cold."

"Your nipples state otherwise."

She actually glanced down to look at her own tits. "They're not cold, they're just having a perky morning, unlike me." She turned back to the stove and he almost shed a tear at the loss of that glorious sight. "I think I overdid it last night."

"You think?"

"Thank you for putting me to bed. That was kind of you."

If you only knew my thoughts while I did it, you wouldn't be thanking me.

She continued, because, of course, the woman liked to hear herself talk. "Do you normally sleep in? I figured you'd be up at zero-dark thirty."

He was late coming down for breakfast because, while he resisted relieving himself last night, this morning's wood wouldn't go away until he took action. So he pulled up her photos on her Facebook page—he needed to tell her about the dangers of putting her life out there on social media—and took care of business.

Once his clogged pipes were clear and he could think a little straighter, he then dug deeper into her online presence. After that, he texted Hunter and got him to hack her social media accounts, instructing him to change all her public posts to private instead. When this current situation was over, he didn't give a shit what she put out there for the world to see, but while she was in Shadow Valley, he did.

His job. His rules.

His bonus on the line.

But he didn't tell her any of that.

Instead, he muttered, "Jet lag," and took another swig of water.

She approached him carrying a mug, then offered it to him. Black coffee. When he didn't take it, she put in on the counter near his hip and moved back to the stove. He had no idea what she was doing over there, because he was too busy watching her round ass cheeks wiggle back and forth under the soft cotton of those PJ's.

Then, not a minute later, she sauntered back over to him and shoved a plate into his chest, which he had no choice but to accept.

Egg whites and two slices of what looked like dry whole wheat toast.

"The cook made you breakfast." She smiled up at him and then moved away once again to her own mug of coffee. She picked it up and turned to face him, lifting the coffee to her lips. He watched her delicate throat undulate as she swallowed some down.

Putting his water bottle on the counter next to the ignored coffee, he went over to the nearby trash can, stepped on the foot lever to lift the lid and dumped the contents of the plate into the garbage.

"Going for a run. Not leaving the compound, but you *do not* leave this house, you *do not* unlock or open the door for anyone. Tell me you heard that and will follow those instructions."

Her blue eyes lifted from the now closed trash can and hit his. She pursed her lips and it took her a few long moments before she said, "Got it."

He turned away and dumped the empty plate into the sink. "No, say it."

He heard a sharp intake of breath behind him. He

waited. Finally, she muttered, most likely through gritted teeth, "I heard you and promise to follow instructions."

That had to be painful for her. He nodded in satisfaction. "Four pancakes with butter and maple syrup, along with six strips of bacon when I get back in forty-five."

Without waiting for her to respond, he walked out of the kitchen, his lips twitching as he went.

"Asshole wants pancakes. Four. With butter *and* maple syrup. Bacon. Not two pieces but six. If I ate like that I'd look like Humpty Dumpty. He eats that, he looks like freaking Adonis. Eats two burgers and almost two orders of French fries. Again, I'd be looking like the Goodyear Blimp." Parris puffed her cheeks out like a chipmunk and flipped another pancake. It was done perfectly, of course, so she threw it on the stack of awaiting pancakes. "His ass better appreciate the hard work I'm putting in making him this breakfast after I already made him one earlier. If he doesn't, he's getting this spatula shoved up his ass."

She froze, her head snapped up and her nostrils flared as she picked up the smell of a man. Not just any man. A hot, sweaty, slightly musky one. Who was very, very, *very* close.

Her heart flipped, then began to beat like one of those wind-up toy monkeys playing drums.

Maybe if she ignored him, he'd move away.

How did he get so close without her hearing him, anyway? The man was, like, huge. How could he be so quiet?

She turned and glanced down to see what shoes he was wearing that made him so stealthy. However, on her travels south, she got sidetracked and saliva went down the wrong pipe, making her cough. As soon as she could breathe somewhat normally again, she waved the spatula in a circle, indicating a certain area of his body, asking, "Um, what happened to your pants? You seemed to have lost them."

"Went running."

"Yes, I know. That's obvious since you said you were. And you're sweaty." His drool-worthy chest glistened since he apparently lost his shirt, too. "But you're... almost naked." *Yes, he was!* "Did your pants just break free and run in a different direction? You're now wearing..." Her gaze raked over whatever he was wearing. Which wasn't much. And definitely didn't leave much to the imagination. *Um, hello there!* "Panties or something," she finished a little breathlessly, much to her chagrin.

"Ranger panties."

Did he just say... Ranger panties? Did he say he *was* wearing *panties*? Was she right? She blinked. "Say what?"

"Running shorts."

"Okay." They were certainly okay. Like very okay. Extremely okay. Any male with his physique should be required to wear them when working out. Hell, twenty-four hours a day. "They... um..." Emphasized a *lot*. A lot. *Holy shit. A lot.* "You don't worry about... things breaking loose in them? Escaping? Scaring women and children with..." That monster?

And didn't his hand slide down there to cup himself? He certainly did. And now she knew he was more than a handful. One of his hands, too. Which was *not small*. "It's under control."

That was too bad. "So, did you have a herd of women chasing you around the compound ripping off your clothes?"

He almost smiled. She swore the corners of his eyes at least crinkled the slightest bit.

"Removed my track pants before I walked out the door. Usually take my shirt off midway through my run once it gets soaked."

Parris bit her bottom lip, willed her nipples not to ache so badly, and squeezed her thighs together as she turned back to the frying pan to not only gather the bits and pieces of her exploding ovaries, but to remove the pan from the heat. Because things were too freaking hot in the kitchen as it was. She turned off the burner and wiped the back of her hand over her forehead. "Well, you're just in time. Bacon's in the oven, pancakes are done. Butter and maple syrup are on the table. Your coffee got cold, so I tossed it. Get yourself a fresh cup."

She sensed rather than heard him move away. She opened the oven, used tongs to snag six pieces of bacon for him, two for her (because there was no way she was going out running for forty-five freaking minutes so she could eat four extra pieces), and tucked them next to the pancakes. When she turned with the plates in her hand...

She gasped and her heart stopped. At first, her mind couldn't make sense of what she saw.

She put the trembling plates back onto the counter with a clatter before she dropped them and they shattered on the tile floor. With one hand pressed to her mouth, she approached him as he poured himself a fresh cup of coffee, most likely unaware of her approach.

Oh no, he was aware. His spine snapped straight, his dark head lifted and every muscle in his body went tight.

He became a statue. She didn't even think he was breathing. Nothing on him moved. Not his ribcage. Not his hands. Nothing. He was frozen in place.

His skin was warm and still damp as her trembling fingers traced one thick scar, then the next, then the next.

Another.

And one more.

Finally, the last one she could see, which was close to the waistband of his shorts.

They were white and, for the most part, raised but

smooth, so they weren't fresh. They happened years ago. All of them close to the same length, the same width.

The same weapon.

The same hand had held that weapon.

The weapon being the same knife that sliced open his face?

How had he survived this many stab wounds?

She finally released a shaky breath and when that breath swept over his skin, he jerked.

A strangled, "Rissa," filled the air around them.

She ignored it and, from the small of his back, worked her way back up, smoothing, touching, experiencing each one of those scars again.

Each one. Six that she could see.

Six times he'd been stabbed. From behind.

Someone tried to kill him. Extinguish his life.

Remove him from the earth.

Why? Had he been a threat? Was it self-defense? What had he done to deserve something so violent?

What caused someone to cut open his face?

Where had this man been? What had he done? Why had he even been in that type of situation?

She lingered on the one on his back nearest his heart. The one that could have been instantly fatal.

She was jerked out of her thoughts when he spun on her and grabbed her wrist in a hold so tight, she cried out in surprise.

His silver-gray eyes were no longer icy. Not unless ice seared. No, something else flickered behind them. Blistering, blazing, but barely restrained.

"Rissa," came from deep within his chest, almost like a lion huffing.

Goosebumps exploded over every inch of her skin. Her nipples puckered so hard, the ache from them shot through her and landed in her core.

"Parris." Did her lips move? Did that come from her? Why would she feel the need to correct him at this very moment?

"Rissa to me," he growled, dropping his head low.

Now his eyes held a new look. Dangerous, unrestrained. Similar to that lion he sounded like, only now she had become his prey.

His target.

So maybe this wasn't the best time to argue about his use of her name.

Right now, he was on the edge of something.

It could go either way. Something disturbing and violent, or...

If she pushed him the wrong way things could end up badly for her.

"Mercy." His name caught in her throat. But she needed to talk to him, see where his head was at. She cleared her throat. "Mercy—"

"Two ways to shut you up. Both ways, I could lose my bonus and possibly my life."

A shudder swept through her.

"One will definitely suck for you. The other..."

The hand not gripping her wrist like a vise curled around her throat.

She should be very scared.

Very, very scared.

Especially when those long, strong fingers began to squeeze.

Chapter Five

His eyes narrowed as hers widened and her mouth opened, a puff of air escaping.

She should be scared, very scared, but there was no fear behind those baby blues.

None.

Her pulse raced wildly under his thumb and when a groan slid up her throat, he felt the vibration against his palm.

Yeah, there were two ways to shut her up. From talking, at least.

With a tight grip on both her neck and wrist, he bumped her backwards using his body. One step, two steps, and with the third, her ass hit the center island. Now she was trapped.

Now he had complete control of her, had her pinned in place.

His eyes raked over her lipstick-free lips, ones he imagined stretched around his cock when he jacked off this morning. Then they slid down to her heaving chest. The elastic fabric of her snug pink camisole did nothing to hide how hard those tips were. So puckered that he could even see the outline of her areolas. Her nipples were substantial in size, perfect for his mouth.

There wasn't anything delicate about this woman.

She was unbreakable.

She was the type who could take a pounding and would ask for more. That was the kind of woman he liked. One who wasn't afraid to mess up her hair or break a nail when things got a little rough.

He jammed a knee between her thighs, holding her in place as he released her throat and her wrist before wedging his hands behind her to grab generous handfuls of her ass. So much to grab, so soft. He wanted to bury himself there, too. His mouth, his fingers. His cock.

He lifted her up and slid her ass onto the counter, hooked his fingers into the waistband of her PJ's and heard them tear as he yanked them down her hips, over her thighs and off her bare feet.

Surprisingly, she wore plain peach cotton panties instead of some expensive, lacy ones. He wanted to shove his nose against the darker center, where it was damp and clinging to plump lips barely contained within the fabric.

"Mercy." His name came out on a hitched breath.

She should be scared.

She wasn't.

And he liked that.

Her hands were planted on the counter behind her and she leaned back, offering herself with a groan.

She belonged to someone else, but at that moment, he didn't give a fuck.

His cock was hard, throbbing, as his fingers slid over the breadth of her hips, over the tuck of her waist, along her sides, skimming the heavy curves of her tits.

She was now panting, her head falling back. He reached up, yanked the elastic band out of her hair, the thick, light brown strands falling loosely, pooling on the counter beneath her head. He slipped her glasses from her face, brushed a thumb over her plump bottom lip, her warm, damp breath beating against his fingers. His fingertips traced her feminine jawline, down her throat once more. He didn't pause there. Though he wanted to.

He kept going. Over the hollow of her throat, a very vulnerable spot. A place where he could easily crush her windpipe with a well-placed two-finger jab. He curled both hands to either side of her neck, stroking his thumbs up and down her pulse points before sliding them over her shoulders, slipping his fingers under the straining spaghetti-thin straps of her top and snapping them both at the same time with a jerk.

Her sharp intake of breath made him lift his eyes to her unfocused ones. Her makeup-free face was flush, her lips parted. He took advantage of that, leaning over, crushing his mouth to hers, capturing her moan, finding her tongue, forcing her to submit to him with just a kiss.

He worked the cami down, over the swell of her tits until the fabric was gathered at her waist like a belt. He deepened the kiss as his fingers explored the fullness, the weight, the heaviness of the tits he wanted to get lost in. Both palms brushed over the diamond-hard tips, invoking another moan he captured and kept for himself.

Using his thumbs and forefingers he plucked, twisted and pulled. Her back arched, her tongue tangling even more frantically with his. He couldn't wait, so he broke the kiss and sucked one nipple into his mouth, not being gentle. Showing her who he was, what he was.

He was not going to woo her. He was not going to whisper sweet nothings in her ear. He was not going to be gentle.

He was going to fuck her. Deep. Hard. Fast. Until they both came. Both collapsed.

That's what he'd give her.

No flowers. No chocolate. No breakfast in bed.

He scraped his teeth over the taut nipple and her whole body flexed as he did so.

A low growl escaped him as he did the same to the other one before moving down her belly, nipping at her flesh as she quivered beneath him.

Fuck yes, she liked it.

She hadn't said no yet. She hadn't tried to push him away. She wanted exactly what he was giving her.

She made a little sound of complaint when he released her tits and grabbed both her wrists, pulling her hands free from the counter, forcing her to recline on the granite counter top. Her legs automatically circled his waist. Slipping his hands between them, he found her panties and ripped them apart with a jerk so hard, her whole body shifted.

His fingers found her hot, slick, and open. She ground down against them as he inserted two inside her, finding her ready and willing.

So fucking wet.

He wanted to taste her, suck on one plump, juicy fold then the other. But he didn't have the patience to wait.

Shoving his shorts down and tucking the elastic waistband under his heavy, aching sac, he freed himself, sliding the head of his cock along her slick slit. Her hips lifted slightly, enough to encourage him to take that next step.

His dick was right there. Another inch and he'd be inside her. But she belonged to another. A powerful man with a lot of money.

She didn't belong to him.

He had no right to do what he wanted to do. He shouldn't even be thinking about it. He shouldn't be considering it.

This could change everything.

He curled over her and growled in her ear, "You belong to Paranzino."

"No," she breathed, her head thrashing back and forth. Her hands wrapped around his bare shoulders, her nails digging in.

He liked it. The pain. The discomfort. The sharp reminder that he was alive. "Yes."

She arched her back again, her hard nipples pressing into his chest. "No. Michael... Michael is gay. I... I don't belong to him. I don't belong to anyone."

Michael is gay.

I don't belong to him.

With a grunt, he thrust his hips forward and slid deep inside her. No resistance from her or her body. The slickness, the heat, the tightness surrounding him, making him grunt again in her ear.

I don't belong to anyone...

Now you fucking do.

Her head slammed back into the counter and she cried out as she clenched tightly around him, drawing him deeper, encouraging him to fuck her harder.

Her hips rocked against him and he couldn't get deep enough.

Not fucking deep enough.

He lifted himself up, so he could watch her tits sway heavily with each thrust of his hips. He curled his fingers around the front of her neck once more.

His fingers flexed and squeezed, released and curled. His other hand found the soft skin of her inner thigh, and he dug his fingers into her flesh, spreading her wide, encouraging her to pull her legs back even more. To give him everything she could.

Every powerful pump pushed the air from her lungs and, along with it, a groan. Her fingers shifted from his shoulders, down his chest, her nails raking along his skin.

Her hand dropped to where they were joined, and his pace hitched when he felt her touch him there. But it was only for a brief second before her own fingers pressed on her clit and began to work it.

He didn't know where to watch first. Her pleasuring herself, making her clench tighter around him. Her tits sliding back and forth, begging for his mouth. Or those lips of hers, open, releasing an endless stream of groans, moans and gasps.

Or maybe her blue eyes, which were not closed, no. They were watching everything happening between them. This was not a fantasy for her. She knew exactly who was inside her.

Fucking a scarred freak wasn't on her bucket list unlike most of the other women he'd been with in the past few years. With her career, she dealt with men like him every damn day.

She recognized how dangerous he could be. He had seen it in her eyes. It didn't scare her. She didn't see him as an oddity. She didn't fuck him out of curiosity.

He uncurled his fingers from her neck and after tracing his thumb around her lips, dipped it inside. The tip of her tongue played along it for a few seconds before she sucked it hard, then bit it even harder.

His hips stuttered once more at that. The bite, the suck, the pure ecstasy on her face as she played orally with his digit. He hooked his thumb inside and yanked her mouth open wide, growling, "I'm going to come in your cunt this time, in that mouth next time."

Her pussy rippled around him at his words and a loud rush of air escaped her.

He was right. Fucking her shut her up.

And was much more pleasant than strangling her.

"Hold on," he growled, and wrapping his arms around her back, hauled her up, making sure she stayed seated deep on his dick. He carried her the few feet to the nearest wall and pressed her against it. Holding her up with his hands, he bent his knees and powered up into her over and over, hitting the end of her each time.

For once he wanted to hear her say something, but she was remaining too quiet. He only heard their ragged breathing in his ears, those invisible words driving him on, but he wanted more.

Then he heard it. The cry. Along with the tightening of her muscles around him as an orgasm ripped through her.

He gritted his teeth and digging deep, slammed her even harder, expecting the drywall behind her to give way, to crack with the force. Somehow it miraculously held.

Grabbing her hips, he lifted her off him, dropped her feet to the floor and spun her to face the wall before sliding inside her from behind.

She was so fucking wet, he had to hesitate for a split second to keep from losing it. *Jesus.* He couldn't remember being inside pussy this good in a long time.

Maybe even never.

He snagged both of her wrists in one hand, raised her arms up and pinned her restrained hands to the wall. He wrapped an arm around her chest, grabbing one of her tits, squeezing hard, finding the nipple and pulling even harder.

She gasped and slammed her hips back into him. He shoved his mouth to her ear, growling, "Like that? Like to fuck hard?"

Still, she said nothing.

Fuck the words, he didn't need words. He needed what she was giving him. Just soft grunts, moans and groans, along with the rapid pants escaping her.

The wet heat tightening around him, milking him, driving him to the brink.

"That's it, squeeze me tight."

Her head tipped back, hit his shoulder hard, then fell

forward, her body heaving. Her skin was almost as slick and hot as her pussy.

The pressure in his balls was becoming unbearable. His cock twitched inside her. But he wanted to make her come once more. He needed to feel those strong ripples, he needed to hear the hitch of her breath as her body spasmed around him and spun out of control.

Keeping her hands pinned, he released her tit, dropped his hand to her pussy and pinched her clit hard.

"*Ooooh fuuuck.*"

She liked it. The pain with the pleasure.

"Do it again."

She ate that shit up. He complied, pinching her delicate clit, which he desperately wanted to get his mouth on. She shuddered around him, against him.

"*Yesss,*" hissed from her as he felt the start of her next orgasm.

"*Yesss,*" echoed through this head. Nudging her hair out of the way, he shoved his face into her neck, and nipped sharply along her skin until he reached her shoulder. With a low grunt he sank his teeth into her flesh as he came forcefully inside her.

From a distance, he heard her cry out once more. On the edge of his consciousness he recognized that she came again just as fiercely at the same time he did. He released her wrists, released her clit, but kept a hold of her shoulder within his teeth as he struggled to catch his breath. His right palm smoothed up her belly slowly, the fingers of his left hand curling around the front of her throat. The pounding in her neck even faster than ever.

He unlocked his jaws to release her shoulder, slid his left hand even higher until he held her under her chin and pulled her head back, stretching her neck in an arch.

Her breathing was rapid, ragged and loud.

He could feel himself slipping out of her. Not his cock. No.

His cum.

He hadn't used a condom. He'd broken his own strict rule.

And he didn't even fucking care. Not one bit.

It was a discussion they should have, but most likely wouldn't. Parris stood in the upstairs hall bathroom, naked in front of the sink, studying the teeth-marks left behind on her shoulder. The area was already starting to bruise, to turn various shades of colors. She tilted her head, lifted her fingers to it and prodded it with a wince.

Then her pussy clenched in response and she smiled.

Her hair was a wild mess, her cheeks still held color and her eyes were the brightest they'd been in a while.

She had been coasting through life recently, which had consisted of work, work and more work. Occasionally she'd meet Michael and his husband for dinner.

Her girlfriends had stopped calling and asking if she wanted to meet, go dancing, grab a bite to eat, or go see a movie.

They got sick of Parris's excuses.

Since Londyn moved from Nevada to upstate New York a couple years ago, Parris spent a couple nights a week on the phone with her younger sister. They had always been close but became even tighter after their father died of a stroke ten years back. Then her mother went to sleep one night and never woke up. Parris swore it was from a broken heart since there was no other medical explanation than "heart failure." Especially when her mother never had a heart condition prior.

However, talking on the phone with Londyn wasn't the same as living nearby.

And besides her friends encouraging her to hit the dating scene before she was past her "prime," Londyn encouraged it, too. Her sister had moved across the country for a man she'd met on the Internet. For now, that relationship worked. Whether it would last, Parris didn't know. Either way, she just wanted her sister to be happy.

And in turn, Londyn wanted Parris to have what she had.

She sighed. She was thirty-eight and a sex therapist that hadn't had sex in a couple years. Okay, maybe three years. Four? *Ugh.*

She was beginning to feel like a fraud. She knew that was ridiculous. Not having sex didn't make her unqualified to do her job, but still...

Anyway, every time she met up with her girlfriends, they pestered her to get back out there, to get back on the market. Hell, just pick up some random guy, do him all night long until her thighs quivered and she could no longer walk, then kick him out the door afterward.

Get some guy to "knock the bottom out" of her and clear out the cobwebs.

She'd had no desire to do that. One reason was, she'd watched too many shows on the Investigation Discovery channel late at night.

Which meant she didn't want to pick up some random stranger. Or join a dating website since she liked her body all in one piece. Not hacked into hundreds of bite-sized bits.

Also, most of Michael's closest friends were gay. So, they were out (literally).

All that didn't matter at the moment, anyway.

What mattered, and what they probably wouldn't discuss, was she just let a man, who she was sure had a few deep-seated issues, a man she didn't even know his real name, fuck her in the kitchen in a house outside of Pittsburgh. And the only reason she was there was due to her life being in danger.

But he didn't only fuck her. He fucked her on the counter and against the wall, from the front and back. *And* it was the best damn sex she'd ever had. Not to mention, the most spontaneous, too.

He spoke no bullshit words, told her no lies to try to get her into bed. He didn't have to, he just took what he wanted.

Thinking back on that, her toes curled once more.

The two orgasms she had were so freaking intense, they made her see spots.

Now she wanted more.

Oh, yes, please. Many, many more.

It wasn't like they had anything else to do while they waited in the house for word from Michael. They would be bored, right?

She had no access to the Internet, her phone, her laptop, nothing. Something needed to keep her occupied, besides her steamy romance novels (that gave women unrealistic relationship expectations, but she still devoured them anyway).

However, there was a slight problem. He hadn't worn a condom.

Not that she stopped him.

She wasn't worried about getting pregnant. She had that covered. But she worried about... *other* obvious things when it came to unprotected sex.

Including the fact that she was stuck in this house with the man for who knew how long. Were they just supposed to ignore the massive elephant in the room?

Even though she took a shower earlier that morning, she now needed a second one. Her inner thighs were slick with his DNA, as well as her own.

What they did was stupid and reckless.

But... And it was a big but, those men who were searching for her could find them tomorrow and put a bullet in the back of her head, too. She mentally shrugged. So, she might as well live dangerously, right?

Make the best of her situation?

Sure.

Her eyes slid toward the closed bathroom door. She wondered if he now regretted their spontaneous combustion.

She was probably not his typical sex partner. He probably preferred women who were fitness freaks like him. She dropped her hands to her belly and pressed on her pooch.

Women who had six-packs and walnut-cracking muscular thighs. Not soft and doughy like her. Breasts that were perky and hardly shifted when they went for a five-mile long run in their short shorts.

She had booty, she had boobs, she'd never be petite. If she went for a run, she'd need to wear three layers of sports bras so she wouldn't cause an earthquake. If she wanted a flat stomach, she'd need to squeeze into a pair of Spanx. A very tight pair.

She accepted her body a long time ago. It was what it was and unless she was willing to spend hours at the gym, it wasn't going to change.

She loved to swim in her pool, walk around her gated community, and sometimes dance late at night while music blared through her whole-house speaker system as she cleaned.

She ate healthy for the most part, but she didn't deny that she liked to eat. She also appreciated a good glass or two—or, apparently, a whole bottle—of wine.

She also loved to eat in Michael's casinos because he had the best restaurants and top chefs, who he hand-picked himself. Plus, Michael spoiled her. She could enjoy a gourmet meal on the house in any of his restaurants any time she wanted. One of his high-profile chefs often texted, asking her to stop in and try a new dish before presenting it to his boss.

So, yes, she liked to eat. She enjoyed good food. And she wasn't ashamed to admit it.

Mercy hadn't closed his eyes once while he fucked her. Not once. Because of that, she assumed he wasn't imagining anyone else. He had actually looked at her, really *looked* at her while she was naked. He wasn't fantasizing he had some hot chick on the counter beneath him. He was fucking *her*. Parris.

But that's what it was... *fucking*. Nothing more, nothing less. Two people finding sexual satisfaction with each other. Even if only momentarily.

Nobody had to be a runway model for that. She wouldn't be on his arm, nor would she be introduced to his friends.

While they were hidden away in this house, he merely took advantage of an available female to get his rocks off.

Simple.

Just like she had taken advantage of his impressive cock wrapped up deliciously in little olive green "Ranger panties."

So... whatever.

It was done. They both were satisfied with the results.

Their pancakes were left forgotten after he'd pulled out, stared at her silently for a few moments (which kind of freaked her out), then yanked his shorts up with a jerk and left the kitchen.

When she followed his path a few minutes later, she heard the shower running in the master bathroom and figured she should clean up before going back downstairs to reheat his breakfast.

Maybe they'd just act like what happened hadn't.

She was fine with that, too, but the truth was, she would be a bit disappointed.

Again, there wasn't much to do in the house while they waited, so why not just have copious amounts of gratuitous sex? She was all for it. If she had enough in the next couple days, it might keep her satisfied for a while once she got back home.

Maybe she'd suggest it.

She snorted, then sobered quickly as her fingers traced the bite once more.

She had to admit, that shit was hot.

While the sex was great, she had a feeling the man himself was a ticking time-bomb.

But as long as she didn't snip the wrong wire and accidentally make it detonate, she'd be fine.

Chapter Six

He'd been quiet since coming back downstairs with his dark hair damp, wearing another sinfully tight black T-shirt over muscles she'd now seen up close and personal. He was also wearing soft, worn jeans. She mourned a little about the loss of the "panties," but he was just as drool-worthy wearing jeans and going barefoot. He had nicely shaped feet and long toes. No cloven hooves like a couple of the men she had dated in the past.

"I thought about getting a breast reduction," she stated after swallowing a mouthful of reheated pancakes.

He lifted his gray eyes from his plate and they landed on her breasts. Not that he could see much since she now wore a bra, a cotton top with a modest V-neck and a pair of yoga pants. Since she wasn't leaving the house, there was no point of dressing up, putting on jewelry or makeup or even spending a half hour on her hair. Instead, she had pulled it back into a ponytail after her second shower.

After their late breakfast, she planned on grabbing her e-reader and curling up on the couch to catch up on her TBR pile, anyway.

If it wasn't for the scar marring his face, Mercy could be

the perfect alpha hero in some of the steamy, toe-curling romances she enjoyed reading. Or the villain in some of her favorite romantic suspense.

He'd probably prefer to be the villain.

She certainly couldn't imagine him desperately running through an airport chasing down a woman who he'd fell deeply in love with and dropping to his knees in a crowd of hundreds to declare just that.

She rolled her lips inward.

"Why the fuck would you do that?"

What? Oh, right. "They're heavy."

He still stared at her breasts but said nothing. Was he trying to imagine them smaller?

She added, "Too much to deal with."

He let his gaze drop to his plate and stabbed a piece of pancake, then shoved it into his mouth. "You do that, every man in the world will weep."

"I probably won't do it because I've been told they're my best asset," she murmured, watching him carefully.

He grunted and forked another piece of pancake into his mouth.

This man kept himself detached and distant for a reason. But deep down, something burned hot. Like the scorching depths of the earth's core. While she'd told herself not to provoke him, she couldn't resist scratching at the surface a little to feel some of that heat.

She took a sip of the fresh coffee she had brewed and stared at him over the rim of the mug. "What do you think?"

He sat back in his chair, his brows furrowed deep. "Why the fuck do you care what I think?"

She lifted a shoulder. "I was just curious, since you saw them." And it had been a while since anyone else beside her gynecologist had seen them.

He dropped his fork to his empty plate and shoved it

away, shaking his head. "Don't take you as a woman who'd give a shit about what other people think."

She didn't normally, she only cared about what he thought since it might give her an idea of how he'd respond to her proposal. "I was thinking—"

He sighed loudly.

"That maybe we could... you know..." She tilted her head in silent invitation.

He lifted the dark eyebrow with the scar running through it. "What?"

Apparently he didn't understand the head gesture. So much for being coy. Since the man liked direct, she was going to be direct. "Have sex again."

He shook his head. "No. Fucked up. Lost my shit. Not doing that again."

She made him lose his "shit?"

That was promising.

"Mercy..." Frowning, she plunked her coffee mug onto the table. "For goodness' sake, do I have to call you that? Can you tell me your actual name since we'll be roomies for a couple days?" *And* they actually had intercourse? Official introductions were probably in order.

"Told you what my name is."

It was her turn to release an exaggerated sigh. She pushed up from her seat, snagged her plate and his, stacking them on top of each other, and moved over to the sink to rinse them.

She turned on the water, began to rinse off the remaining syrup, lifted her head to say something else to him and jumped.

Out of nowhere he was pressed to her back. His chest was hot and broad and so very solid.

"How the hell do you move so quietly?" she asked in a shaky whisper.

"Practice." His deep voice rolled through her and made

a few things on her quiver. "Don't have any condoms. Used the last one in my wallet the night before coming to Vegas."

Oh sweet. That's what every woman wanted to hear. That the man she wanted to do on every surface and against every wall throughout the house they were standing in, just had sex with another woman a couple days earlier.

Wonderful.

"Well, I have my vibrator, then. I'll be fine," she forced out because she was suddenly having a bit of difficulty breathing. Maybe because it wasn't only his chest against her, his hips were also jammed against the top of her ass.

And even through his jeans, she could feel how hard he was. *Hmm.*

"Do you wear a condom every time you have sex?"

"Apparently not."

Heat swirled through her and landed in her belly, after taking a few turns like a tornado in Kansas. "Besides earlier."

"Yeah."

Things were looking up again. Before she could continue on that topic path, he continued, "Guys are coming over for poker night. Would ask one of them to bring some, but the boss said to keep my dick out of you and having them bring over a Costco-sized box of condoms might be a tip-off that I failed that order."

There were so many things she needed to analyze in what he just said. So. Many. Things.

First, he probably had the perfect stony face for poker. And his expressionless eyes would never give away the hand of cards he was holding.

Which meant he probably cleaned up on poker night.

Second, who were these *guys*? He must trust them enough to invite them over when they were supposed to be keeping a low profile.

Third and most importantly, *Costco-sized box of condoms.*

She pursed her lips, wondering how many condoms were in that size of a box. Probably a lot. Which meant if they set a goal to use them all, she might be set with sex *for life.*

He also might have to pour her back onto the plane when she headed home because she doubted she'd be able to walk.

But she was okay with that.

Very okay.

"Maybe one of the neighbors? Go knock on a door and ask to borrow some, like a cup of sugar?"

"The compound's full of Dirty Angels MC. My boss is the enforcer for the Angels. That shit gets back to him, I'm pulled from this operation and I lose that fucking bonus."

Bonus? She wondered what that was about. She'd have to circle back to that. "This neighborhood is full of what?"

"Bikers."

"Huh." She blew out a breath as his hands landed on her hips and worked their way up her sides. "Well, then I guess I'm just back to using BOB."

He jerked behind her, and she pinned her lips together when he growled, "Bob?"

"My battery-operated boyfriend."

His body jerked again. She twisted at the waist in his arms. He couldn't be biting back a laugh, could he? But his arms tightened, preventing her from seeing his face. She was pinned tightly between him and the sink.

"Are you over here to help me with the dishes?"

"No."

"Then what?" She held her breath in anticipation. Were they about to have more kitchen sex? She wouldn't be opposed to that. She'd take it wherever she could get it.

His hands now spanned her rib cage on both sides, his thumbs sliding along the outer curves of her breasts. Her breathing shallowed and her nipples pebbled painfully. He needed to shift his hands over a little more...

"Mercy," came out on a breath.

Instantly, he had her ponytail wrapped in his fist and roughly yanked her head back. She gasped at the sting of her scalp, the over-arch of her neck. His eyes were dark, not the normal silver ice shards, instead they were like storm clouds. He dropped his head until his lips were right above hers. His warm breath, a heady combination of coffee and maple syrup, swept over her mouth and she licked her lips in preparation.

But he didn't close that gap. That slight gap. It wouldn't take much.

She couldn't read anything in his eyes, his face. Did he war with himself deep down inside? She could see him having sex with a woman once and only once before moving on. Anything more than that could be dangerous for him. Or the woman.

When it came to sex, most women got attached too easily. Sex brought out the oxytocin in their body, which caused them to want to bond. Mercy wouldn't want a woman becoming attached. Once and done was probably another of his many "M.O.'s."

Cut ties before the strings tightened.

Be as cling-free as a dryer sheet.

"Mercy," she whispered again. How long were they going to stand there like this? How long would he make her wait?

"Ryan," came out so quietly she thought she imagined it. Until his face changed. His jaw shifted, his nostrils flared and his eyes turned to ice once more. "Fuck!" he barked, making her wince.

He released her so quickly, she lost her balance and had to catch it by stepping back into the empty space where he'd been previously standing.

He was gone.

That quickly. That quietly.

Poof.

Parris shivered as she turned and stared at the doorway where he had to have disappeared. She held up her hand. It was trembling.

She didn't know what just happened, but now she knew one more piece of him.

It was a tiny shard, but it was something.

Mercy aka Ryan Mercer.

Ryan.

She liked it. And it made him seem a little more human.

Chapter Seven

MERCY SQUINTED as the smoke from the cigar swirled into his eyes. It wasn't just his, though, the room was full of it. He'd crack the sliders open to vent the area where the table was if it wasn't so goddamn ball-sweating humid outside.

He clamped his teeth down on the stogie and reached for the hand of cards that Brick just dealt to the five of them. They tried to have a poker night at least once a month, for not only down time, but to catch up on shit. Diesel sometimes joined them, but since the girls had been born, that was few and far between. Besides, they'd all told him under no circumstances were babies welcome at the poker table.

In the middle of the table sat a bottle of Jack, three cans of Iron City beer left in the plastic rings, two ashtrays, five cell phones and a few poker chips, which were the minimum buy-in for the round.

Walker held his hand of cards close to his chest, his chin pinned to his neck, peering at what he had. He slammed his cards back on the table, scratched his balls and shook his head. "I hate when you deal, asshole."

Brick smiled big around his cigar and gave Walker the finger.

Hunter downed the rest of his beer, crushed the can in his hand, then belched so loudly, Mercy swore he saw the glass in the sliders vibrate.

Mercy snorted, and then cursed silently at his shitty hand. He threw his cards on the table and leaned back, scrubbing a hand over his hair. "You do suck at dealing, Brick."

"Motherfucker's probably sitting on a royal flush," Steel grumbled around his cigar, throwing his cards down after sorting them.

"Heard he's sitting on some hot piece of ass. Why the fuck does he get the fucking sweet jobs, when the rest of us get stuck with the shit?" Walker griped.

Mercy slid his gaze to Walker. "Babysitting some woman ain't a sweet job. There's no fucking action."

Or at least not the kind of action he normally got off on.

"So you get a short vacay with eye candy. D said her tits are—" Brick's eyes lifted to something behind Mercy.

Mercy's spine stiffened, and he knew exactly who was behind him. He hated people approaching him from the rear.

He couldn't fight the sneer as he noticed Brick eyeballing Rissa up.

It wasn't a threat assessment, either. Mercy knew exactly when Brick's gaze followed the curve of her tits, the tuck of her waist, the flare of her hips. Mercy tipped his head left, then right as his fingers curled into his palms and every muscle in his body went solid.

A breathy "Hi, boys," came from behind him and he shot to his feet, almost knocking his chair backwards to the floor.

Fucking motherfucker.

He spun on his heels and took two long strides to where she stood, wearing those black fucking yoga pants that were like a second skin. And now she had on one of those camisole thingies again, one that was as tight as the casing around an overstuffed sausage link.

"I was just upstairs reading and I heard—"

She *oofed* when Mercy grabbed her arm and began to drag her backwards through the kitchen.

"Yo, Mercy! Dude! What the fuck you doing?" Steel yelled, jumping to his feet.

Mercy stopped short and glanced down at Rissa. Her face was pale, her blue eyes wide. Those lips of hers parted.

Did he scare her?

Good.

She shouldn't be interested in having more sex with him. They were in that house for a reason, and it wasn't to play sexual romper room.

Or sexual roulette since he had been a stupid fuck and fucked her without a condom.

He was there because she was a goddamn job. That was it. A fucking job.

"Brother," Steel rumbled low next to him.

Mercy sucked air through flared nostrils and forced himself to release her arm. Steel knew better than to touch him, so he didn't, but he stood close. Within arm's reach.

Ready in case he was needed.

He wasn't.

Mercy gave him a sharp nod, indicating shit was under control. Spinning on his heels, he went back to his seat, grabbed the Jack, twisted off the cap and poured about an inch in the glass that had been sitting empty in front of him.

It had been empty because he was in the middle of a job and he shouldn't be drinking.

But now he needed a fucking drink.

And there were four other Shadows from his team sitting in that kitchen. If shit hit the fan, that shit was covered like flies on roadkill.

Brick, Walker and Hunter settled back into their seats, their eyes pinned on him. Ignoring them, he knocked back the whiskey and slammed the glass on the table. "We've got poker to play."

As one, the rest of the guys visibly relaxed and he heard behind him, "I... I'll just head back upstairs. I didn't mean to interrupt. I was only going to ask if you could crack the window because of the smoke."

All eyes slid from Mercy back to the woman behind him.

"You don't need to go back upstairs. You don't need to hide," Steel told Rissa, his normally gruff voice uncharacteristically smooth and soft.

Mercy gritted his teeth.

Yes, she fucking did. She needed to go back the fuck upstairs to get away from these dogs who probably all had bones.

Steel continued, "We don't bite... at least most of us. We'll crack open the sliding glass door."

Suddenly Hunter was up from his seat doing just that. *What the fuck.*

Mercy scrubbed his hands over his face, and by the time he was done, he made sure his expression was blank. He was not giving these assholes any fodder to bust his balls. "Are we going to play poker or what?"

As Steel and Hunter settled back in their seats, the hair on the back of Mercy's neck stood.

She was still behind him. Standing there. Breathing. Why didn't she go back upstairs to read?

Why was she letting them all fuck her with their eyes?

"You done?" he barked, not turning around.

"I'll just grab a glass of wine first, if that's okay with

you, boss," she said. While the words were said softly, they held an edge.

Steel snorted and jammed his cigar back between his lips. Hunter dropped his head and studied the back of his cards intently, since they were lying face down on the table. Walker rubbed a hand over his lower face, trying to hide a grin. But Brick didn't even bother hiding his huge smile.

Mercy shot him a glare, but Brick ignored it, continuing to stare at Rissa.

He forced himself to stay in his seat, not to jump back up, throw her over his shoulder, carry her upstairs and lock her in her room. Especially since he'd never hear the end of that, either. They'd ride his ass so hard, it would become chapped.

He listened to her move around the kitchen, opening a cabinet, getting out a glass, sliding a bottle out of the fridge. Did she plan on getting just as trashed tonight as she did last night?

"Like big guns?" Brick called out as he lifted his beer to his lips. Then he cocked his eyebrow at her.

The fuck if he didn't.

Suddenly, she was at the table—the fuck if she wasn't—with one of those stemless glasses full almost to the brim with some sort of pink wine. Her gaze slid over the cards and poker chips and then landed on Brick at the other end of the table.

And, *fuck*, if she didn't give him a sultry smile in return. "No, but I like to play poker."

"Ain't no room at the table," Mercy grumbled. Because fuck him if she was going to sit with them all night while the rest of his team ogled her. Flirted with her. Took mental pictures of her to use later tonight when they were alone with their five-fingered fists.

Fuck that.

The squeal of chairs scraping along the tile floor caught his attention.

"We can make room," Walker spouted helpfully. Him and Brick had parted like the Red fucking Sea to make room at the table.

"Yeah, we're missing our sixth, anyway," Steel stated. "We love strip poker, don't we, boys?"

"Oh! So do I!" Rissa exclaimed as Steel shot to his feet, grabbed a spare chair that had been pushed against the wall earlier and slid it in place next to him. He swept a hand out and Rissa settled into it with a smile and a wiggle as he pushed in the chair like the gentleman he fucking wasn't.

The man's eyes just happened to follow her ass until it reached the seat. When he lifted his gaze, he met Mercy's and the grin on his face said it all.

"I'll redeal the cards," Brick said around his cigar, the corners of his eyes crinkled.

"Stogie?" Hunter asked her.

She shook her head, her long pony tail sweeping over her bare shoulders and she lifted her glass. "I'm good."

Yes, she fucking was.

"That's Brick dealing the cards, by the way. I'm Walker. The fucker next to me is Hunter, the fucker next to you is Steel and you know the grumpy asshole at the end of the table."

"You boys all work together?"

"Something like that," Brick answered as he dealt a new hand around the table. When he was done, he asked, "Sure you don't like big guns? I got a really big one I can let you shoot."

"Brick," Mercy growled.

Brick chuckled and shrugged. "It's true." He cocked a brow at Rissa again. "So since..."

"Parris," she answered his silent question.

"Parris doesn't have any chips, we changing this to strip poker?"

Mercy took a handful of his chips and slapped them on the table in front of Rissa. "She got chips."

A snort came from Walker who sat to his right.

He only gave her enough so she'd quickly run out and be out of the game. Mercy frowned as the rest of the guys shoved chips her way, too.

"Okay, ante up, fuckers," Brick said loudly. "And Parris. Sorry."

"Don't change your evening for me. I won't be offended by colorful language. I've only played strip poker. Is it the same as using chips?"

Hunter threw a chip into the center of the table. "It is. When's the last time you've played strip poker?"

"Grad school. We got a little wild on the weekends sometimes to blow off steam."

"Sounds fun," Hunter said around his cigar.

Everyone else anted up by throwing a chip onto the pile.

"How 'bout we just play for chips," Mercy suggested, staring at his shitty hand. It was no better than the last one Brick dealt.

"Yeah, and once you run outta chips, you bet a piece of your clothes," Walker announced all too helpfully.

All eyes landed on Rissa once again because she was hardly wearing anything, and she probably knew shit about playing real poker if she only played it in college. They all expected her to lose her chips quickly and then have to bet the three pieces of clothing she wore. Three, *if* she wore panties. Which he hadn't noticed any panty lines, so she probably wasn't. That meant two losses and she'd be naked.

He had no doubt the guys were going to bet big until that occurred. All of them had been playing poker for years. All were good. She was no match for any of them.

"That's how we played for the most part. Sometimes we

didn't have any money since we were students, so we just played with clothes. We'd come to the game wearing fifteen layers, I swear." When she laughed, her tits jiggled and Mercy swore Brick wiped drool off his lip.

Fucker.

Mercy cleared his throat loudly and got Brick's attention. He raised his eyebrows in a silent warning.

"I bet that was a lot of fun," Hunter murmured, giving Rissa a predatory grin.

"Anyone look at their fucking hand yet?" Mercy growled. "Or are we just gonna sit around chit-chatting like a bunch of b— *women*?"

"I'm ready to play," Rissa announced glancing at her cards, sitting in between Steel and Brick. Her expression was excited like she had a great hand. So much for a poker face.

These guys were going to wipe the floor with her.

She put her cards down and after taking a sip of her wine, asked, "So there's just five of you who work for this Diesel?"

"Six," Steel grunted as he concentrated on his cards.

"Ah, yes, you said your sixth player was missing. I just figured it was Diesel himself."

"Our boss is too busy with his babies. Ryder's the sixth. He's off dealing with a job who shall remain nameless," Walker said, then did the sign of a cross in front of himself as if he was trying to ward off some sort of evil spirit.

A groan rose from the table.

"Poor fucker keeps drawing the short straw," Walker continued. "Thank fuck it ain't me. D needs to give it up and just let her crash and burn, then move in to pick up the pieces."

"He ain't gonna do that," Hunter said, slapping his cards on the table.

"Oh, is this *job* trouble?" Rissa asked.

"With a capital fucking T," Brick muttered, putting his cigar down and sorting the cards in his hand.

"She's Diesel's cousin," Hunter explained. "He's not going to give up on her. He does and something bad happens like... well, you know what the fuck I'm talking about... then he won't be able to live with it."

Head nods went around the table.

"If you need me to talk to her, I can. I'm a therapist."

With a silent groan, Mercy shut his eyes and slammed back in his chair. *Jesus fucking Christ.*

"A therapist?" Brick asked.

When he opened his eyes, all of his fellow team members were now staring at him again with amused expressions.

He never should have agreed to poker night.

"Yes, a sex therapist," she clarified, but kept going, much to his irritation, "but I have my Master's in Psychology and could help. I don't always just deal with sexual issues. There's underlying causes for most sexual problems."

Steel's cigar fell out of his mouth. He quickly grabbed it off the table and threw it into one of the ashtrays. "Holy fuck," he mouthed.

"Rissa," Mercy growled.

"Rissa?" Walker echoed.

"Yes, he insists on calling me Rissa. Not sure why, but no one's ever called me that before."

"Already had that discussion," Mercy muttered.

"That's right. *He* had that discussion. Normally a discussion involves at least two parties, but his 'discussions' seem to be one-sided."

Hunter turned his head away, but his whole body shook.

Walker barked out a laugh. And Steel...

Didn't Steel put his fucking arm around her shoulders, squeeze and say, "We're used to it. Nothing new."

Rissa gave him a smile. "Frustrating, right?"

Steel winked at her. "Right."

Rissa clapped her hands together. "Okay, boys, let's get to it. Let's play some freaking poker! Maybe you'll teach me some tricks tonight."

"Fuck yeah," Brick shouted.

Not even three hours later, Rissa had the majority of the chips in front of her. She still wore her camisole and yoga pants. *Thank fuck.*

Mercy was about to lose his shirt. He'd already gambled away his boots and socks. Oh, and his fucking jeans. He sat at the table in his boxers and T-shirt wondering what the fuck happened.

Everybody else at the table was shirtless, bootless, sockless and a couple of them were lucky to still be wearing their boxers.

"Hustler," Hunter grumbled as he pushed away from the table. "Not only am I out of fucking chips, I'm down to my skivvies."

Rissa leaned over the table and, after giving everyone a healthy eyeful of her tits as she gathered the pot in the center of the table, dragged the last of the chips toward her. No wonder everyone lost. Who the fuck could concentrate with that?

"Who taught you how to play poker?" Steel asked, sitting back in his chair, his thick arms crossed over his bare chest. He only wore a pair of jeans. They were all lucky because he'd stated if he lost those, he wasn't wearing anything underneath them. Mercy wasn't about to play poker with Steel's junk hanging out.

Rissa lifted a shoulder and smiled. "I only played in college."

Bullshit. She was a card shark. She had played them all.

She reached for the three-quarters empty wine bottle that now sat near her elbow to fill her once again empty glass. Before she could snag it, Mercy did and put it out of her reach.

"You've had enough," he grumbled. "Ain't carrying you upstairs like last night."

Everyone's ears perked up. He also didn't miss the looks shared between all the men. He might as well grab a vat of lotion since his ass was going to be thoroughly ridden raw.

"I'm out, anyway," Brick sighed. He leaned toward Rissa. "Unless you *do* want to see that big gun I was talking about."

Rissa sat back and her gaze roamed around the table. "You guys are probably good with guns. You're all wearing dog tags."

At least she wasn't falling for Brick's not-so-subtle sexual innuendoes.

"I'm much better than them," Brick said with a grin. "Former Navy Seal sniper."

Jesus fuck, since the flirting wasn't working, he was now attempting to impress her.

"Is that how you all met? In the Navy?"

"Fuck no," Steel answered. "I'm a Marine. I ain't no pansy Navy or Army like the rest of these fucks."

"Pansy. Right," Walker barked. "Night Stalkers are no fucking pansies. We can fly *and* shoot. Plus, blow shit up."

Rissa tilted her head as she studied Walker. "Night Stalkers?"

"Airborne," Steel added. Mercy swore the man's chest puffed up like a fucking peacock's tail.

"Green Beret," Hunter announced, catching Rissa's attention. "The rest of the branches don't got shit on us Army men. True soldiers."

Brick snorted and shook his head. "Yeah, I can shoot a fucking grape off your head from a mile away."

"Maybe we should test that," Mercy muttered.

Rissa turned her bright blue eyes to him. "And you?"

"Just a simple Sergeant Major in the Army. A grunt. Nothing exciting like the rest of these assholes," Mercy grumbled.

"Somehow I don't believe that," she murmured, her gaze landing on the chain around his neck that held his dog tags, which were hidden under his tee. "Not with those scars."

Of course she went and made that plural so the men once again shared glances now knowing she saw the scars on his back, too. He was royally fucked.

"Hey, I got shot. Twice," Hunter announced like he was proud of it, standing up and pointing to the gunshot wound that had healed into a thick, puckered scar on his left lower side. "That's one. Wanna see the other one?" He gave her a toothy grin.

"She don't wanna see your fucking pussy-assed wounds," Walker grumbled.

"Think we're done here," Mercy forced out between gritted teeth.

Brick shot him a grin across the table. "Don't wanna compare war wounds, *Sarge*? You got us all beat with that ugly-assed puss of yours."

While the crew normally rode each other hard, he didn't want the night to go down the shitter quickly in front of Rissa.

Things could get crude and rude real fast. Sometimes it even got physical. Though, they never held grudges afterward, *thank fuck*, because in the end they were a team. Once tempers cooled, they shook it off and moved forward.

No matter what, they all had each other's six, like it should be when complete trust was needed.

Brothers for life.

That's why they all worked for Diesel. Unlike their boss, D's Shadows all came from highly specialized military backgrounds and were extremely loyal to each other. But it was a brotherhood just like an MC, and Diesel understood the need to have each other's back. D's club brothers had each other's six the same way, with the same type of fierce loyalty.

Though, when it came to their women and children, it was even more intense. And that might surprise a lot of people on the outside looking in.

You didn't fuck with a biker's family. Blood or otherwise.

He watched his own "brothers" rise from the table, gather their missing clothes and pull them back on.

Brick was still trying to work Rissa with his charm, taking his time and making a show out of pulling up his jeans. Acting like he was struggling to tuck his dick in because it was too big. It wasn't.

"...your number."

Mercy caught the last of what Brick was saying. Did he just ask Rissa for her number?

"She don't have her cell phone," he announced, like Brick was going to care. Mercy pushed away from the table and stood.

Rissa made an exaggerated sad face, and that was goddamn cute, too. "No, I don't. The boss says I'm not allowed to have any outside contact. Even with my sister."

"You got a sister?" Hunter asked, jerking his T-shirt over his head.

"Yes, Londyn lives out here on the east coast. She's probably worried why I haven't called her in the past couple days."

"She'll get over it," Mercy grumbled as he pulled on his own jeans.

Rissa rolled her eyes.

Brick smirked. "Still... If you give me your number, next time I'm in Vegas we could hook up. Get a drink or something."

Or something. "No." Mercy grabbed both overflowing

ashtrays and dumped them into the nearby trashcan as Walker collected the playing cards.

He grabbed the remaining wine and the half-kicked bottle of Jack, shoving the whiskey at Steel as he left. Mercy did not want that shit left behind.

He'd be too tempted to hit it and he was on a job.

He was on a job, he reminded himself once more.

And that job was in the middle of flirting with Brick.

For fuck's sake.

Chapter Eight

Why did Mercy care if she gave her number to Brick? The guy was way more personable than him. He said they wouldn't be having sex again, so what was the big deal?

And this Brick was hot. Like *smoking* hot. Like her panties might have become a little damp type of hot. If she was wearing any. Which she wasn't.

"Want me to call your sister for you? Let her know you're okay?"

"No," Mercy said again, shooting Brick a look. "Phone might be bugged."

Brick stared at him for a minute, his face becoming way too serious for Parris's liking. "That bad?"

Mercy gave him a sharp nod. "Yeah."

Her sister's phone might be bugged? She felt the blood drain from her face. "Is my sister in danger?"

"Just precautionary."

"That's not what it sounds like. Does Michael know?"

"He's got an eye on her. She'll be fine."

Holy crap! Did her sister even know someone was watching over her? Of course, she didn't. She was just going about her life, clueless that she could be in danger. "Ryan..."

Brick's head snapped around, his blue eyes slid from Parris to Mercy and back, then he scraped fingers through his hair.

With a frown, Mercy pointed a finger at her. "Stay here and listen this time." Then he jerked his chin at Brick and they both headed toward the front door, which slammed a few seconds later.

Parris pursed her lips and stared at the deserted table. Brick had been the last to leave, but the table wasn't empty. It was a disaster area. Spilled cigar ashes, ring marks on the table from beer cans, dirty glasses, and her large pile of chips remained behind, among crumbs from some of the snacks they'd been eating.

Plus, the room still reeked of cigar. With a sigh, she pushed the slider open farther and stepped out onto the large, wide furniture-free deck.

The cloudless night was still a little too warm, and since there were no nearby neighbors and the deck faced a patch of undeveloped woods, when she looked up she could see a million bright stars.

She wondered where her sister was at that very moment. Maybe even looking at the same stars. She was Londyn's rock. To be cut off from her younger sister... And worse, unknowingly put her in harm's way...

She worried.

She had left the slider open to air out the house a little, even though the air conditioning was running. Maybe it would push some of that acrid smell out. She felt sorry for the new owners. Hopefully they didn't mind the horrible stink of cigars.

She didn't hear him, but instead sensed his presence behind her. It still amazed her that a man that big could move so quietly.

"Where'd you learn to play poker?"

While he wasn't touching her, he was so close his heat

still seared her back. Her nipples tightened and her pussy clenched hard. She had no idea why. He was miserable and emotionally unavailable and didn't even want to have a little sex for fun. *And* she just spent the evening with four other very handsome, muscular, almost-naked men who probably would've been more than willing.

At least she had plenty of fodder for her date with her vibrator later.

Hell, she might not even need her vibrator if he wasn't such a Debbie Downer. *Womp, womp.*

She sighed. "College. Though, Michael taught me to excel at it. When he was old enough he became a dealer at one of the older casinos up on Freemont Street. That's where he got the start to his empire."

"As a poker dealer?"

Did he really care? And if not, why was he pretending to be interested? "Black Jack. The man was on a mission to become a somebody. And he did." Michael was a driven man. He worked his way up from almost living on the streets to owning several successful casinos. He was a true rags-to-riches story. However, now she knew it wasn't only hard work that helped him rise to the top.

"A somebody who ended up in bed with the wrong folk."

She couldn't argue that. Unfortunately.

She turned and leaned against the railing. The light from the kitchen through the open doorway illuminated only one side of his scarred face making him look not only dangerous, but brutal.

Like a cold-blooded killer.

Neither said a word for a few minutes. They only stared at each other in the dark.

"You shouldn't be out here," he finally said, his voice low and rough, causing a ripple to go through her.

"I know. Rule number four hundred and fifteen. Thou shall not step outside of one's jail cell."

"Just trying to keep you safe."

"Yes, I'm your *job*. You've made that clear more than once." She tilted her head as she stared up at him. "What's with the bonus?"

"We need to get inside."

Oh no. She could be just as bossy as him. "No, you need to answer my question. You're probably used to people taking orders from you, but—"

"Rissa," he cut her off.

"What?" she huffed.

"Shut the fuck up." His order held a tinge of impatience, but it wasn't harsh. No, his tone was softer.

"What's with the bonus?" she asked again. She wasn't spineless. She wasn't going to collapse with the vapors if he got angry with her. Yes, there was an undercurrent of danger, some violence even. But for the most part, he was a man who knew how to keep his cool. There were times he could be pushed to the point of exploding, but she figured those times were few and far between.

This man liked control. Craved it.

And letting anger take over was the opposite of that.

"Get a bonus if you're still able to run that mouth of yours at the end of this job."

She pursed her lips for a few seconds as she let his words sink in. "But you get paid even if I'm not alive at the end of this job?"

"Yeah. Getting paid whether you live or die."

Damn.

"But the bonus is worth keeping you breathing."

Well, that was reassuring.

"Need to get inside. Could be eyes in the woods."

A shiver shot down Parris's spine, causing goosebumps to break out all over her body. He knew how to ruin a moment.

Womp.

Womp.

"I just needed some fresh air, but now you've creeped me out."

"Good."

Parris rolled her eyes, though she was pretty sure he couldn't see it.

With an exaggerated, very loud sigh that he certainly couldn't miss, she headed back inside with him on her heels. He slid the glass door closed, locked it, jammed a piece of wood in the bottom track, and drew the curtains closed.

"You think there's somebody out in those woods watching us?"

"No. But it got you to listen."

Her mouth dropped open and she spun on him, only to gasp as his body hit her with a force that knocked her not only backward, but the air out of her lungs. He fisted her ponytail, yanked her head back and took her mouth before she could even catch her breath.

A whimper slithered up her throat and into his mouth as his tongue tangled roughly with hers. Her eyes watered at how hard he was pulling on her hair. Her hand went automatically to his stomach and instead of pushing him away, trying to break free, she fisted her fingers into the soft, worn cotton and held him there.

He stepped forward, forcing her backward until her ass hit the table, then before she could react, he had her spun around, bent over the table, her yoga pants ripped down far enough to give him access and he was inside her with one hard thrust.

With one hand on her back, pinning her down, and the other still fisting her hair, he slammed against her over and over. The only noise in the room was their ragged breathing, his deep grunts and the slap of their skin.

While she didn't do anything to discourage him because she wanted this as much as he did, she also didn't encourage him with words or actions. She let herself be used because that's what he needed at that very moment.

This wasn't about sex; it was all about regaining control for him. Over her. Over himself. He must have been unraveling all night. And he was doing his best to gather those loose threads into some semblance of order.

Come morning, she may have bruises on her hips from the edge of the table, her scalp might be sore, but she didn't care. Hell no.

She'd never been with anyone this rough before. With someone who treated her like she was unbreakable. Never.

She needed that right now as much as he did. She'd been doing what he did naturally, what was second nature. Hiding.

She was hiding her worry, her fear, her concern over herself, for Michael. And now for her sister.

She tried to be brave. To pretend that the grave situation she was in didn't bother her.

But it did. And she couldn't ignore it any longer. The look exchanged between Brick and Mercy said it all.

"That bad?"

"Yeah."

Obviously, as all former military—and it also sounded like they were all Special Forces—these guys had seen shit, been through shit. But she had a feeling for Brick, a former Navy SEAL, a former sniper, for goodness' sake, to ask that question was telling. Then the concerned look on his face made it even more worrisome.

If Mercy thought it was "that bad," then it was way worse than she thought. Michael had kept things from her. She realized it now. Not just about her situation, but his business dealings as well. Only she never realized just how much.

Michael owed her nothing. He didn't answer to her.

He was a powerhouse in Vegas. Hell, most likely in all of

Nevada. But she didn't realize just how powerful he was. She thought it was just due to his wealth, but there was so much more behind it.

Probably things she didn't even want to know.

Only now, those things were like an octopus's tentacles, trying to reach out to touch her, wrap her up and drag her under.

As she came back to the here and now, to what was going on in that very room, on that very table, she pushed the rest of that aside.

For now.

Because now... she was getting what she asked for.

Not quite in the manner she had hoped, but maybe in the only way he could give it to her.

He was emotionally crippled. She doubted he could let himself be tender or caring. Having sex was just like any other mission he'd been on.

A means to an end.

A way to get it done. Over with. No lingering. No whispered words. No passionate kisses.

Sex, like control, was a tool for him. To cope. To keep the gunpowder that was tightly packed in that stick of dynamite from exploding.

To keep it from destroying him.

She could help him. Not just with the sex. But with disassembling that explosive device.

It would take time, persistence and caution.

He would need to not shut her down, shut her out.

But he would.

He would resist her at every turn.

However, what was happening on that table showed her that he might not be able to resist for very long.

He intrigued her.

And she was affecting him in some way, too.

His pace had slowed, their skin was no longer slapping

loudly, his grunts had softened, so she let herself relax a little more. Now he was having sex and not just taking back control.

Because he now had himself under control. Maybe just barely, but it was there.

His fingers released her hair and curled around her hip instead, supporting her. The hand on her back was no longer pressing her to the table, instead it was sliding up her spine to the back of her neck. His fingers traced the bruise on her shoulder, the one he'd left behind yesterday. Good thing it only ended up being a slight discoloration and not a bite mark, or that would have sparked a whole bunch of questions from his "team."

Questions he would've wanted to avoid.

But him touching that spot, with more tenderness than she expected, made her remember the exact moment he bit her and once again, just that memory made her clench tightly around him.

Suddenly her hips were jerked back from the edge of the table and he was free of her. But neither of them was finished. Not even close.

Would he just leave her hanging like that?

Yes, he would.

He reached down and yanked her yoga pants back up over her hips, then jerked his jeans up over his own.

He raked fingers through his hair. Fingers she swore held a tremble.

"Ryan," she whispered, searching his face. Unfortunately, it gave her nothing.

A complete blank. His eyes shuttered. His body stiff.

"Rissa, go upstairs."

She reached out to touch him, but he stepped back. "Ryan—"

"Rissa, go the fuck upstairs," he roared and spun away. His whole body heaved, and his raw voice was forced when he ordered, "Go the fuck upstairs *now.*" He turned his head, not enough to look at her, but enough so she could see his profile. A muscle flexed in his jaw. "Now!"

He needed to talk this out. He was so used to burying shit, tightly tamping it all down like that gunpowder.

But dynamite was volatile.

He needed to learn a better way to deal with his shit. Those demons he fought. Whatever they were.

But now he was shut down, closed off.

There was no point in beating her head against a wall with him.

She felt filthy. Not because of what he did, but because she'd been pinned to the dirty table. She had cigar ashes and crumbs stuck to her damp skin.

Without another word, she headed toward the stairs. She needed a shower anyway. She wasn't going upstairs because he ordered her to. *Fuck him.*

She was doing it because she needed to rinse the debris off her skin.

Womp freaking womp.

PARRIS LAID IN BED, staring up at nothing. Her room was dark. The house was quiet. She leaned over and picked up her e-reader off the nightstand where it was plugged in to charge, hit the power button and looked at the time. 2:00.

She never heard him come upstairs, but that didn't mean anything.

Hell, he could've been standing outside her door after she showered and dug out BOB, closed her eyes and finished what he'd started.

Twice. Because when she caught her breath after the first orgasm, she did one more for the hell of it.

Funny, in those fantasies, Mercy wore a smile and his

gray eyes were warm when he looked down at her and made love to her like she was the best thing since sliced bread.

Fantasy is freaking right.

Anyway, she hoped he was listening in. She didn't bother to muffle the sounds she made each time she came. In fact, she made sure she was extra loud. Nor did she care if he heard the hum of her little powerhouse of a vibrator bringing her to that point. *Twice.*

She had even considered a third time.

She thought having two orgasms would help her sleep. It didn't.

Hell, he owed her an orgasm.

At least one.

You don't start things like that, get a woman's hopes up, and then pull out and pull up your freaking jeans. Just like that. Tuck away the goods and leave her hanging.

Nope.

She blew out a breath as she touched her shoulder where the mark remained of his bite.

He owed her.

He not only cock-blocked Brick from getting her number but didn't finish what he started.

That was not acceptable.

She shoved the covers off her now overheated body and dropped her feet to the floor, staring at her closed bedroom door.

Did she dare?

He probably wasn't someone to wake up unexpectedly. He was the kind of guy who would lash out when startled from his sleep. Was it worth the risk?

She stood, left her pajama bottoms on the end of the bed where she threw them earlier, and took determined strides to the door. Yanking it open, she rushed down the dark hallway in just her panties and cami to the master bedroom on the other side of the house.

The door was wide open, and the room dark. She poked her head in and saw the bed was made up perfectly and with precision.

Figures.

But he was not in that bed.

There was no way he left the house, no way he'd leave her alone. He was too dedicated to his job. Too hungry for his "bonus," which she still had no idea just what it was. Just how much her life was worth.

However, going on a run in the daylight around the gated community was one thing, just leaving was another. Plus, it was the middle of the night in an undeveloped neighborhood. So, he didn't go out for a run.

She quietly descended the stairs. She could never be as quiet as him, though. She winced when one of the steps creaked under her weight.

Once she hit the foot of the staircase, she glanced down the hall toward the kitchen, finding it dark.

She moved to the entrance of the living room and froze.

Did he fall asleep sitting up?

He was on the couch. The room was in shadows since the only light came from a small lamp in a far corner that didn't reach the whole room.

He faced straight ahead, staring at the empty, cold brick fireplace. His hands where curled into fists as they rested on his bent knees, his feet were propped on the edge of the coffee table.

A black handgun sat in between his bare feet on the table. Within reach.

Why did he have his gun unholstered?

Was there a threat?

Or was the threat him?

Was he tortured enough that he'd thought about turning that gun on himself?

What had he seen? What the hell had he done?

His scars told one story. His mind held another.

Shutting down and shutting people out was common among soldiers who'd seen action. For military personnel who'd been front and center in war, death and destruction.

She might be a sex therapist—a career some might scoff at—but she'd seen how PTSD affected relationships. How it had torn couples and families apart. How it could even destroy intimacy with the one they loved.

PTSD affected everyone differently, every person handled it in a different way. There was no simple or easy way to deal with it.

Some went searching for a "fix," but more often than not, an easy solution was impossible. Either way, it had to be dealt with or it could destroy a person from the inside out.

Chapter Nine

He sensed her there. Hell, he heard her footsteps coming down the stairs, even though she was barefooted and trying to be quiet.

When he sat in the dark, when he tried to turn the rest of the noise off in his brain, his senses were amplified.

He was trained to hold still for hours. Keep total control of his body. When needed, he could lie in wait.

In the desert heat, under the blistering sun, in frigid temps, during torrential downpours, whatever the conditions, he'd done it all. No matter how harsh the environment, he could remain silent. Still.

Waiting for his target.

His prey.

He knew how to disable a threat just as quietly. To take out a target without anyone else aware of what was happening until it was all over, and he was gone.

Ghosted.

Being a part of a Delta Force team had taught him to blend in wherever he was. Whatever country he was in. Whatever culture. Whatever terrain.

Now, with a big fucking scar crossing his face, he was too recognizable. He caught just about everyone's attention.

While the scar was good for intimidation, that was about it. And to use it as such you had to be exposed, out in the open, facing your threat or target head on.

That was not how he liked shit to play out.

But now, he didn't have much of a choice. Disguises didn't help much since his face attracted so much unwanted attention. Unfortunately the scar tissue was thick, so even using any kind of makeup or cover-up was usually ineffective.

His career had been over before he was ready to give it up. He didn't fucking like it, but he had to accept it.

Shit happens.

But that's where that fucking sentence should stop.

"Shit happens *for a reason*" made him want to throat punch anyone who said that to him.

Her soft question, her throaty voice twisted something inside him. "Couldn't sleep?"

Hell, he didn't even try. He knew laying in his bed with his eyes closed wouldn't have brought sleep. Fuck no. There was something about Rissa that was pulling shit he'd buried so deeply long ago, to the surface. And how could he sleep when he was feeling so restless?

He'd only known the woman for two days and was now worried that if this job went for any length of time, things would only get worse for him. For her, too.

If things got worse, he'd end up being the bigger threat when it came to the job—the woman—he was supposed to protect. Not some highly paid goons belonging to a powerful, ruthless sex trafficker. One who was going head to head with *her* Michael.

How the fuck did she ever get tangled up with Paranzino in the first place?

"Why are you up?" His voice was rough, and he

wondered why he even bothered to ask. Did he really care why she was awake in the middle of the night? Or was he more bothered she had come downstairs to find him?

To poke and prod at him. Until he lost his shit again.

Hell, she was a therapist. Had a fucking Master's in Psychology, which she announced when she offered to help Kelsea, Diesel's train wreck of a cousin.

If he had known all of that before he took the job, he would have said no.

A million "fuck no's" to be more exact.

He could still demand that D swap him out with one of the other guys. Not Brick, though. Fuck that.

Fucking motherfucker. Not any of them, because not one of those assholes would say no to lying between her soft thighs. Fucking her against the wall. On a kitchen table. On a center island counter.

Or on the living room floor in front of a cold fireplace in the middle of the night.

Fuck.

Just thinking of Brick or Steel, or any of them, sticking their dick in her made him want to smash shit.

He shouldn't care. He really fucking shouldn't.

And it irritated the fuck out of him that he did.

Women were trouble. And a woman who was also a therapist? Double fucking whammy.

He had a perfectly good reason to fuck a woman only once. He was not a project. He was not a broken fucking vase they needed to glue back together.

Sex needed to remain just that, sex. An activity tied to a bodily function that relieved the load in his balls when he got sick of his own fist.

However, earlier, after pulling out before either of them finished, he hadn't even resorted to self-help. Not like Rissa had.

As he listened to her taking care of business upstairs

without him, it took everything he had not to take those steps two at a time and finish what they'd started on the table.

Or what he'd started.

When he realized what he was doing, how he had manhandled her, he stopped immediately. He already had hurt her once when he bit her the first time they fucked.

He didn't hurt women. He fucking disposed of people who hurt women.

While she hadn't mentioned the bruise and she didn't tell him to stop when he took her forcefully on the table...

It wasn't fucking right.

This woman shouldn't be taken like some street whore in a back alley. She might be close friends with a man who didn't deserve her, but she was no trick like he originally thought.

She was intelligent and successful, and she was well-off because she'd built all of that herself. She was no gold digger. That was clear when he dug deeper into her background once he found out about her occupation.

She didn't need a man.

Not for money. And apparently, from what he heard earlier, not to orgasm.

The woman was self-sufficient. And while he liked that, he didn't like the idea of getting involved with her and going down that long, dark rabbit hole.

She was a job.

Only a job.

"Shouldn't hafta say it but keep your dick outta 'er, too. Got me?"

He'd already broken his own rule, as well as Diesel's.

Why was she just standing there in the middle of the living room now, staring at him?

Fuck. He had asked her a question.

She probably answered and then asked him a question

and was waiting for his reply. Because that's what women did, asked too many fucking questions.

"Yeah," he grunted, because that usually covered most questions they asked favorably. If you agreed with them they were usually good with that.

She put her hands on her hips and... *Jesus fucking Christ*, he just realized she was only wearing that *about-ready-to-split-its-seams* camisole and panties!

"Yeah what?" She wrinkled her nose. And, fuck him, if that wasn't cute, too. He was never into cute. But she made cute sexy as fuck.

"If the question was if you need to put on some pants, then, yeah, you need to put on some fucking pants."

She shook her head. "That wasn't the question."

"Then, yeah, you need to go back upstairs to bed and leave me the fuck alone."

"That wasn't the question, either."

"Don't matter what the question was, that's my answer."

There was a long pause filled with awkward silence.

"You owe me."

His nostrils flared as she stepped closer. His heart began to thump as he sat up straighter and dropped his feet to the floor when she pushed the coffee table out of the way.

What the fuck. He watched his loaded weapon slide out of reach.

However, that wasn't the only fucking loaded weapon in the room.

His dick was now on the rise once more. Especially when she took one more step forward to stand in between his spread thighs. She even kneed them open a little farther to make room for herself. The fuck if she didn't.

He would have to tilt his head up to look at her. But he kind of liked staring straight ahead at her panties. In the limited light, he guessed they could be nylon. They weren't a sexy, expensive kind, either. Just plain ol' panties she must've pulled on after pulling one off. Or two. Or however many orgasms she had when she was howling like an injured cat upstairs.

She probably had a lot of practice with that toy she called BOB.

"What do I owe you?" he stupidly asked in a murmur, curling his fingers tighter into his palms to fight from touching her. To fight from checking whether those panties *were* made out of nylon.

She had showered after the earlier table sex SNAFU. But she hadn't showered again after the date with her vibrator, which meant he could pick up the resulting musky scent of a woman's orgasm.

It wouldn't take much effort to lean forward and press his nose to the soft mound that was covered by that thin fabric.

It wouldn't take much to yank those panties down and put his mouth to her there. To taste what remained after she came at least twice.

It wouldn't take much to slide his fingers through her soft, plump folds and check to see if she was still wet and responsive.

He only had sex with women once. Then he was done.

He had Rissa once. Almost twice.

There should be no third time.

Fucking her again would be like quicksand. He'd get stuck and slowly get pulled under until he couldn't escape. Until he suffocated. Drowned.

This job shouldn't last long. With a little willpower, he could resist her for another night or two. At least until he could break free and go on the hunt for some nameless, random snatch in a bar somewhere. Hell, at a fucking grocery store. A single mother just looking to blow off some steam in the backseat of her minivan in a dark parking lot.

Fuck the freak for a thrill, then go home and feed the kids.

That was fine with him.

When Rissa reached out, he didn't catch his flinch in time.

His lungs seized, and he stopped breathing when she slowly traced his facial scar with the tip of her finger. From the top edge at his hairline to the very bottom, ending at the corner of his lip.

He didn't know why he allowed her to do it.

He shouldn't.

Especially with the expression she was wearing. Full of care and concern. The soft look to her eyes unmistakable. Her lips slightly parted. Her breath smelled faintly like mint toothpaste.

Fuck.

He snagged her wrist and pulled it away from what she did next, which was running her thumb across his lips. By her doing so, it allowed her to gauge his reaction to her touch since his breathing had become ragged.

Whatever she wanted from him, whatever he "owed" her, he couldn't give her.

Nor did he want to.

Because to give her anything opened himself up. She was looking for a way in, the slightest crack. And once she found that crack, she was going to pick at it until he was cut wide open and his guts spilled out of that gaping wound.

That could never happen.

He could easily snap her wrist within his fingers, so he released her abruptly. "Step back."

She shook her head again. She no longer looked cute. No, now she looked fucking determined. "No. You owe me."

"Don't owe you shit."

"Sex shouldn't scare you."

"It's not the sex..." he trailed off. It wasn't the sex that worried him, it was all that went along with it. For a woman, it tended to be more than just about the act.

"Tonight it would only be sex. Nothing more."

"Bullshit," he growled.

She lifted a bare shoulder. "How about if I promise you that?"

"Not sure I would believe you."

"You said you had sex with a woman a couple days before you went out to Vegas. Were you planning on seeing her again?"

For fuck's sake, she was good. She knew how to ask an obvious question to get the hidden answer she really wanted.

He wasn't falling for that, either. "No."

"Why?"

He gritted his teeth. When you can't sneak in the back door, just walk through the front. *Fucking goddamn.*

"Because you probably don't want to make a deep connection with anyone and seeing someone on a regular basis, or even more than once or twice, would threaten that, right?"

He needed to push her away, get the fuck off that couch, head upstairs into the master bedroom and lock her the fuck out.

He needed to get her out of his view, out of his head, out of his life. She could easily destroy him. "Don't need my sex life analyzed."

"I'm just making an observation."

Yeah, right. Sure she was. "You're a fucking sex therapist. When my dick can't stand up, then help me fix it. But anything else? I don't want fixed."

"I might be a sex therapist, but, like I told you, I have a master's degree in psychology, Ryan."

Fuck me. He never should have slipped and told her his name. He already fucked up one too many times on this job.

He was slipping. This was supposed to be a simple and quick job for a boatload of cash.

The curvy, outspoken woman standing in between his thighs in just panties and a camisole was not making this simple.

Not at fucking all.

He needed to shut this shit down now.

"And I'm a master at fucking death and dying."

Her brows knitted together. "Are you trying to scare me?"

"Fuck yes." He met her gaze directly. "Are you scared?"

"No." Her eyes steadily held his and she now looked more determined than ever. That did not bode well for him.

"You should be."

"Why?"

Because you don't want to peel away the layers, woman. You don't. You might have nightmares for the rest of your fucking life if you do.

He had done shit, seen shit, the rest of the Shadows didn't even know about. Shit that would never pass his lips, and not because it was classified information, either.

"Rissa, you need to go back upstairs."

"No, I'm not going upstairs because you said so. I'm staying right here until I get what you owe me."

"Jesus fucking Christ," he muttered under his breath. "What do I owe you?"

"Two orgasms. Two." She emphasized the number by lifting two fingers up. "Normally, I'd say one would suffice. But no, after you left me hanging earlier, I want two. I'm sure you can muster through paying me what you owe me."

This woman was bat-shit crazy. He should've let Brick have her.

He kept his expression blank when he asked, "Is there any particular way you want payment made?"

"Whatever you're good at."

He flattened his lips because he almost smiled at that.

Almost. It was a close call. He finally let himself touch her by pressing his palms to her hips then sliding them around to grab her ass. He ran a finger over the nylon (he was right) fabric at her ass crack. “Anything?”

“Not that. You’d have to be *really* skilled at that to make me orgasm that way and I doubt you’re that good. In fact, from what I’ve experienced so far, I know you’re not good enough to make that worth my while.”

His head snapped back, and he stared up at her. *Say what?*

With a growl, he surged up, was on his feet, and not a second later all the oxygen whooshed out of her lungs as she landed on her back on the couch.

He had her panties ripped down her thighs, her knees shoved into her chest and his mouth on her clit before she probably knew what hit her.

Her hips shot off the couch and she cried out as he sucked her hard. With two fingers in a V, he spread her open and tasted the results of her earlier orgasms.

Fuck, that shit could be addicting.

Whatever you’re good at.

He would show her how good he was with his mouth on her pussy. For once, he cared more about the woman coming than his own release.

She wanted two? She was getting at least four.

She didn’t think he could make her orgasm when he fucked her ass?

That sounded like a challenge.

Then it hit him.

Just like the poker game, she played him. She knew exactly how to get what she wanted.

She was a natural-born hustler. She was skilled with manipulation.

And he, fucking fool that he was, fell for it.

But if she thought she had the upper-hand, she was so dead wrong.

He was onto her.

He could turn this around in his favor. He was used to making himself impenetrable. He'd been an expert at it for so long, it came naturally.

So she could scratch at his barriers with those long painted nails of hers, but she wasn't getting farther than the outer edge. He would only give her what he wanted her to see. Which wasn't much.

But she might give up if he tricked her into thinking that she was successful.

Fuck yeah, that would be the plan.

Give her what she thought he "owed" her. Also let her think she was getting a peek inside. Then shut her the fuck out.

Once this job was over, her ass was getting back on a plane back to Vegas and *her Michael.*

She'd be none the wiser.

Plus, he'd end up with a nice bump in his bank account.

He needed to pay attention to what he was doing if he was giving her at least four orgasms. Though, he must be doing what he was doing good enough for her. If his hair was any longer, she'd be ripping it out of his head. Instead, she had a hold of his ears and was holding them like handles.

Fuck. His ears needed to stay attached to his head.

He knocked her hands off, then lifted it just enough to order, "Top off. Now."

He went back to sucking on her clit and flicking it with his tongue as she scrambled to raise her upper body enough to peel off that camisole. He lifted his eyes and met hers once she was naked. Then he grinned against her pussy at how she had obeyed.

Luckily, she'd never see that grin since he kept his lips busy on hers.

Sliding two fingers inside her, he was not surprised how wet she was. There was no doubt she liked sex... good sex... and wasn't ashamed about it one bit.

He groaned silently as her fingers slid to both of her nipples and she began to tweak and twist.

Oh... fuck... yeah...

There was not an uptight bone in her body. She oozed sex. She exuded confidence.

This woman enjoyed a good fuck and an even better orgasm.

And he was going to give her both.

Two when he was eating her, two when he was fucking her.

Finding her G-spot, he stroked it until she clenched around his fingers, and her core began to convulse. Peering up her body, he noticed her head was thrown back, her mouth open, her fingers twisting her peaked nipples at a feverish pace. She bucked and wailed his name.

His name.

The name no one who knew it used.

And before the ripples of her muscles ceased, he slipped his fingers free. Making sure that they were slick with her wetness, he trailed them down her pussy and before she could stop him, if she even wanted to stop him, he took her ass with his long middle finger.

She gasped and then groaned as he worked his finger in and out of her. Feeling how tight she was. Feeling how hot. His mind spun as he imagined his dick replacing his finger instead.

She didn't think he could make her come like this. He was about to prove her wrong.

With one hand continuing its sensual assault on her ass, his mouth busy on her sweet, sweet pussy, he blindly reached up and knocked one of her hands off her tit. He snagged her tightly beaded nipple between his fingers and twisted.

Since she wasn't gagged, she was capable of telling him when, and if, it was too much. Until then, this was his time to show her how wrong she was.

He had been played, she was getting what she wanted.

But right now, he didn't give a shit.

All he wanted to do at that moment was to sink into her wet heat and forget everything that swirled in his brain.

Forget she was a job.

Forget that he would regret this afterward.

Forget that he was fucking a woman more than once.

Forget that he was taking that dangerous step into the quicksand.

But one thing he'd never forget, was the sound she made as she tightened around his finger, ground her pussy into his face and slammed her hand on the couch so hard that it startled him enough that his heart stopped for a second.

He squeezed his eyes shut and tried to slow his racing pulse.

He was safe. She was safe.

Even better, she was going to orgasm for the second time.

Her hips shot up again as she did just that.

Before she could recover, before she could catch her breath, before the last wave of that orgasm, he surged up off the couch, stripped himself of his clothes in record time and settled in between her soft thighs.

When he drove hard and deep inside her, a shudder went through him, not just because her pussy felt tight, and wet, and searing hot.

Fuck no. Because as his mind cleared, his senses all focused on her. The scent of her multiple orgasms, her face twisted with ecstasy, the sounds that rose deep from within her throat.

He curled over her, one palm planted in the couch cushion and his hips driving forcefully, using his knees to power deep.

He dropped his head because he needed to suck the nipple he had twisted so hard it was now puckered and swollen, deep into his mouth.

Fuck. She tasted so fucking good.

Too good.

She wasn't fast food, she was a gourmet meal.

She wasn't a quick fuck, she was a woman to savor.

She wasn't someone he'd want to kick out of bed the second he came, she was one he'd have a hard time letting go of.

She wasn't a nameless, faceless snatch; he knew her name and Rissa was someone who was complex and a challenge.

She wasn't a woman overwrought and afraid of her circumstances, she was facing it head-on.

She hadn't fallen apart, she remained brave.

And, for fuck's sake, he couldn't ask for anything more from a woman.

With a last lick at her nipple, he took her mouth, which was open, her breath hitched, but he wanted to capture the sounds she made when she came for the third time.

Once he did that, once she began to melt into the couch once more, he slowed his pace. Told himself to take his time.

Savor that gourmet meal.

Enjoy the sensuality she exuded.

Appreciate everything about the woman beneath him, the one whose little moans and mews made his chest ache. The one whose pussy fit him perfectly.

The one who responded to his touch like he wasn't simply a check box on her bucket list.

The one who kept whispering his name against his lips.

The one who wrapped her legs tightly around his hips like she never wanted to let go.

The one who saw past his outer scars to his inner ones.

The one who was the most dangerous woman of all.

He needed to fight the pull of that quicksand.

Otherwise, he was fucked.

Chapter Ten

He was spooked and trying desperately not to show it. But she could feel it in the tension of his body as they laid on the couch together. Sticking around with a woman after having sex most likely went against the very fiber of his being. He probably itched from it.

She wanted to turn within his arms to face him, but every time she tried, he tightened his arm around her and forced her to remain where she was. Which was him lying on his side wedged between her and the back of the couch, her back pressed to his chest.

Admittedly, her ass settled nicely against his hips. Perfectly, in fact.

Even so, she was surprised he hadn't bolted from the couch yet. After her fifth—*yes, fifth*—orgasm, and after he came deep inside her—again, surprising her that he hadn't pulled out before doing so—she expected him to jump to his feet, give her a chin lift, an *oorah,* maybe a two-finger salute and then head upstairs to his bedroom, slamming the door shut, and even locking it.

He didn't.

After he came inside her, he remained deeply seated

within her, had pressed his forehead to hers, their panting the only sound in the room. In fact, he stayed that way for so long, she began to worry.

She wondered if he'd had a mental break, if something had snapped inside him during the sex that, she had to admit, was freaking awesome.

Of course it was awesome, she had orgasmed *five times*.

But then, he was the type of man that when you threw the gauntlet on the table, he was hard pressed not to pick it up and accept that challenge. And, of course, exceed it just to prove a point.

So, he had added a few extra orgasms onto the two she demanded. Which made her appreciate his drive to succeed.

Normally, she'd find it amusing that she'd gotten what she wanted out of him if she wasn't so worried about his psyche right now.

This man was not typical in any sense of the word.

She had to remind herself that he could potentially be a ticking time bomb.

Facing away from him, she couldn't read his expression —if he even had one—or his eyes. She only could read his body language. Which was stiff.

And she wasn't talking about his cock, either. No, that was now soft and warm against her ass. His steady breath blew across her ear, making a strand of her hair tickle her cheek.

They could be any couple in Anywhere, USA, right now who had just had spontaneous sex on their living room couch.

But they were far from that.

She'd only known him for a couple of days and she trusted him. She probably shouldn't. He could end up being more dangerous than the individuals who shot Michael's men in the back of the head without hesitation.

Pop. Pop. Pop.

She squeezed her eyes shut as that scene played out in her head once again.

How many times had Mercy killed someone just like that, without a thought, and simply walked away?

Did she even want to know?

Some people could take a life and it never affected them. Or at least, on the surface it seemed like it didn't affect them. After a while that had to rot a person from the inside out.

Unless they were a psychopath. Someone who lacked any type of empathy at all.

She didn't think he was like that. He was compensating for something by keeping himself distant and closed off.

He'd built a wall of protection.

She knew the signs to look for. She caught it when his face would change, his eyes would melt from their normally icy appearance, before he would quickly rebuild that stone divider again, shutting everyone out.

She was sure he was dedicated to his job, to his boss, to his team. He wasn't a complete loner. Though, he most likely preferred it.

Her gaze slid to the gun on the coffee table that was out of reach. She never owned one, never shot one, was never against anyone having one until she saw the effect it had on someone's cranium up close and personal.

Even so, she would rather die quickly with a shot to the back of the head than be tortured. Get it over quick-like, not slow and dragged out while begging to die.

That had her wondering about his scars. Had he been captured and tortured? Had he been in a fight for his life?

She couldn't imagine him being sloppy enough to allow himself to be in a situation like that. It was on the tip of her tongue to ask, but she knew he wouldn't answer.

She was probably a double threat to him.

Not only a woman—a potential noose around his neck

—but a therapist. Someone he'd think would push him to tighten that noose, throw it over a tree branch and kick the stool out from underneath himself.

She had no doubt he'd be a man who would die before exposing his secrets. His failures. His weaknesses.

He might not realize it, but that didn't make him strong, that made him vulnerable. It was better to face failures and weaknesses head-on instead of keeping them hidden where, if exposed, could be used as a weapon.

However, right now they were on a couch in a living room in the middle of somewhere called Shadow Valley, and he wasn't on her couch in her office back in Vegas.

He didn't want help and would resist any effort if she tried to give it to him.

She wasn't sure how long they'd be holed up in this house. But for the time they were, she'd do what she could and try not to be too obvious about it.

He needed to be handled like an untrusting stray cat. She could put out a dish of food and stand closer to that dish every day until, maybe, the cat would let her pet him. Even just a quick stroke of a tail or a scratch behind the ears.

She glanced down to where his heavily muscled arm circled her middle and fought her grin. He'd probably hate that she compared him to a feral kitty. He undoubtedly likened himself to a mature lion who was a protective leader of a large pride, not afraid to use his deadly claws and teeth.

She started when his soft, but rumbling, words came unexpectedly, and he tightened his embrace.

"I don't apologize for anything I do. Instead, I own it. I fucking own it. When I do wrong, I fucking admit it. I don't coat it with bullshit like 'I'm sorries.'"

She remained quiet, because he wasn't done. Clearly, he needed to get out whatever he needed to say without interruption. From experience, she knew to stay silent and simply listen.

His next words surprised her, though. They were raw and an emotion existed behind them that twisted her gut.

This was not the type of guy who did "emotions." Why now?

"I did you wrong, Rissa. Did you fucking wrong."

He did? Why would he think that? She couldn't remain silent anymore. He was beating himself up about something. Something she needed to correct him on. She placed a hand on his forearm and squeezed. "How?"

She thought he might not answer, because he'd be opening himself up to her. So she didn't prod him, she simply waited patiently.

"That bruise on your shoulder. The way I took you in there," his body jerked behind her, "on the table. It was wrong."

Oh no, not for the reason he thought. The only thing that was wrong with what happened in the next room earlier was him pulling out and leaving her hanging. "And the way you took me here?"

"Not sorry for that, either."

"Good. You shouldn't be. That was freaking amazing."

Suddenly, he relaxed against her. Or at least relaxed as much as a man like him could. But it was something. A step forward quite possibly.

Maybe she could keep him talking. She wanted to know about his scars, but she had to work up to that. Start somewhere simple.

"Don't you agree?" she asked carefully.

"Freaking amazing," he echoed her, almost in a Neanderthal grunt. Like he was proud of himself.

"Don't worry, I'll let you know if you're hurting me. You weren't. I enjoyed it. Even when you got rough." *Especially when you got rough.* "I'm not into erotic asphyxiation or anything, so just don't choke me out. But otherwise...?" She let that hang out there between them.

"Not supposed to be fucking you."

"Yes, well... that horse left the stable."

"Shouldn't be fucking you without a condom."

That steed galloped out of the barn and kicked his heels up while doing so. "Yes, well... That's stupid on both of our parts. But again... too late. So, it is what it is." She winced. *Ugh*, she hated that saying. It was such a Band-Aid phrase.

"Your Michael didn't stock the house with them because he didn't plan on me fucking you."

She sighed. "Will you please stop calling him *my* Michael?"

"He'd probably be pissed."

"I doubt he would care. He doesn't monitor my vagina. He doesn't even like vaginas."

Parris heard him make a noise which may have been a snort or a curse or a combination of the two. She smiled.

Uh huh. He had a sense of humor in there somewhere. He wasn't as dead inside, or as cold, as he wanted people to believe.

"I like vaginas," he stated matter-of-factly after a minute.

"I hope so, since I have one." She twisted in his arms and this time he let her turn enough to face him. "And I have to say, you did all right with it."

They were practically nose to nose as his gray eyes met hers. "You said the sex was 'freaking amazing.' Exact quote."

Ah, he was proud of his sexual prowess. "Well, sometimes I exaggerate in the heat of the moment."

"It wasn't the heat of the moment."

"In the afterglow, then. I really won't know for sure how freaking amazing sex is with you until I get a good sampling and can average out the results."

"How many times do I have to fuck you to get a *good sampling*?"

"Oh, I don't know... a dozen?"

Did his lips twitch?

"But also, a good variety is needed. To get the complete picture."

"I see," he answered, his voice low and deep.

Did he actually purr? Heat rushed through her and landed in her core, making her insides clench.

Here, kitty, kitty.

Now she just needed to try for a quick scratch behind the ears.

His head jerked back when she traced her fingertip along his facial scar. Since he was wedged between her and the couch, he couldn't escape her touch. She expected him to grab her hand and stop her again. But he didn't. Instead, he stared at her, his nostrils flaring slightly. His gaze was so intense, she avoided it, her eyes following her finger as she moved down over his forehead, over the line of missing hair at his eyebrow, across his nose. Once she got to the bottom, she whispered, "How did you get your scars?"

THIS WAS the second time she touched him like that. If he was smart, he'd roll her out of his way, get off the couch and go upstairs. She was too close.

Way too close for his liking.

She seemed fascinated by his scar. It didn't gross her out. It didn't turn her off.

But it was a story he wasn't sure he wanted to tell. Especially to a woman he'd only met a couple days ago.

She lifted her gaze to his, her sky-blue eyes once again way too warm, too curious.

The woman was persistent. That was easy to see.

Because if she wasn't persistent, then they wouldn't both be naked on the couch, her legs tucked between his, his arm wrapped around her to keep her from tumbling to the floor and, more importantly, her pussy full of his cum.

Two broken rules now.

He fucked her more than once.

He didn't use a condom.

He was on a fucking roll.

And if he told her the story of how he got his scars, he might as well crack open his little pink diary, the one he wrote in with purple ink and made little hearts over the i's.

"Combat," slipped past his lips. That wasn't telling her anything she didn't know. The dog tags he still wore, which he considered his lucky rabbit's foot, made it obvious he was former military, even if they hadn't discussed it while playing poker. So, that was no secret and his simple answer might satisfy her curiosity.

Or not.

"Hand-to-hand combat," he clarified, not that he needed to.

Her warm fingers trailed down his throat, dipped into the hollow at the base then continued following the path of the metal chain. She found his tags which had been sandwiched between his chest and her tits and lifted them. "What were you fighting over?"

She didn't study them; she didn't read them. Her thumb brushed back and forth absently over the raised lettering. Why was that getting him hard again?

Possibly because those tags were a part of him. They were who he used to be. They were what made him who he was now.

They were also a reminder.

With zero interest in college, from eighteen on, the Army had been his life, his focus. It gave him a structure and purpose he longed for which had been missing during his childhood.

He ended up *living* for that shit. He also would have died for that shit. But not willingly.

It was in his blood and when he was forced out due to his injuries, and for his mental state at the time, he had nothing.

Absolutely fucking nothing.

He'd never felt so fucking lost.

He no longer had a purpose.

Nothing to live for.

He was not wired to live a normal civilian life. He wasn't going to find a good woman, put a ring on her finger, and give her babies. Buy a house, work a nine to five, save for retirement so him and the missus could travel.

Fuck that.

After his discharge, he'd been courted by a private military company and after some negotiation, he was about to accept the offer and go back to the locations he knew best, where he knew the people and cultures inside and out, when Hunter approached him. Fresh out of the Army himself, restless and looking for action, he'd stumbled across a small town in Pennsylvania named Shadow Valley. A town full of a motorcycle club called the Dirty Angels. It just so happened that their enforcer, Diesel, was looking for some heavy hitters to work for him. Men who weren't afraid to get their hands dirty. Men who were skilled enough to take out threats in any manner necessary without getting caught.

Men who also had no problem taking out a rival MC because of the heinous shit they'd done and the threats to the DAMC women. And now children.

Mercy instantly liked Diesel the first time he met him. The man didn't give two shits about what was in Mercy's file. He didn't give a shit what Mercy did in his past. He didn't chit-chat like a couple of women sitting around drinking tea. He was direct, to the point, and took no bullshit.

He also didn't mind getting his own hands dirty when needed.

And he had no qualms when giving the order to take a life in order to save another's.

Diesel was fiercely loyal to his brotherhood and Mercy respected that.

By working for D, he wouldn't be working under any bullshit rules that went along with a contracted military company. He'd answer to no one except D. No one would be sitting in a bullshit boardroom somewhere safe in the States while he was putting his ass on the line out in some desert, sweating his balls off and trying not to eat a bullet.

It was a no-brainer. The money was good, and with the team D built after weeding out some pussies he'd previously hired for bullshit work—like being bouncers at bars—his reputation grew. And grew rapidly simply by word-of-mouth. His "security" business became known to the people who needed the job done quickly and efficiently without blowback. His clients had money and paid well for what they needed.

Even so, there were always jobs D turned down. He usually didn't discuss them. Sometimes if it was questionable, he'd call a meeting and run it past the Shadows first. They all had a line they wouldn't cross. D knew what those were, for the most part, for each of them. But he still respected his crew enough to run it past them if he was on the fence.

That's when he noticed Rissa's eyebrows were furrowed.

Fuck. She had asked a question again and he never answered.

He wasn't used to this shit. This question and answer kind of thing with a woman. Normally, the less they talked, the better.

What was the damn question again?

Oh, right. She wanted to know what he was fighting about when he was almost fatally injured. Hell, that answer was simple. "My life. Asshole wanted to take it and I wanted to keep it."

Her brow stayed wrinkled. "Well, you apparently won."

Mercy grunted. "That I did."

Her eyes traced his scar again slowly, then paused on his lips. "Does he look worse than you?"

Does he look worse than you?

Maybe the scar bothered her more than he originally thought.

"By now, I'd say so." He left it at that. He didn't think it was wise to tell her that he unarmed him by taking the man's own knife and sinking it deep into his soft belly, sawing it upward until he was filleted like a fish. No, he'd keep that to himself.

Especially since a lot of females were squeamish.

He also wouldn't tell her how his own face looked filleted open. How he attempted to sew the two halves together himself with a dirty needle and some thread he normally carried on missions until he could get medical attention, which wasn't for another eight hours. Or so he'd been told. He hadn't stayed conscious long enough to watch the time.

Fuck no, telling her all of that would be completely unnecessary.

"Does it bother you?" *Goddamn it.* Why the fuck did he even care?

"What?"

"The scar."

"No, not at all. It tells a story."

Yeah, not a pleasant one. And that *story* was the beginning of the end for him. A story he had *what if'd* to death.

"You need to talk about it."

"No, I don't."

"Ryan," she began.

His jaw tightened and he frowned. "Past is the past." Unless you couldn't let it go.

"The past shapes your future. Your past is holding you back."

Her words reminded him of what he told Jazz. *"What we experience throughout our life makes us who we are. Good or bad. It shapes us. No one needs to be fixed. We just need to embrace who we are and how we ended up that way. Every situation we survive makes us stronger. It teaches us how to deal with the next one."*

"I'm doing just fine."

She pressed a palm over his heart. "On the surface. At least, you want people to believe that. You have an expensive SUV on steroids, but what else do you have? Family? Friends?"

"Got brothers."

"You mean your team? The men you work with?"

"They're more than that."

"Are they?"

Yeah, they were. His fellow Shadows, along with Diesel... There wasn't a group of men he trusted more to be at his back. It was the way it should be with any kind of true brotherhood.

"Are you done?" he asked.

No, she wasn't done. She wouldn't be done until she cracked him open and poked around inside. If she was wise, she'd stop trying to do that, because she might regret what she finds.

"Yes, I'm done."

He lifted his gaze from where her hand was over his heart. From where her tits were pressed against his chest.

She was done? His eyes narrowed. Was this a trick?

"As much as I enjoyed having sex on this couch, I'd prefer it in a bed where I'm not worried about crashing to the floor and getting a concussion."

"It's the middle of the night, you don't want to go upstairs and get some sleep?"

She pursed her lips and tilted her head. "Mmm, no. I'd rather go upstairs and have sex again. It's not like I have anything pressing tomorrow—unless Michael calls and says it's safe for me to come back home—so I can sleep in. You'll just have to deal with the cook making you a late breakfast."

"Of steak and eggs." He had spotted some fat steaks in the fridge.

She bit her bottom lip and the corners of her eyes crinkled. He wanted to bite that bottom lip for her.

"Of steak and eggs. No ketchup allowed, though, or you'll insult the cook."

"Gotta have ketchup. It's the American way."

She *mmm*'d with a look of disgust. "And you are a patriot, right?"

"You mean the missile? Yeah, I got a missile."

She rolled her eyes and laughed. "Well, let's go launch that missile."

And didn't he follow her naked ass up those steps and have sex with her for the fourth and fifth time?

Amazingly enough, not once did he have a failure to launch.

Chapter Eleven

PARRIS'S EYES popped open and it took her a few seconds to figure out where she was. She rolled to her side and stared at the empty side of the bed.

Of course. Because one, the man didn't sleep regularly. And two, she couldn't imagine he'd sleep all night, or even a partial night, with any woman.

No, that would go against his grain.

She didn't even bother to look for a note. Since he answered to no one, leaving a message about where he went would be a completely foreign idea to him.

The sneakers she had noticed when they had come upstairs hours ago—because they had been tucked *too* neatly in the corner of the room and lined up against the wall—were missing, but his perfectly aligned black boots remained.

Which meant he'd probably went for a run. She sat up with a groan, because although the sex had been freaking awesome, they'd had a lot of it and her body wasn't used to it, even if it had been sweet or gentle. Which it wasn't.

She was sore in places she hadn't been sore in for a very long time.

That made her smile, but it quickly turned upside down when she wondered what time it was.

Scrambling out of bed, she hurried over to the window, peeked between the drawn curtains and saw the sun was up. Since it wasn't too high in the sky, that was a good sign it was probably late morning.

She wondered how long she had before he returned, which got her wheels turning. She dashed naked down the hall to get dressed and was thankful nobody had witnessed that maneuver.

If she was ever going to get a message to her sister, now was the time. Even if Londyn was being bugged, Parris could at least send a text from a borrowed phone, just to let her younger sister know she was okay. As well as check on her well-being.

If she was lucky, she may be able to send Michael a quick text to get an update on the status of her coming home.

Not that she minded a few more nights like the one she had last night, but she had patients she was ignoring. A business to run. A life to live.

She couldn't be just lollygagging around a house in Shadow Valley, Pennsylvania, having sex with a man she hardly knew.

A man she was sure most other people didn't know much about, either.

But that was neither here nor there, right now. Now, she had to get her ass in gear, find an occupied home nearby and borrow a cell phone from, hopefully, a kind neighbor who wouldn't look at her like she was some mental hospital escapee.

She just hoped whatever house she picked wasn't that Diesel's house. She didn't think it would go over well when the door opened, and she ended up face to face with Mercy's boss. That could get awkward.

Plus, he'd probably not only drag her back to this house—most likely by her hair, grunting all the way—he'd tattletale on her.

And Mercy probably wouldn't find a lot of joy with her actions.

In fact, none at all.

After that, she could kiss any more of the freaking awesome sex they could potentially have goodbye.

Which might make her shed a tear. Maybe even two.

So, she had to be careful and smart about it.

She pulled on her pair of black yoga pants, some slip-on sneakers (did the person who packed for her think she did anything that actually entailed wearing sneakers? *Fsst),* a bra, and dug in her bag until she found a casual top. She rushed into the hall bathroom, quickly pulled her hair back in a neat ponytail—since she was going for the "Oh yes, of course I power walk on a regular basis," and not the "Hi, stranger, I'm a complete loon" look.

Forget makeup or anything like that. Time was of the essence. And since she was rushing around, she was probably going to get sweaty anyway. With a quick sniff to her pits (no, they wouldn't kill anybody, thankfully) she hurried out of the bathroom.

Parris jogged down the steps, took a quick glance at the alarm system by the front door to make sure it wasn't set, then moved toward the kitchen and out of the back sliders. Standing on the deck she glanced in both directions. The neighborhood wasn't fully developed yet, but she could see a house in what looked like a cul-de-sac a few lots down.

And was that...

Yes, someone was out on the back deck of that house. Bingo!

She leaped (sort of) from the deck to the dirt—since no grass had been planted yet—like a pole vaulter (sort of) and then sprinted (sort of) toward a woman who was sitting outside playing a guitar.

In fact, the closer she got she could hear the music over her wheezing. She really needed to start doing more than swimming. Point taken.

When she got close enough and caught the woman's attention, she flapped a hand around in the air in a sort-of greeting. Unfortunately, she was struggling to find enough oxygen to shout a "hello."

By the time she got to the steps of that woman's deck, she leaned over and pushed a hand into the stitch in her side. She finally gasped a "Hi!" because that was all she could manage without too much effort.

The woman's fingers had stilled on the strings of the guitar and she only blinked at Parris. Was that shock? Horror? Surprise?

She hadn't split her yoga pants during that Olympic-worthy athletic leap, had she? She peered down. No, all her important bits were covered. *Phew.*

"Hi," she attempted again, trying to actually form words. She sucked some air and tried again. "I was just out exercising and heard your beautiful guitar playing."

The petite blonde woman with great big green eyes just continued to stare at her.

So much for not looking like a loon on her part. Obviously that was a major failure.

"Uh," the younger woman started. "How did you get into the compound?"

Parris straightened since she'd been bent over trying to catch her breath and slow her runaway locomotive heartbeat. She waved a hand absently in the direction of the other house. "I'm staying down there."

The woman's head twisted in that direction, then quickly back to her. "With Nash?"

It was Parris's turn to blink. "Nash?"

"Yeah, that's Nash's house. I didn't think he moved in yet."

"Oh, uh, yes, in Nash's house. But not with Nash."

The woman's eyes narrowed. "Wait. Are you the woman who Mercy is babysitting?"

Oh shit. "Well, I'm kind of old to need a babysitter... but, yes, I'm staying with Mercy."

"You're his current job. The package he picked up in Vegas."

Sigh.

"Uh... sure," Parris said slowly. She climbed the three steps from the yard (they actually had grass) and approached the woman who couldn't be older than her upper twenties. Parris wondered if she still lived with her parents. When she got close enough to where the woman was sitting, she offered her hand. The other woman stared at her outstretched hand, then after a few seconds, took it, giving it a firm shake. "I'm Parris."

After releasing her hand, the woman pulled the wide guitar strap over her long, blonde hair and propped the instrument against a small table. "Jazz."

Parris pasted on a smile. "Oh, how fun. Do you play jazz?"

"No."

"Oh... Well... I..."

"Are you supposed to be out of the house?"

Parris sucked in a breath and tried not to curse. "Um... like I said, I was out exercising."

"Why isn't Mercy with you?"

"Because I can't keep up with him, so I go at my own pace." Right. He probably ran like a rabid cheetah next to her snail crawl.

"So, he knows you're not in the house right now?"

"Of course." Holy crap, she hated lying. "I, uh, just have a favor to ask. My cell phone got lost at the airport and

Mercy's isn't charged. I really need to get a message to my sister. Just a simple text. So I was wondering if I could borrow yours? She's... She's having surgery in a couple hours and I want to wish her good luck. I... um... am worried. And she'll never forgive me if she doesn't hear from me."

Jazz's cell phone was sitting on the little table next to where she had been playing guitar. It was *right there.*

She could dive for it, grab it and run away. But that would involve running again. And that wasn't going to happen anytime soon.

"Are you supposed to be contacting anyone?"

Damn this woman and her blasted questions! Had someone given her the heads up?

Parris swatted a hand nonchalantly in the air. "Oh, yes. I was told just no phone calls in case... I can text, though. No problem."

Jazz's gaze slid to her cell phone, then back to Parris.

She wrung her hands and put on her best award-winning concerned face. However, she never won an award for acting, not even when she took part in a play during high school. The teacher had actually asked her to never sign up for any plays or musicals again. What a way to crush a blossoming child's dreams. "I'm really worried about her. I'm the only family she has left. And unfortunately, due to my current circumstances, I couldn't be there with her. I could never live with myself if something happened while she was under the knife and I didn't get to tell her how much I loved her before... Well, *you know.*"

She was going to hell. She glanced up at the sky to make sure there weren't any clouds and there was no risk of lightning striking her.

"Is Mercy going to kill me if I let you use my phone?"

A little nervous laugh bubbled out of Parris before she

could stop it. "No... No. Not at all. Like I said, he forgot to charge his phone... and..."

Jazz was reaching for it... Parris held her breath and her fingers twitched. The woman hit the power button, plugged in her password, then held it out to her.

Parris breathed with relief as she snagged it quickly, turned away, pulled up the text app and entered Londyn's phone number. "Thank you," she said over her shoulder as her fingers quickly moved across the keyboard.

She typed, "Hey, sis! Just checking in. Everything's fine with me. My phone's broken and I'm waiting for it to be repaired. Hopefully everything's fine with you." *Send.* "I love you and miss talking with you. I'll call you soon! Promise! Just be careful and stay safe!" *Send.*

Shit. She heard the whoosh of the sliding glass door being opened behind her and her heart began to race. She quickly typed one more message. "I'm borrowing someone else's phone, so don't bother to text me back. Love you!" *Send.*

She gripped the phone tightly, hoping her sister wouldn't listen and instead respond quickly with a return text so Parris could see for herself that she was okay.

But before she could turn, the phone was plucked from her fingers. By fingers which weren't Mercy's. After last night and many, many naughty things later, she'd recognize those fingers. The ones taking the phone from her were slightly darker and not quite as long as his.

She slowly turned... and lost her breath.

Oh...

Wow...

What looked like a Native American man frowned at her. One who had sharp cheek bones, almost black eyes, and long black hair held in a tight braid down his back...

Even wearing a scowl, he was...

Stunning.

While not as tall or even half as muscular as Mercy, he was lean, and his skin tone looked like a burnished gold. He seemed to be a lot older than Jazz, who was now standing next to him, looking slightly worried.

"Hi," Parris managed, a little breathlessly. Her excuse wasn't overexertion this time. "You are?"

The man shot her one more scowl before scrolling through Jazz's phone to read what text messages Parris sent.

"This is Crow, my ol' man."

He was what? "He's your father?" They definitely didn't look related. Not even distantly.

Jazz's eyes widened for a second, then she shook her head. "My *ol' man*."

Okay, she still didn't get it.

But before she could get a clarification, Crow's annoyed gaze dropped to the smaller woman next to him. "Don't have to ask if you got Mercy's number in your fuckin' phone. Know you do." He shoved the phone at her. "Call 'im an' tell 'im this woman was here an' I'm takin' her back."

Say what?

Though his voice was as smooth as melted butter, his speech pattern didn't match his looks. He had to be one of those bikers Mercy had mentioned who lived in the neighborhood.

That was confirmed when he turned enough so she could read what was on the back of the black leather vest he wore.

DIRTY ANGELS was curved downward at the top, PENNSYLVANIA curved upward at the bottom, with some sort of skull insignia in the middle. It was similar to the one that Diesel was wearing the first day she arrived in Shadow Valley.

"His phone isn't charged," Parris panicked and fibbed.

Onyx eyes turned back to her. "Right," he grumbled before ordering Jazz, "Call 'im."

Jazz glanced at Parris, mouthed a "sorry" and then went into the house with her phone to her ear.

Shit!

"I can find my way back," she quickly reassured Crow. She swung an arm blindly toward the house where she came from. "Look, I can see it from here. I promise not to get lost."

Crow shook his head and jerked his chin up at her. "Let's go."

She sighed and walked down the steps and back toward the house. The closer they got, she began to walk like a death row inmate on the way to the electric chair, because now on the back deck was a very tall man only wearing a pair of those Ranger panties and a pair of sneakers, standing with hands on his hips and wearing a very perturbed expression. It might be *possibly, slightly* a bit more than perturbed.

"Shit," she whispered under her breath.

"You lied to my woman," Crow growled.

"Sorry," she whispered again.

"By leavin' that house, you coulda put her in danger."

"I was desperate," she kept whispering while her gaze remained on the man whose hard, gray eyes were fixed on her. Fury visibly rolled off him in waves. "My sister could be in danger."

"Sure Mercy's got it covered."

"I'm not so sure about that." He'd stated that Michael had someone watching Londyn. But since she hadn't heard a word from Michael, she couldn't confirm that.

Mercy walked down the steps and met them in the yard. No pleasantries were exchanged between the two men. In fact, they both scowled and seemed to have a clear dislike of each other. "Got it from here," Mercy growled.

"Keep 'er on a leash," was Crow's return growl before he spun away and headed back to his own house.

Parris had a hard time pulling her gaze from the retreating man since his gait was smooth and, she had to admit, pretty damn sexy.

When Mercy ordered, "Get the fuck inside," much louder than necessary, she reluctantly turned her attention back to him.

She shivered because his voice, no longer growly, was sharp and chilling. "I—"

"In..." he said slowly and with tight control, "...side."

She huffed out a breath. "Fine." She hauled herself up the steps and through the open glass door into the darker, cooler interior of the kitchen.

Behind her, she heard the slam of the slider, the click of the lock and the whoosh of the curtains being jerked closed.

Without turning around, she began, "Sorry I risked your *bonus*, but—" Her words were cut off when all the air left her lungs in a rush as Mercy snagged her around the neck and pinned her against the wall.

"You think I'm fucking worried about my bonus?" came out in a roar. "You fucking not only put yourself in danger but Jazz, too. You were not to leave the fucking house. I was very clear about that."

"It was only for a few minutes." *Lame. Lame. Lame.*

"It only takes a split second for a sniper to put a bullet between your eyes. You'd never know he was out there."

Why did he assume all snipers were men? There weren't any women snipers? *Not the time, Parris, not the time.*

Her eyes slid past him toward the woods, even though she couldn't see them through the curtains. "You think they hired snipers?"

"I don't know who the fuck they have looking for you. I have no way of fucking knowing because I'm stuck the fuck here with you."

Parris winced because he was still roaring, and his face was now only an inch from hers.

A face that was red, twisted and his eyes burned hot.

Oh yes, while maybe not the best time to notice it, this man was not all ice. Oh no, he was not.

"Are you more worried about your bonus or the fact you can't handle the idea of failing at a job?"

His nostrils widened, and she swore little puffs of smoke shot out of them.

"What you did was fucking stupid. Reckless. You texted your sister using Jazz's phone. You not only put your sister at risk, you put Jazz in danger, too." A muscle popped in his jaw. "That woman has been through enough shit in her life that she doesn't need more. You compromised three people *and* you lied to do it."

"I needed to check in with my sister. I'm all she has."

"I don't give a fucking shit. You're no good to her if you're dead. And you won't ever forgive yourself if something happens to her when they use her as a pawn to get to you. I've seen shit, woman. Situations you wouldn't wish on your worst enemy, especially your sister. These fuckers aren't playing, Rissa. They got money and resources backing them up. This isn't a fucking game. I thought I could trust you to stay in the house when I went on my morning runs. I was wrong. Guess I can't trust you at all."

Parris opened her mouth to say something, but she wasn't sure what. She didn't know how to fix the mistake she made. And a simple "sorry" wasn't going to cut it. So she shut her mouth.

His whole body heaved as he sucked in an audible breath. His fingers relaxed a little bit on her neck and he pulled his head back enough so they were no longer nose to nose.

Some of the red in his face had dissipated, but she could still feel the tension, the anger he held onto.

"Paranzino told me what you witnessed. Then he told me what you know. What he wanted you to know. He didn't tell you shit. He kept things from you. Whether to protect you or to protect himself, I don't fucking know, nor do I care. It could even be that he was afraid of what you'd think of him if you knew the complete truth. But, Rissa, this shit is way more serious than you can imagine and because of that, I'm going to tell you everything about your *friend*, even though I agreed not to."

None of this sounded good. And she wasn't sure she wanted to hear it all.

"All I know is there's a war over some sort of territory. I thought it had to do with real estate, so I didn't question it when he glossed over it," she admitted. "I should've demanded he tell me everything."

"Even if you did, he wouldn't have. We need to move, but before we do, I need to tell you the complete background that I demanded from him. I needed to hear it all so I could protect your ass successfully. He does love you, Rissa, and I could see the real fear he had for you, so there's that. But that might not be enough after I tell you the rest, so you'll have to decide if you still love him."

Her head spun with everything he just said. The situation she was in was worse than she thought, even after Michael explained it to her. Or told her only the minimum. Then they had to leave this house because she'd put not only herself in jeopardy but others. Including her sister, who she was sure had no clue that she was in danger. "Where are we going?"

"Somewhere other than here. But we need to move. You might not think what you did could come back to you, but I've been on the other side of the hunt. I could find you just by those three fucking texts you sent to your sister from someone else's phone."

"How?" she asked surprised, feeling the blood drain from her face.

He shook his head. "Doesn't matter how, just know it can be done. I can do it and any of my team could, too. I'm gonna call Steel, have him bring my bike, then you and I are taking that while he takes my RPV back to the warehouse. You're gonna pack your shit and he'll take it with him until we settle somewhere safe."

"When is this going to be over?" she yelled in frustration.

"When you're dead or they're dead. My preference is the latter."

Hers, too.

He let her go abruptly and then pointed at one of the chairs at the kitchen table. "Sit."

She considered her options, then decided it was best to sit. Her gaze followed him as he went over to his cell phone on the counter, picked it up and made his call to who she assumed was Steel, giving him orders about swapping out the vehicles.

When he was done, he threw his phone back on the counter and pinned his gray eyes back on her. "Do us both a favor and keep your mouth shut 'til I'm done. Yeah?"

He was dead serious about whatever he was about to tell her, so she simply nodded.

"Prostitution is illegal in Vegas's city limits. Know you know that. Paranzino didn't build his fortune with casinos. That shit's a front and a way to launder money. I'm sure it makes him some nice scratch, but that's not where he started. Ever wonder how a practically homeless black jack dealer ended up being so fucking rich he now owns three successful casinos?"

Was she supposed to answer that?

Apparently not, since he continued, "Paranzino owns and runs underground brothels within the city limits."

She opened her mouth, but quickly shut it because of the look he gave her.

"Some right outside of the city, too. That's where he began to make his real money which he invested in real estate and, eventually, started a legit corporation to build those fancy casinos. His empire was built on the backs of women. Once his brothels were established, he began taking girls, who were drugged and beaten by their pimps, off the street. He got them clean and, if they chose to continue with their career, he put them to work in his brothels where they kept more of their money, had protection, free health care and financial help. Real noble, right?"

She opened her mouth again, but quickly shut it when he cocked a brow at her.

"He gave them the option to leave at any time and would even foot their tuition at the local community college. However, he ain't the only game in town. Before he got into the sex business, there was someone already established in Vegas. Actually more than one, but the little guys were easy to deal with. His main competition, someone who ran a prostitution ring, not so much. A war began over, not only territory, but the fact that Paranzino was always stealing from his stable. Paranzino had, and still has, men searching the streets looking for prostitutes who are ready to 'better their lives.' However, 'better' is fucking subjective, depending on who you are and whether it's you on your back with your fucking legs in the air letting strangers shoot their loads in your cunt or your mouth or even up your ass."

Parris winced.

"That ain't it. He didn't just steal, or what he calls 'save,' women, it was males, too. By taking both in, he doubled his money by offering a nice selection to anyone who wanted it."

She lifted shaky fingers to her mouth. "He found his husband on the street after he'd been beaten almost to death, hooked on heroin by his pimp and was nothing but skin and bones. Michael had taken him into his home, got him healthy, drug-free and Joshua never left."

"Right. Now the guy only gets one dick up his ass in payment for living large."

"Michael loves Joshua," she whispered. Joshua was the reason Parris met Michael in the first place. Michael had been in denial about his sexuality, until he "rescued" Joshua. She'd also met with the both of them to help Joshua to deal with his abuse at the hand of his former pimp.

Had Joshua been used and abused by the man, or whoever it was, behind what Mercy called a war?

"Sure he does. Just like he loves you but kept you in the dark. It wouldn't have affected you if you hadn't stumbled across the situation you did."

The situation.

"Take a sex trafficker with a fat wad of cash in his pocket watching his assets disappear. Then those assets resurface making money for another trafficker. He's going to get itchy fingers and start taking a fucking stand against it. Which he did after several warnings that Paranzino admittedly ignored. And worse, was too arrogant to care about, thinking he was untouchable. News flash, money don't make you Teflon. Shit can stick to anything it's thrown at. So, the three men you saw get popped were supposed to be a warning to Paranzino. Only problem was, you wore a ridiculous pair of fucking high heels, tripped and caught their attention. You witnessed the act. Of course, Paranzino's not going to any authorities to report his men being whacked, but you? No guarantee. You're the wild card. You could cause more trouble than Paranzino if law enforcement starts digging into a report of a triple murder, and then finds out where it stemmed from. It's not only bad for Paranzino, but for his competition, too."

"How could I be so stupid? Why didn't I know any of this?"

"Because he didn't want you to know. He has some sort of sense of loyalty to you. Don't know where that comes from, he only said you helped him out and that's how you first met. He didn't go into details. Whatever you did for him, he's truly grateful. He mentioned that a couple times. Doesn't mean it's right that you're stuck in the middle of his shit. He was able to keep this from you because he's got enough men under him that he doesn't even know who's the lowest hanging fruit at the bottom of that fucking tree. He rules from the top branches; the roots don't dirty him. Which means at his level, it's easy to keep any talk of business in his underground brothels to a minimum. Paying people very well makes for extremely loyal employees. Though, some of those employees may be getting a little restless since three of his work-force were popped. Some jobs ain't worth dying over."

"He told you all of this?" she asked in surprise, trying to beat back the panic that was bubbling up from her churning gut. This situation was so much worse than she could ever imagine. And Michael had lied to her. Or omitted the truth. Which might as well be the same as lying.

"Like you, he told me what he wanted me to know. Though, it was more than he told you. The rest I had my own crew dig up. I wasn't gonna trust some man with a fuck-ton of cash and very dirty hands to tell me the truth. And I was right."

Mercy knew all of this and kept it from her as well. Both Michael and him kept her in the dark. For what? Her safety? If she would have known...

"Maybe if one of you were upfront with me from the beginning, I never would've stepped outside this fucking house!" she yelled.

"For fuck's sake, Rissa! You saw three men shot execution style. Plugged point blank right in the back of the head. That should've been enough," he yelled back.

Parris lifted shaky fingers to her lips, "Oh my God, they're never going to stop searching for me until I'm dead! It's not like if any length of time goes past they'll just forget about me and move on, right?"

"No. I told you what will end this. And if Paranzino doesn't make it happen soon, then we will."

We will.

"But you're not getting paid for that." And wasn't it all about the money? And his big, fat bonus?

Or was she missing something?

He said nothing, his jaw moving as if he was grinding his teeth.

After a few moments, he relaxed his jaw enough to say, "I'm getting paid to keep you alive. And, right now, that's my focus. So, go pack your shit and get back down here double-time. I'm gonna go shower. *Do not leave this house.*" The last was a low, dangerous growl as he spun on his heels and strode out of the kitchen. She heard him jog up the stairs and slam his bedroom door shut.

He didn't have to worry, she wasn't planning on leaving the house until he said so.

She had messed things up enough already.

Chapter Twelve

HAVING his girl between his legs felt good. And it also felt way too fucking good to have Rissa plastered to his back on the ride through the warm night to their next safe house. With her big tits pressing against him, and her soft thighs sandwiching his hips and ass, he could imagine her riding with him on a regular basis. Though those rides might get cut short, since he'd have to take her home or pull over somewhere where he would fuck her until she rumbled as loudly as his straight pipes.

They had headed out of the DAMC compound a lot later than he wanted. Even though it didn't take long for Steel to bring over Mercy's Harley and swap it out for his RPV, it took a while for Diesel to find another place outside of Shadow Valley for them to hole up in. A last minute rental hadn't been easy to find.

When he stopped in, Steel took their bags and also brought helmets for both him and Rissa. Even though he normally didn't wear one, he figured it couldn't hurt to wear full-faced brain buckets to help disguise who they were.

He doubted anyone was watching them yet. Yet being the key word. But he'd rather play it safe anyway. Even if those texts could be traced back to Jazz and Shadow Valley, it would take time for men to get into place. That was if they didn't have a bead on Rissa already. He had no idea how skilled Paranzino's competitor's men were or if he'd hired someone, or even a team, as skilled as D's Shadows, to hunt her down.

If he did, they could be fucked.

He was tempted to fly her out of the country to one of his Delta Force buddies who retired down in Panama. But time wasn't on his side right now and to get her a fake passport, and whatever else needed, could be time-consuming and get sticky. Plus, he wasn't letting her out of his sight.

No, he fucking wasn't. Not even for his morning runs, which helped keep him sane.

He was also waiting for word from Paranzino himself. He had Diesel get a message to him, to update him on the situation and also ask what the fuck was taking so long out in Vegas.

Mercy's patience was wearing thin. Diesel's, which was never abundant in the first place, was now non-existent. But his boss wasn't at the point where he'd send his own crew out to Vegas to get this over and done with. Until Paranzino asked for assistance with that part of the job, and then forked over a healthy chunk of change, D would let Mercy continue to babysit a woman who was driving him fucking nuts.

He had just walked into the house from his run when he got the call from Jazz. At first, his only thought was how her voice in his ear didn't affect him as much as he thought it would. She was Crow's woman now, he had no choice but to accept that. Then it hit him what she was saying and why she called him.

It took every ounce of control not to run over to Jazz's house to drag Rissa back by her fucking hair. After that, teach her a lesson she wouldn't soon forget.

When he stepped out onto the deck and saw Crow escorting her back... he had to remind himself once again, he couldn't drag her back to the house by her ponytail, carry her upstairs and tie her to the bed, so she wouldn't do stupid shit like she just had.

Not only did she not fucking listen, Mercy had to go face to face with Crow, which he enjoyed about as much as a kick to the nuts.

And worse, she believed he was pissed because she had risked his fucking bonus.

At that point, he almost did something unthinkable, so he had to dial back his fury and take a breath, then another before he did something he'd regret.

Unfortunately, the very woman he was trying to protect jeopardized her own safety as well as Jazz's. And to think about Jazz being in a situation like she had been when she had been only twenty-two, one that fucked her up for years, had nearly sent him over that thin edge he always skated along.

But it was more than that. In those few minutes it took for Crow to escort Rissa back to him, he had a flashback of Jazz and Kiki in that abandoned house, bound, bloody, bruised, and broken. And during that goddamn flashback, he couldn't stop picturing Rissa in Kiki's place.

He also couldn't stop reliving the bone-chilling and hair-raising reaction Hawk, the Angels' VP, had when he saw his woman like that on the filthy floor.

Mercy knew his own reaction would've been much worse. But he wouldn't have made any noise, had no outward reaction. Instead, he would have only focused on finding those motherfuckers who kidnapped Kiki and Jazz.

Black Jack and Squirrel had been lucky they got away that day. However, he, and the rest of the Shadows, made sure those fuckers weren't so lucky when they were finally caught. But it had taken too long to find them for Mercy's liking.

Locating those two motherfuckers had been his sole mission and he didn't stop until they found them. If something like that happened to Rissa...

He released a slow breath and tried to shake that image.

Mercy needed to talk to Diesel again. He needed a deadline on Paranzino "cleaning up" his problem. If it didn't happen soon, he'd personally take Paranzino's competition, and every single one of his heavies, out himself. He was pretty damn sure the rest of the Shadows would help. They'd just do it off the clock if the "casino mogul" wasn't willing to fork out the dough to pay them.

His teammates would do for him what he would do for them.

They had each other's six.

For life.

About twenty minutes east of Shadow Valley, Diesel found and booked a "rustic" vacation rental that included only the basics. Luckily, it was available immediately. Though the place was isolated, it was fully furnished. Even better, it didn't have Wi-Fi, so Rissa couldn't contact anyone with her e-reader.

The only thing Mercy didn't like when Hunter texted the pics of the cabin was that it was surrounded with woods. Being summer, that meant good cover for someone wanting to approach the place without being spotted.

Mercy turned his bike up a rutted dirt lane, taking it slow and careful so he didn't dump his girls. Both of them.

At that fucking thought, he almost rolled his eyes at himself.

He had seen a lot of the DAMC brothers fall hard for their women. With that came the loss of their independence. That even included the big guy himself, Diesel, and that wasn't going to ever happen to Mercy.

Pussy was never going to rule his life. Or change it, either. No matter how good it was.

Damn right.

He'd been told the property had a shed large enough to store his bike for the time they'd be there and one of the guys would drop off their bags, along with some boxes of food and basic supplies.

He should have whoever was doing the shopping throw in a box of condoms, but at this point that ship had already sailed. Plus, it could've been Jewel doing the shopping. At least he hoped it was, otherwise they were getting a box full of beer, Pringles and beef jerky to live on for the next who knows how many days.

And, once again, asking for condoms was evidence he was doing something he shouldn't be doing with his *job*.

Diesel would blow a gasket.

Truth was, no one wanted to be around Diesel with a blown head gasket. Certainly not Mercy.

He blew out a breath in irritation.

Fuck, he hated full-faced helmets and couldn't wait to take it off. He drove his Harley around to the back of the cabin, which he hoped looked better in the daylight than the dead of night. If it looked that bad in the dark, he couldn't imagine it would look any better when the sun was shining.

No surprise why it had been immediately available for rent. But they had to take what they could get.

He'd survived staying in many rat holes throughout his life. Hell, there were many times he'd slept out in the open without shelter. So, he could deal with it. Rissa? Not so much.

This was no Four Seasons with a spa and turn-down service. Mercy just hoped they had running water and it was hot when they showered.

He stopped in front of the shed and yanked off his

helmet, grateful he could now breathe. He hated confining shit like that.

He barked, "Off," to Rissa and without hesitation —*thank fuck*—she gingerly peeled herself from his back, grabbed onto his shoulder for balance and climbed off his bike. After she unstrapped and pulled her own helmet off, she stared at him. "Open the fucking door."

Even in the dark, he could see she shot him a frown and probably mentally gave him the finger. But he didn't give a fuck.

The woman needed to listen.

Whether she wanted to or not.

When she shoved her helmet at him, he took it and watched as she approached the rickety shed. The headlight from his bike lit up her generous ass as she bent over to grab the garage door handle and attempted to pull it up.

He pursed his lips and watched as that ass wiggled enticingly as she struggled to open the piece of shit door.

She was one determined woman. She didn't give up, turn to him and whine about it. Nor was she worried about breaking a nail as she kept working at it until finally the door freed unexpectedly and she fell backward onto her ass in the dirt as the door sprung open.

He was sure she couldn't hear his chuckle over the rumble of his exhaust as he drove his Harley into the shed and shut it down. After dismounting, he stacked the helmets on the seat and turned to see she had risen to her feet on her own power and was brushing the dirt off that sweet, fuckable ass of hers.

He schooled his face as he stepped back outside and slammed the overhead door closed. The springs probably hadn't been greased in decades, no wonder she had struggled.

He stepped toe to toe with Rissa, who now stood glaring at him with her hands planted on her hips.

"Hands off your hips. Hands on mine," he demanded.

Her eyes widened for a split second, then she stepped into him, close enough her tits were pushing against his chest. Yeah, that's exactly where they belonged. Pushed into his back while on his bike, pushed into his chest when she wasn't.

Swinging like pendulums when he was fucking her from behind.

She curled her fingers around both of his hips and tipped her face up to him, her eyes now hooded. "You're hard."

No shit. He'd been hard almost the whole ride. How could he not be with her warm pussy shoved against his ass?

Then when she had bent over...

Instead of answering her, he dropped his head and took her mouth. He'd been wanting to do that since he had pinned her against the wall by the neck at Nash's house. But he'd resisted because he'd been seeing red and that kiss would have been nothing but brutal punishment. Neither would have enjoyed it.

It was stupid for them to be standing out in the open, even in the dark, but he couldn't not take a quick taste. It would have to hold him over until he got to fuck her in whatever disaster of a bed was in the cabin.

Because no matter what, he was fucking her tonight, and every night, until this job was over.

His tongue slid through her mouth and tangled briefly with hers before he pulled away just enough to ask, "You wet?"

She nodded. He shoved a hand between them and down the front of her yoga pants. Since she wasn't wearing any panties, his finger hit that slick slit and slipped inside her.

She gasped, which made his dick even harder.

"How close are you to coming?" he murmured against her lips.

"I already came once on the back of your bike."

He pulled his head back to stare down at her. *Fuck*, his dick was throbbing now. "When?"

She lifted one hand from his hip and waved it absently. "Like halfway through the ride... The vibrations..." she drifted off.

He smiled.

Her eyebrows lifted. "Are you smiling?"

"No," he answered, then stepped back from her. "We need to get inside." He grabbed her wrist and pulled her along through the small overgrown patch of weeds to the backdoor of the cabin. He found the key hidden where the owner said it would be. Which turned out to be a shitty hiding spot. For fuck's sake, people were careless with their safety.

Unlocking the door and stepping inside, Rissa followed on his heels. Before he could find a light switch and Rissa could turn up her nose with what they saw in the light, he had her pinned against the door, his mouth on her again, and his hand back down her pants.

She was more wet now than a few moments ago. With a thumb on her clit and his middle finger moving in and out of her slick heat, he captured her cry in his mouth and it didn't take long for the pulsations around his finger to start and her body to go limp against him.

He broke the kiss, pressed his forehead to hers until they both caught their breath. He was fighting a raging hard-on that he couldn't do anything about at this point. Once he was breathing a little more normally, he slipped his fingers from her and raised them to his own mouth, sucking the middle one clean.

She tasted so fucking good.

When she was gone, finally safe and back in Vegas, he'd never forget the taste of her. Her scent. Her cries of "Ryan" when she was about to come. No other woman called him that. They never even knew his name. Or even his call name.

She was the only one who used the name he was born with.

What he was doing with her was beyond careless, it was dangerous. He was getting addicted to something he shouldn't because once this was over, he was going to have to quit cold-turkey.

And she would be a hard habit to break.

He knew he should stop. Leave her alone. Follow his own rules about once and done. He was being stupid and being stupid got people hurt.

Even so, he couldn't leave her alone. He'd never done a drug in his life, but he could imagine his pull toward Rissa was similar to an addict chasing that next high.

He needed to let her go, turn on some lights, inspect the property, make sure everything was satisfactory and safe for the most part. Especially before one of the other Shadows showed up with their supplies.

But he couldn't move away from her. Not yet.

"Ryan," she whispered, one hand gripping the front of his tee, the fingers of the other sliding over his cheek. Those fingers slid lower and curled around the side of his neck as she released his shirt and dropped her hand to his erection.

Her fingers moved up, quickly worked the button of his cargo pants and slid down the zipper. She released his neck and used both hands to lower his pants down enough to circle her fingers around his dick. He swallowed the groan that began to rise.

He needed to stop her. This was not the time.

Later, once things were settled, he could give her what she needed and wanted, then he could take the same. But right now...

Fuck, right now, she was going to her knees and circling the head with her hot, wet tongue. He grabbed her ponytail to stop her but ended up yanking the elastic band free that was holding her hair back. Before it could fall around her shoulders, he took two fistfuls of it and helped guide her head back and forth as she took him almost completely into her mouth.

Well, not completely. But with her fingers circling the root and her mouth performing the magic it was doing, she might as well be deep-throating it.

"We don't have time for this," he managed to get out without groaning. His fingers flexed in her hair as he fought the urge to take over and fuck her face.

Of course, she didn't answer... Her mouth... and lips... and that wicked, wicked, tongue were way too busy. While he wanted to drop his head back and close his eyes, he bent it forward instead, so he could watch her. Even in the dark, because his eyes had adjusted, he could see her expression, the heaviness of her eyelids, her chest rising and falling rapidly.

He curled his fingers around her throat and pressed a thumb to her pulse. It was racing. He was sure her nipples were beaded, her pussy getting even wetter. Rissa wasn't sucking him off because she felt obligated, she was doing it because she enjoyed it.

A man could always tell the difference. The way she worked his dick made it clear that there wasn't anything she didn't like about taking him into her mouth.

For fuck's sake, this woman was determined to take him to his knees. To make him feel something. Anything.

Even if only for her.

Maybe that wasn't her actual goal. Maybe she simply wanted to use him like the rest of the women he'd been with.

They used him, he used them. Means to an end.

But the woman on her knees before him drudged up feelings he hardly recognized anymore, shit he hadn't experienced since before he enlisted in the Army. Since before he'd seen and done things that made him build those barriers. The ones that he needed to keep him a functioning man. Ones he needed to prevent him from eating his own gun or going on a killing spree. Barriers that helped him cope with normal people who hadn't done or seen what he had. The ones who lived their lives clueless on the realities of war, death and dying. Of every kind of injustice known to man.

How could one woman get past everything he built? One woman who'd been thrown into his path due to her situation? A woman he never would've met otherwise?

He needed this to stop. He needed to draw back. Remember who this woman was. Why they were here.

He couldn't let her make him forget his training, his mission, or even his past. He needed to remind himself this would soon come to an end.

He couldn't allow her to draw him under until he began to tumble out of control.

Because if that happened, he was fucked.

He didn't know what would happen if she found that crack in the dam and dug at it until it began to leak. The whole dam could very well collapse and cause a devastating flood.

He needed to patch any weak points before it was too late.

But right now, it was too late. What she was currently doing was making him forget, if only for those few moments when she cupped his balls, squeezed his dick tighter at the base and then sucked him as hard as a Hoover.

He forgot everything as his hips drove forward, stilled, and he shot his cum down her throat. A groan rose up between them that didn't come from her. Fuck no. It came from him.

Her eyes tipped up and even though he couldn't see the

color in the dark, he knew what they were. That blue like the sky on a clear summer day. Those eyes that somehow touched his fucked up soul. Then those lips curved around his dick in a smile, no doubt with satisfaction. He wondered if he wore the same satisfied expression. At the moment, he didn't even fucking care.

His fingers were still gripping her hair tightly, so he relaxed them and combed through her long strands.

She hadn't gagged once, she hadn't spit out his load. She kept him in her mouth, almost as if she was savoring him, or at least the taste of him. That in itself made him want to bend her over and fuck her hard, but they didn't have time and he wasn't capable of that right now, anyway.

As he began to soften, she let him slip from between her lips, and her smile was still there, her eyes soft. Which scared the living fuck out of him.

He couldn't allow her to share that softness because he couldn't allow himself to accept it.

He released her hair and reached down to help her to her feet. When she stood, she pressed both palms flat to his pecs and he knew what she couldn't miss, his heart wanting to escape his chest.

It was no longer pounding due to his orgasm, but because the darkness was rushing in, the panic starting to seep into his bones, the cage starting to close.

If it did and became locked, he'd never escape.

"...an... yan... Ryan... Mercy!"

He shook his head and focused on Rissa. An overhead light now lit up the dank kitchen and he realized the switch had been right inside the door within reach. She didn't even have to move to turn it on.

He blinked at her and the softness in her face was gone, her brows were furrowed with a look of concern. Her lips were moving, and he had to concentrate to hear what she was saying.

"Someone's beating on the door."

Fuck.

He heard it then. The noise finally sank into his foggy brain. He jerked up his cargo pants and fastened them.

His cell phone vibrated in his back pocket. He pulled it out to answer it. "Yeah," he barked into his phone as he strode to the front of the house. Which wasn't that many steps, apparently. With a quick glance, he realized the cabin was one big room and it was like he feared...

Dated and unkempt.

"I'm outside, asshole. Open the door and help me bring the shit inside."

The phone went dead at the same time he twisted the lock in the knob and yanked the front door open. The place didn't even have deadbolts.

Fuck me.

He hit a switch by the front door and a bare bulb lit up Ryder as he stood with a shit-eating grin on his face and a large box in his arms. "About time. I texted you like five thousand times. Been pounding on the door for—"

He knew the exact moment Ryder spotted Rissa.

Mercy's lip curled as Ryder let his gaze slide from the top of her light brown hair, pause at a few extra curvy spots, slide the rest of the way to her toes and then back up where it again hesitated on her rack. "Damn," he murmured, his eyes landing on Mercy before he smiled big.

Mercy grabbed the box from him and dropped it to the floor. He shoved Ryder outside and slammed the door closed behind them.

"Thought you were handling DC?" Mercy growled.

They had several reasons why they'd given Kelsea the call name "DC." One, it was short for "Diesel's cousin." Two, the acronym meant disorderly conduct in law enforcement circles, and if Kelsea was anything, she was disorderly. The third? The woman had been doing so much dumb shit lately that... Hell, the last reason wasn't kind but it unfortunately fit. D wouldn't be so happy about the last reason. But then they tried not to use her nickname around him. Because, fucked up or not, Kels was still Diesel's blood.

"Was. Handled it. Just waitin' for the next time, which I'm sure I'll get the fuckin' call. *Again.*"

Mercy shook his head. "Fucking bitch is gonna end up dead, or something will happen to her and she'll be wishing she was dead."

Ryder, with his jaw tight, didn't say anything as he strode back to what looked like a full-sized rental van. The sliding side door was open and at least half a dozen more boxes of supplies could be seen inside. Plus, Rissa's luggage and his duffel.

That seemed to be way too much stuff for one or two nights. "What the fuck? We need all that shit? The boss didn't get an update from Paranzino?"

They both grabbed a box and headed back to the cabin.

"Oh, he heard from him."

Mercy stopped at the front door and, using his body, blocked Ryder from opening it. "Leave it there. I'll bring them in once the van's unloaded." He did not want Ryder eyeballing Rissa again.

Ryder stared over his shoulder at the door for a second, then looked up at Mercy with a twisted grin. "Got it, brother. Stakin' your claim."

"Ain't staking shit."

"Right. It was pretty fuckin' obvious in there. You lookin' like you were about to rip my head off with just me checkin' her out."

"You were seeing things."

"The fuck I was."

They dropped their boxes and headed back to the van. "So, what's the news?" They each grabbed another box and headed the short distance up a brick walkway that should've been replaced twenty years earlier. There wasn't one evenly set brick. It was a broken neck waiting to happen, especially in the dark.

"Once D stopped his bellowin', he said that Paranzino's men lost track of about half of this other asshole's men. Nicco, I think his name is. Though, D was yellin' like normal, so I couldn't be sure. Paranzino took out about five. Thinks there's at least another five but doesn't have a good number. Nicco went to ground and could've taken some of his men with him. Also could've put some of them on the woman's trail. Thinkin' we need to step in and get this job over with."

Mercy nodded. "Yeah. Me, too. Gotta run it past D first."

"He's not gonna wanna do it without some sort of payment from Paranzino."

"Then someone needs to convince Paranzino to pay up. You get what you pay for. Fucker should know that."

"Maybe your woman can call and convince him." Ryder eyed the cabin. "I'm sure after a couple nights in this shit hole, she could be very convincin'."

"First off, she ain't my woman. Second, not sure if I want her in direct contact with Paranzino."

"Why? Is the asshole gonna be pissed that you stuck your dick in his piece?"

"He might be if he didn't have a husband. And he only swings that direction."

Ryder stopped in his tracks, then laughed and nodded. "Yeah. Guess he won't care that much then. Just gotta deal with Diesel if he finds out." This time they were headed back with the bags. "Though, not sure why D would care as long as he's gettin' paid."

"Once he's got the scratch in his hand, he probably won't." Or at least, Mercy hoped that was true. He didn't need to go a few rounds with Diesel. They'd probably be evenly matched, but he liked his job and wanted to keep it, especially since it paid well.

"But you aren't gonna wait until the job's over to bone her." Ryder stopped on the cracked concrete stoop in front of the door. "*Daaamn*. You broke your own rule, didn't you?"

Mercy ignored his question. "Thanks for the delivery. Got it from here." He adjusted his duffel bag's strap more securely over his shoulder and took one of Rissa's suitcases from Ryder.

"Brother, you're allowed some fuckin' happiness. And from what I saw, that would make me pretty damn happy. Again, I saw your reaction. You might wanna ignore it but it was as plain as day. You laid your claim."

"This conversation's ending right now."

Ryder laughed. "Hey, maybe me and a couple of the guys should stake out this place. Grab some tents, set up in the woods, keep an eye out. Haven't slept in a tent for a while. Though, I'm sure any tent's nicer than where you're gonna be sleepin'. But then, you're gonna have a nice piece sleepin' next to you. Did notice there's only one bed." He snorted. "Doubt you're gonna get any sleep, anyhow."

"You fucking done?"

Ryder shot him a smart-ass grin. "For now. But, seriously, if you think it's smart, we could break out the campin' gear and make a vacation out of it. Wouldn't mind some shootin' practice on some actual movin' targets. It'll get me ready for buck season."

"Think I can handle it. Unless D gets an update that indicates they got a bead on us. Then whoever's available needs to haul their asses in this direction as backup. Got me?"

"Yeah, brother, got you." Ryder paused as he began to return to the van. "At least you're gettin' a piece of tail out of this job. My recurrin' nightmare of a fuckin' job only gives me a fuckin' headache," he muttered over his shoulder.

Ryder calling Rissa tail made Mercy's whole body go tight. He waited until he saw the taillights of the van disappear before he opened the front door and began to haul the delivered shit inside.

He dumped their bags next to the one and only bed that sat along one wall in the wide-open space of the cabin. It wasn't even a fucking big bed. It might be a queen, which sucked since he was six-foot-three and two-hundred and sixty pounds. He doubted he was going to sleep anyway, but still...

He had plans for that bed. He eyed the ratty couch that sat in front of a pot-bellied wood stove.

Rissa's husky voice came from behind him. "I can't find the thermostat for the air conditioning."

He turned. She had her long hair piled on top of her head, which made her look really cute as she fanned herself with her hand.

Fuck with this "cute" shit. He hated "cute."

Fucking motherfucker.

He unclamped his jaws to ask, "You see any vents that indicate this dump has air?"

She glanced around, then pursed the lips which had so expertly sucked him off just a little while ago. "Not even a window unit!"

"There's a fan sitting in the corner."

"We're going to need that pointed at the bed," she murmured.

Yes, they were.

"Otherwise, I won't be able to sleep," she continued. "I'll be melting all night long."

"Sleep naked," he suggested.

She arched an eyebrow in his direction. "Is that what you plan on doing?"

"Yep," he lied as he eyed the bare mattress. "Gotta bring in the rest of the supplies. Find some clean sheets and make the bed. Check to make sure the bathroom has a toilet that flushes and hot water to wash my cum out of you when I fuck you hard later."

Her sexy little mouth dropped open.

One side of his mouth curled up. "*Now,* I'm smiling." As he moved past her, he smacked her ass hard enough it had to sting. Then he brought in the rest of the stuff that would have to tide them over for the next couple days.

Chapter Thirteen

MERCY AND PARRIS – 0; rickety bed – 1.

Of course, they already broke the unstable bed. It didn't take more than two nights of heavy activity. In fact, she was surprised it lasted even that long. And until Mercy could find some cinder blocks or bricks, or whatever, to brace the corners of the bed frame that could withstand their non-stop sexual escapades, they had to make do elsewhere.

Since they had been five minutes into their latest round of sex when it finally collapsed, neither wanted to take a break for him to do just that.

Which meant Parris now had her ass planted on the counter (after she cleaned it) with her back pressed against the top cabinets (with a knob jammed into her shoulder) and he was pounding her so hard her head kept bouncing off the cabinet door.

It was a small price to pay since she didn't want him to slow down or be more gentle. She liked it just the way he was giving it to her. She'd been with too many men who had treated her like she was breakable. It was refreshing that Mercy didn't treat her as if she was, since there was nothing fragile about her.

Every time he pounded his cock deep, Mercy grunted, and her pebbled nipples brushed against the hot, damp skin of his very muscular, very lickable chest. She found this was a very good use of a kitchen.

Kitchens seemed to have become their theme, though she wasn't complaining. Cooking, eating, fucking. The perfect multi-purpose room.

However, this kitchen wasn't really a "room." The whole rat trap of a cabin had an open floor plan. Privacy was nil unless you went into the bathroom since it had a door. Unfortunately, it was only about a third of the size of her walk-in closet at home. On the plus side, the toilet flushed without issue (so far) and there was hot water for showers. While the shower curtain did have mold along the bottom edge, she ignored that (pretending it didn't exist).

The sheets she found in the cabin's one and only closet had smelled like moth balls. The fridge stank like it had stored a dead body for over a week. And she couldn't forget the trails of mouse droppings (at least she hoped it was a mouse and not a rat) along the edges of the walls. Joy.

This was no romantic getaway. But then, it wasn't meant to be. The purpose of their stay was to keep her breathing. And anyway, Mercy probably didn't have a romantic bone in his very powerful, very orgasm-inducing body. Plus, the only bone that mattered right now was the one he kept thrusting into her.

His face was buried in her neck, his breath warm and damp as it beat along her skin. She had one hand wrapped around his neck to hold him there, and another along his back, where her nails drilled into his skin. She had discovered the deeper she clawed him, the more he liked it. While he didn't come right out and say it, she could tell by his response.

With a hand cupping one of her ass cheeks, he held her right where he wanted her and the other squeezed her breast firmly while his calloused thumb scraped back and forth over the very sensitive, tightly beaded tip.

Since this was the second round of sex in the span of an hour, this time he had amazing endurance. They'd been at it for a solid ten minutes, in which she had already came twice. Once in the beginning, a second time a few minutes in. And now she felt another building. It was the perfect angle and the right hip action that was pulling these multiple orgasms from her. He could power up and into her like nobody's business. Add those low, caveman-like grunts...

A tremble began deep inside her, then she gasped as her third orgasm shattered outward from her center. Her back arched and her fingers, her muscles, her pussy convulsed, but he didn't let up and continued to use his powerful thighs to drive himself up and into her.

He pulled his face from her neck, sliding his cheek along hers until his mouth was at her ear. He growled, "That was five."

Like she hadn't kept count on her own.

"Three," she gasped as the waves rocking her still had her quivering like jelly.

"Two earlier."

"One wasn't an orgasm; it was the bed crashing to the floor."

His hips stilled. "Bullshit."

She was about to smack his delicious ass to get him moving, but he began to pump again. She smiled because she knew he couldn't see it. "I'll give you credit for four."

"If I give you another one, you'll let me take your ass."

She sucked in a breath. "I counted wrong. It was five."

"Yeah, thought so." The "so" was drawn out and his warm breath tickled her ear, making her shiver. He drove into her again and again until finally a "Rissa" escaped him on a breath.

She shivered once more, this time because of how he

said his nickname for her. It came out almost sounding desperate. And that couldn't be right.

"Yes?" she whispered.

Maybe she had imagined it because his next words were back to being a sexy, low growl. "Going to give you another one, anyway, and when I do, I'm going to come deep inside you."

"Yes," she sighed in total agreement. He'd get no argument about that from her.

"Tell me when you're coming this time. Say my name when you do it."

Her heart began to thump wildly at his unexpected request. She didn't think he liked it when she used his real name.

Was this becoming more than "only sex" for him?

They'd only known each other for a few days. It couldn't be more. Could it?

He was a once and done type of guy. No attachments. Cling-free like a fabric softener sheet, she reminded herself.

With a strained grunt (apparently she needed to eat more salads instead of carbs), he picked her up and, amazingly enough without breaking their connection, kicked a chair away from the small 1970s Formica kitchen table, then sat on it with her straddling his lap.

Fear engulfed her as she met his gaze. Not because his gray eyes were burning hot, unlike their normal ice-cold silver, but because she worried that the ancient chair wouldn't be able to hold their combined weight. It was bad enough when the bed crashed to the floor, the chair collapsing could maim them.

She planted her bare toes on the floor to help support her weight and, not breaking his gaze, began to slowly rise and lower herself. How deep he was before didn't even compare to how it was now. It was to the point that she couldn't put all her weight on him because it would be too much to bear. Instead, she found a rhythm and would only lower herself to right before the point where she couldn't take any more comfortably.

He leaned forward to press his face into her neck once more. She pulled back and murmured, "No."

She didn't want him hiding, because she was learning that was what it was for him. He was hiding whatever he was feeling, hiding his expression, hiding the intensity of his gaze. And she wanted to see it all.

He might feel exposed by being forced to face her like he was, but she wanted to be sure about his reactions. To see if she was affecting him in some way she never thought she would.

As she continued to lift and lower slowly, carefully, tenderly, she could see his struggle, his inner turmoil, how he beat back whatever was fighting to surface. She could see it in the sharpness of his jaw, the flare of his nostrils, the thinning of his lips. His fingers dug painfully into her ass, as if at any moment he would lift her up and off him and toss her to the side, so he could simply escape.

She hoped he didn't.

She recognized the signs. They were clear. He wasn't used to making a personal connection with a woman when he had sex with her. It made him uncomfortable.

But even so, his eyes exposed the truth. How hot he burned, how vulnerable he was becoming by keeping that connection. He wanted to break it.

But she refused to let him.

This was good for her. This was better for him.

She smoothed her palms up his broad chest, skimming over his pointed nipples, then she cupped his cheeks, forcing him to see her.

Really see *her*.

Keeping her eyes open, she leaned closer and brushed her lips lightly over his, keeping the kiss gentle, unlike any of their previous kisses. No, those had been more about him showing her that he was in control. He was in charge. He was the boss.

He needed to realize he didn't always need to be hard and remote, that sometimes good things came in soft packages. Not everyone was an enemy to steel himself against. Not everyone was suspect or bad. Some people were good.

And he could let that good in without his whole psyche imploding.

She brushed her lips over his once more, then starting from the top, she pressed butterfly kisses along his scar, down his forehead, his eyebrow, the bridge of his nose, over his cheek, ending at the corner of his lip where it was pulled slightly upward.

She teased his lips with the tip of her tongue, then swept it along his bottom lip, before dipping it inside. She took his mouth again, but he didn't kiss her back at first. He'd become tense, his jaw even tighter, his breathing sharp like it always became when she explored his scar.

The proof of his vulnerability.

She pulled back just enough to whisper "Ryan," before pressing her lips against his once more, not giving up until finally... *finally* he began to kiss her back. They fed off each other, their tongues tangling, their breath mingled. She moaned into his mouth and he accepted it.

His hand slid from her ass up her spine, continued around her neck until his fingers tangled in her hair at the back of her head as he deepened the kiss while she rocked back and forth on his lap. Her clit was so sensitive that the more she rocked, the wetter she became and the closer she got to that precipice.

With a slight tilt of his head, he kissed her like she was the only thing keeping him alive. Like she was his lungs to provide him oxygen, his heart to keep his blood pumping. Spreading her fingers over both of his cheeks, she returned the kiss in a way to prove to him that he *was* alive.

He was very alive.

She rocked harder against him, driving him deeper and their kiss became more intense. After a few moments, they had to break it because neither could catch their breath. Even so, she didn't stop, she continued to ride him as his one hand gripped her hair almost painfully. The fingers of his other hand traced along her crease and she cried out as he slipped his middle finger deep inside her.

She ground down on his cock and his finger, not caring that he was too deep. That slight edge of discomfort had her blood racing, her breath ragged and rapid, his name teetering on her lips. He wanted her to tell him when she was coming. He wanted her to use his name.

There was only one name she would utter when she came. It wasn't Mercy.

"*Ryan...* I'm coming," she said on a hitched breath.

And as she did so, his hips shot off the chair and he spilled deep inside her.

When he lowered himself back onto the seat, she draped herself over his chest and wrapped her arms around his neck.

With her cheek resting on his shoulder and his arms around her waist, they remained there quietly for a long time. Neither wanting to move, to break their connection. Neither wanting to let the other go.

Neither wanting to admit what had just changed between them.

Mostly because neither wanted to recognize the fact that things might have just gotten complicated.

He never should have slept with her and, after he fucked

up the first time, he never should have repeated it. He didn't just repeat it once, he repeated it so many times, he'd lost track.

Lines were blurring, he was losing his razor-sharp focus and he was fighting this addiction to a woman he should have no parts of.

That quicksand he stepped in was now strangling him, and he was desperately trying to claw his way out of it. But he had no grip, nothing to hang onto to haul himself out of the mire.

He just kept sinking.

The only problem was if he went under, things could get dark. And if things went that direction, he might become helpless to protect her.

He needed to remain on the surface, hold onto the light, keep focused on his mission. On the reason they were at this dump of a rental, the reason he'd met Rissa in the first place.

Somebody powerful wanted to keep her quiet. And the easy way to do that was to simply remove that voice by taking her out, silencing her forever.

He could not let that happen. What had started out as a paid job now became a personal mission.

What he needed to do was get one of the other Shadows to take over guarding her, so he could head back to Vegas to wreak havoc on Nicco and his men. He was even tempted to take out Paranzino as well, simply for the fact that he'd put Rissa in this dire situation in the first place.

Fuck that asshole. That man had her complete trust and he'd lied to her. Put her at risk without her knowledge because of how dirty he was.

He allowed that filth to touch Rissa.

Maybe now it was Mercy's job to clean up that mess. It was time to strategize and take action. This inactivity, this waiting, was killing him and the only way to relieve that tension was to fuck Rissa. And every time he did so...

Right. Every time he did so, he was back sinking in that fucking quicksand.

Every time he was inside her, she somehow, in turn, wormed her way inside him.

But here he was, digging around inside the dark, musty, run-down shed, looking for shit to brace the bed, because even though he knew it was dangerous to keep fucking her, that was all he could think about.

Though the cabin wasn't as bad as the abandoned house that the Shadow Warriors MC assholes had taken Kiki and Jazz to, it kept reminding him of that day they found the two women there.

He never told anyone, but he returned a couple times to sit in the middle of that house. A shack with no windows, peeling wallpaper, ratty carpet in spots, broken floor boards in others. He'd sit and focus on how those two fuckers needed to die so they'd never be able to touch another woman again.

So they'd never destroy another soul.

On his third trip back, he had brought an accelerant along with a lighter and burned that fucking place down to the ground, so it could never again be used for that purpose.

He watched it burn for hours, keeping an ear out for sirens. Luckily, they never came, since the house had been out in the middle of nowhere. Or maybe nobody cared enough to call it in.

Either way, it was satisfying and cleansing to watch it be reduced to ash.

Then he turned his attention to taking out the Warriors, one by one, until there was nothing left of them, either. He didn't give one of those damn nomads any mercy. If they wore that MC's colors, they were in his line of sight.

He'd do the same to Nicco and his men.

He'd throttle the threat until it no longer existed.

"What the fuck," he muttered as he used his cell phone as a makeshift flashlight. He pointed it at the dark corners of the shitty shed and found nothing he could use. Not one fucking thing. They needed a place to sleep, or at least somewhere for Rissa to sleep, since he hardly slept. The threadbare couch wasn't big enough for the two of them, and it smelled like cat piss.

He might just have to pry up some of the bricks from the front walk to stack as posts for the bed corners. He'd thought about throwing the mattress directly on the floor, but not only was it too thin, Rissa had shuddered at the thought of being the same level as the resident rodents.

No matter what, this whole thing was a major pain in his ass and it all needed to end soon.

His spine snapped straight, and he stilled as he heard a noise behind him. He hit the power button on his phone, letting it go dark.

He slowly and quietly turned as his eyes adjusted to the dark.

Just in time to see something long and metal swing in his direction.

Then he saw nothing.

Parris's pulse was pounding so hard, it was trying to escape her throat. The blood rushing in her ears was making it difficult to hear.

She couldn't see because she was blindfolded. She couldn't speak because she was gagged. She couldn't move because she was bound.

She had no idea where she was. She had no idea who had her.

Well, she knew who the men belonged to, she just never

got a good look at them as they knocked her to the floor from behind, causing her skin to split open above her eye. Then they had her trussed up before she could get out a scream of warning to Mercy.

She closed her eyes behind the blood-soaked blindfold and remembered the last time she saw him. Mercy had been walking out the back door of the cabin in search of something to brace the bed up. All for her. So *she* could sleep. He went outside to do something for her and was probably now dead.

Because she couldn't imagine she'd be in this position if he wasn't dead or seriously injured. He wasn't a man who would let any of this happen without a fight.

Unless they ambushed him.

If these men had achieved that, then they'd found their location quickly and had been waiting to make their move.

She had resisted crying, but now couldn't stop the first tear from falling. This was all her fault. Her stupid idea of getting a message to her sister.

She had been careless and now both her and Mercy were paying the price.

They wanted her; maybe they'd let him live.

She could only hope.

However, right now she was having a hard time drumming up any hope.

Because this was it.

She was going to die. She just didn't know how soon.

And she could only hope that they wouldn't draw it out and make her suffer.

There was that word again.

Hope.

She needed to stop using it.

Hopeless seemed to be way more appropriate for her current situation.

Chapter Fourteen

MERCY SQUATTED on the concrete floor of the warehouse. He had a blood-soaked towel pressed to the seeping wound at the back of his head.

He was trying not to rage, pace, or scream since he knew that would just get the blood flowing faster.

"Need to get to the hospital," D said in a stream of grunts.

Mercy's fingers clenched the towel tighter. "No."

"Probably got a concussion."

"Won't be the first fucking time."

"Need stitches."

Mercy wanted to shake his head, but he knew better. Instead, he said, "Walker's getting the first aid kit. He's gonna sew it closed."

"Crazy motherfucker," Diesel muttered. "Gonna get fuckin' Paranzino on the horn an' see if he's heard from the other motherfuckin' side."

"You tell him—"

D cut him off by bellowing, "Know what to fuckin' tell 'im!" Then Mercy's boss lumbered away, shaking his head.

Yeah, D knew what to do. That was the only thing

keeping Mercy from detonating like a grenade. Diesel had dealt with this kind of shit before. They all have.

Mercy because, as a Delta Force operator, hostage recovery was his specialty.

The rest of his team had assisted D with recovering not only Kiki and Jazz, but Diesel's own woman, Jewel, when the Warriors had kidnapped her. And again, when D's club brother, Slade, was taken by the same fucknuts.

So, D knew what was up. He'd had experience with this type of shit, though not as much as Mercy. Or even as much as some of the other Shadows.

No, Mercy dealt with hostage situations one too many times. He bore the scars of the last one he'd handled.

Or attempted to handle with some success. But it was that last situation that ended his military career.

Walker was suddenly standing next to him.

How the fuck did that asshole approach him without Mercy knowing? Most likely because his fucking head was throbbing, and he couldn't think straight. Also, because D was right... He was sure he had a concussion. A metal pipe meeting the back of his head pretty much guaranteed that.

They should have killed him. That was their first mistake. He wasn't sure why they hadn't. It would have been easy enough to do once he was down and out.

Maybe they thought he was dead. But if he'd been in their shoes, he would have plugged a couple .45's center mass to make sure.

Maybe they wanted to keep the noise down to a minimum, so as not to warn Rissa or any nearby neighbors. At night sound carried and a couple gunshots might draw some attention.

If it was him, he would have made sure the man down was dead. Even if it meant putting that pipe to good use until he was splattered with brain matter.

Whatever their reasoning was, he hoped they did the same with Rissa.

Not that he wanted her injured, he just didn't want her dead.

So, if them trying to remain on the down low kept her alive a little longer, then he was okay with that.

Mercy just needed to move soon and find those fuckers before they decided it was time to dispose of their hostage.

The only problem was, Mercy needed the gaping hole at the back of his head closed first.

"Need you to sit somewhere or lay down so I can do this. It ain't gonna be pretty. The back of your head might end up matching your fucking ugly face."

Mercy glanced up at Walker as he said, "Why do you think I look like this, asshole? I sewed it closed myself," and didn't miss the other man's wince.

"Yeah, so you said. At least this needle's clean and was made for suturing. Unlike the kit you used that was made to sew on a missing fucking button."

The needle he had used might not have been sterile and the thread not appropriate, but it held his face together until he could get medical help. At the time, that was all that mattered. "Let's get this done. I have shit to take care of."

"*We* have shit to take care of."

Mercy met Walker's gaze and gave him a slight chin lift. "We," he corrected himself. "Get me sewed shut so *we* can go get these motherfuckers."

Not twenty minutes later, with his brains safe from spilling out due to Walker's skill with a needle, they were crowded into D's office. It used to be that all of them fit somewhat comfortably until Jewel squeezed out two babies and D had his girls' baby shit now filling his office, because it was rare that he was more than a few feet away from them at any time.

Mercy couldn't wait until they started kindergarten and

D tried to fit his enormous body into one of those tiny school desks next to them. He'd end up wearing it like a tutu because he'd never get himself back out. *If* it was even capable of holding his bulk.

But while that thought was entertaining, what D was saying was not. Mercy was itching to go find Rissa. However, they had no way to tail her or the men who nabbed her.

At least, not quickly. And time was not on their side.

"He's already in the fuckin' air, on his way," D was grumbling.

"So we gotta sit on our hands 'til he gets here?" Brick asked. Mercy could see Brick was chomping at the bit for some action just as much as Mercy.

"Got a better idea?"

Hunter spoke up, "We need to get Nicco on the phone to get a bead on him. If he contacts Paranzino, I can find him. But if Nicco isn't with Parris, then... *Fuck.*" He scrubbed a hand over his short hair. "Maybe we need to snag Nicco and then have him call his men wherever they're holding her."

"We assume they're holding her. Could be dead and dumped by now," Steel muttered.

The whole room stilled and went silent for a second until Walker exploded, "Fuck! You asshole!" and shoved Steel.

All eyes slid to Mercy. The thin thread that held him together was getting more frayed by the second. It was on the verge of snapping.

"Sorry, brother," Steel said.

The hardest thing he ever fucking said was, "She's just a job, brother." Because fuck if that was true. She wasn't just a fucking job. She wasn't just a package.

She was Rissa.

And Rissa belonged to him.

He forced himself to continue, "Gotta expect that they

didn't waste time. Though, thinking since they didn't pop her right there, they're holding her for a reason."

"Blackmail," Brick muttered.

"Could be a good thing, gives us some time to work with. If they were going to just take her out, this job would be over and done with and I'd be looking for my next assignment," Mercy said with careful control.

He was about to flip the fuck out and if that happened, he might not be able to be contained. And in no way would losing his shit help Rissa. He needed to keep it tight. Needed to keep focused.

He met his boss's dark gaze. It hadn't gone unnoticed that he'd been watching Mercy carefully. D knew more about what was swirling inside Mercy than he let on. Probably because he'd been through the same thing when Jewel was snagged. That man had turned into what Jewel called him: a "beast."

However, Mercy only knew Rissa for a few days. D knew his woman his whole life since they'd grown up together in the MC. Diesel's connection to Jewelee ran a hell of a lot deeper than Mercy's did with Rissa.

Didn't it?

He easily understood why D had never wanted to be saddled with a woman or with kids. It made him susceptible by putting the people he loved at risk, since they could be used as a weapon against him. Used as pawns.

Rissa was a pawn in Paranzino's war, in a game she'd had no idea she was a part of. Now she could pay the ultimate price for being loyal to what she considered a close friend. Someone she trusted because she never knew the truth.

"How soon will Paranzino be here?" Mercy asked, his fingers curling into his palms as the urge to choke that fucker to death surged through him.

"Since he's got a fuckin' private jet, maybe four hours."

Four hours was a long fucking time for Rissa to be in the enemy's hands. Mercy didn't like that at all. Four hours of being unable to do a fucking thing to find her.

He not only didn't like that, it made him cranky as fuck. "Can't wait four hours to start searching."

"What're you gonna do?" his boss asked. "She ain't got a cell phone to ping. She got nothin' to track 'er. Don't even know who snagged her ass. Brick said there wasn't even tire tracks once the vehicle hit the pavement. Unless you got some kinda magic you haven't told us about, not sure where the fuck we're gonna start."

He was going to start by ripping off Paranzino's head. That's where he was going to fucking start.

He sucked oxygen deep into his lungs in an attempt to tamp down his burning rage.

"What if she's bein' taken back to Vegas and our asses are all here, includin' Paranzino?" Ryder asked.

D lifted his shoulders and let them drop heavily. "Then she's that fucker's problem. It's outta our hands."

Mercy closed his eyes. He needed to keep his mouth shut right now because otherwise the shit he was going to spew would be toxic.

"Don't think that's true, boss." Walker's low words sank into Mercy's still throbbing, scrambled brain.

Mercy inhaled slowly, exhaled even slower.

Inhale. Exhale.

Breathe.

Breathe.

Fucking goddamn breathe.

"Out!" D barked. "All of you, get gone!"

Mercy's eyes opened.

"'Cept you," Diesel shouted, spit flying while jabbing a finger in Mercy's direction. "You fuckin' stay."

"We need to get a plan together," Brick said.

"Yep," Diesel barked. "Gonna do that. Right now, fuckin' get gone."

All eyes turned to Mercy and after a few seconds, they filed out of the office, Hunter giving Mercy a shoulder squeeze before shutting the door behind him.

"Went against my order, didn't you? Stuck your dick in 'er after I fuckin' told you not to." Planting his massive palms on his desk he pushed up out of his office chair. "Coulda walked away from this mess, washed our hands of it. He still woulda had to pay our initial fee. Just woulda forfeited the fuckin' bonus. But fuck no. Had to get your dick wet. Now it's fuckin' personal. Now you ain't gonna let it go, even if we're told to by the goddamn client. If you get shit stuck to the bottom of your fuckin' boots from this, it's all on you." He shook his head and crossed his massive arms over his equally massive chest. "Hope that snatch was worth it."

Diesel, like the rest of the Shadows, was like a brother to him. However, at that very fucking moment, he was glad a desk separated them. He had no idea who would win a battle between the two but with a concussion, Mercy was sure today it wouldn't be him.

"Got a cracked-open skull, but you still wanna come at me. Can see it, brother. You're fucked. She got your dick in a sling." Diesel's dark brown eyes narrowed. "Pussy must be good."

Now, his boss was antagonizing him. Trying to get him to snap.

Why? What was the fucking point?

Then something rare happened. Something Mercy hardly ever saw, unless it was directed at Indie or Violet. Occasionally even Jewel, when D didn't think anyone was watching.

Diesel fucking smiled.

Smiled. The big man sank heavily back into his chair.

"Goddamn. Must be good shit since you got it bad after a few days. Seen my brothers go down hard once they found the right one. But *fuck*, never thought you'd fall like that."

Mercy finally unlocked his jaws. "Never thought I'd see the day you'd have not only a woman but two babies."

D sat back in his chair and contemplated Mercy. "Yeah. Sometimes pussy's hard to resist."

"You calling Jewelee pussy?"

Diesel brushed a hand over his short dark hair then down his jaw. "They all start out as just pussy. Got me? But in the end, sometimes that shit's got teeth an' ain't lettin' you go. She got a fuckin' sharp set of choppers down there?"

For fuck's sake.

Diesel was right. He watched the man's fellow biker brothers all get caught one by one. Finding the right woman not only had almost all of them tied down, but the club was beginning to overpopulate Shadow Valley on its own.

Mercy wasn't a part of the MC. He and his crew stayed on the edge, so the club would remain legit. But MC brothers and military brothers were a lot alike. And none of them, except for Jag who'd chased Ivy for so long, had been looking to get snagged.

But they got snagged.

Fuck, Mercy might have stuck his foot in a steel trap. Or his dick, anyway.

"Really wanna let Paranzino handle this mess, but you ain't gonna let that happen. Am I fuckin' wrong?"

"No. But we got nothing."

"Right," D grunted. "Got nothin'. Gotta get somethin' an' get your woman back still breathin'."

Breathing would be great.

Unharmed would be better.

Mercy wasn't asking for too much.

"Call those assholes back in here. Need a fuckin' plan

before that fucker gets off his fancy tin can with wings an' gets here."

That they did.

SHE COULD NO LONGER FEEL her hands. Her ass was just as numb from sitting on some uncomfortable metal chair. She remained bound, gagged and blindfolded. And now, she couldn't hear anything, either. At least the blood from the cut above her eye had finally stopped trickling down her face.

They had left her in a room by herself and closed the door. The lock clicking had been the last thing she heard. Well, except for the pounding of her heart. That was hard to ignore.

The longer she sat there, the more pissed she got. But she was glad they hadn't hurt her in any way. They hadn't struck her or even touched her inappropriately. For that she could be thankful.

Still, that didn't mean it wouldn't happen.

Maybe they were waiting on someone in particular to show up wherever they were. Or she was going to be used as a bargaining chip with Michael.

She preferred the latter, if she had a choice.

Which she didn't.

Her bladder was screaming, but she couldn't call out to anyone with that damn rag in her mouth.

She had no idea if anyone was looking for her. She had no idea where they had taken her. She had no idea why she was alone in a room.

And, worse, she had no idea if Mercy was alive.

If he was dead, would she ever be found? Would Michael have people skilled enough to find her? If he was alive...

For goodness' sake, she hoped he was alive.

He needed to be alive because *she* needed him to be alive. It was selfish, she knew. But since she was currently in a messed-up situation she was allowing herself to have that one selfish thought.

Plus, just sitting there for hours had her mind spinning with all kind of things.

Things like, if they both survived this, she was...

She was...

She wasn't going to do anything, because what she wanted was probably not the same thing he wanted.

He didn't want a relationship. He probably wasn't even capable of a relationship. Not the way he was now. And even if he agreed to sit down with a therapist, someone other than her...

Who was she kidding? He wasn't going to simply agree to therapy. The man was in his late thirties. Maybe even older. He wasn't eager to change anything about himself, especially for a woman.

Ugh. Why was she even thinking about this? She should be more worried about what the men who took her were going to do, rather than Mercy's mental state.

She could be raped, even mutilated. Have fingers or toes cut off and mailed to Michael. They could use her as bait to kill him.

So many things were worse than Mercy not wanting a normal freaking relationship!

She held her breath as the door creaked open and heavy footsteps came in her direction.

Oh shit.

A deep voice, way too close for her liking, made her jerk in the chair. "Your lover boy's on the phone and wants to hear your voice. He wants assurances you're alive before we begin negotiations."

The gag was yanked roughly from her mouth. She

sucked her lungs full of air while she could, then tried to clear her scratchy throat.

"Talk," her captor demanded. A phone near her ear.

"Ryan?" she croaked. Was that her voice? It didn't sound like her at all.

"Parris!" filled the room. "It's Michael."

Michael. While she should feel relieved to hear his voice, she didn't. It wasn't who she hoped it would be. "Where's Ryan? Is he okay?"

"He... uh..." A slight pause. "I don't know, Parris. Are you okay?"

"I... They have me tied up... gagged and—"

The phone was pulled away and she could no longer hear Michael, only the deep voice growling, "You heard her voice. No questions."

Then the gag was pulled back in place, footsteps receded, and the door slammed shut again.

No. Oh no.

Chapter Fifteen

"Ryan?"

That hardly sounded like her through the speaker of Paranzino's cell phone.

Had they hurt her? Had she suffered? Was she in pain?

"Parris! It's Michael," asshole answered her.

"Where's Ryan? Is he okay?"

For fuck's sake, she was more worried about him than her own situation.

Mercy struggled not to assure Rissa that he was alive and sort of well. He wanted Nicco's heavies to think he had been taken out and wasn't going to hunt their asses down.

Which he was. And he would get off on every fucking second of it.

"He... uh..." Paranzino's eyes slid to him. Mercy gave him a slight shake of his head. "I don't know, Parris. I'm worried about you. Are you okay?"

"I... They have me tied up... gagged and—"

A deep voice on the other end of the phone growled, "You heard her voice. No questions."

The sound of footsteps and a door slamming in the background came through the speaker.

They had her in a room. Mercy just needed to figure out where.

Hunter circled his finger in the air, motioning to Paranzino to keep the guy talking. Not that it mattered for tracking purposes, but by keeping the man on the phone, they were simply buying time.

Hunter had a way to geolocate what they assumed would be a burner phone by cellular triangulation. However, that wasn't always accurate. It still left a large area to search. Preferably, they needed to arrange a meet, if the other side agreed.

Nicco would most likely want to meet with Paranzino, not his muscle. He doubted Nicco was stupid enough to be at the same location that Rissa was.

Though, his men were pretty fucking stupid to leave him alive. They couldn't get much more stupid than that.

"I need to speak with Nicco, not his hired help," Paranzino said, his brows furrowed.

Okay, yeah, even though the asshole was worried about Rissa, Mercy didn't give a fuck. He was the one who put her in this situation with his dirty dealings.

"Michael," came a purr through the phone and filled the small room.

When the voice changed on the other end of the phone, Mercy's eyes slid to Walker and he lifted a brow. Walker returned the gesture. Both of them were surprised Nicco was on scene where Rissa was. It could be a good thing, if the man was in town. It would make it easier to take the man the fuck out. Or it could be bad, if they had transported Rissa somewhere away from the Pittsburgh area. Which could be anywhere and finding Rissa would be almost impossible without careful negotiations.

Mercy hoped it was the first scenario.

"I only want Parris safe. She has nothing to do with our business dealings," Paranzino said. "This perceived war of yours is between you and me, Nicco. Not her. She had no idea about any of it."

"Ah, keeping secrets from your lover. *Tsk*, *tsk*, Michael."

"You know she's not my lover. You know my relationship status."

"Then why do you care what happens to her?"

"Because she... She's a close friend who means the world to me."

Mercy frowned. For fuck's sake, now the asshole just made Rissa a more valuable pawn in Nicco's eyes. Stupid fuck.

He wanted to rip Paranzino's head off right then and there and shit down the gaping hole left behind. He couldn't. He needed that asshole for the time being.

"I'm willing to let her go. I only want two things from you."

Paranzino's glanced at Mercy who nodded in a silent answer. "What?"

"One, for you to stay out of my business. Stop stealing my workforce. You're hurting my bottom line. In reality, both of our businesses can flourish in Vegas. *If* we stay in our own lanes, we can run our businesses harmoniously. There's enough clientele for both of us. Two, I want assurances that your girl here isn't going to flap her pretty lips. I want her to forget what she saw. If both you and she agree to those terms, I'll let her go."

Mercy drew a finger over his throat in a slicing motion. Brick stepped up to Paranzino and spoke softly in his ear.

As soon as Paranzino hit the phone's mute button, Mercy growled, "Don't believe it. They're not going to let her go."

He glanced at Hunter, who was behind a computer in their network room where they had gathered. Once he caught Hunter's attention, the man gave him the thumbs up, then turned it sideways.

Fuck. Hunter had an idea where they might be situated, but not an exact location.

Nicco would want a meet, though. He wasn't going to let Paranzino live. Or Rissa. The sex trafficker didn't want to share territory, he wanted to dominate it. He didn't want to "stay in his lane," he wanted to own the whole highway. The sex business was a lucrative one and, if you're willing to kill for it, what was plugging one more bullet into one more brain?

Or two, if they executed Rissa.

He ground his molars at that thought and bit back a growl.

He had to keep reminding himself that he needed the asshole alive and to not snap his neck, even though his fingers were itching to do so.

Paranzino continued, "If I agree, you'll let her go?"

"I need to hear you say that you'll find your own whores and stop stealing mine."

"Maybe you need to stop rounding up teenage runaways and putting them to work like slaves, Nicco. And if you treated the ones who weren't underage better, they wouldn't be so willing to find a new employer who values their hard work."

Mercy's blood was boiling. He was ready to rage like a pissed-off Diesel. The other Shadows were all fighting their reactions as well, with tight jaws, tight lips and tight fists.

"I'll assume you're not agreeing, then," Nicco purred. "That may be to my benefit, Michael. Parris is a beautiful woman. I have a specific client in mind who would pay a fortune for a new sex slave with curves like hers. She would look spectacular shackled with her bare ass in the air, just waiting for her master to do what he will with her. He pays extra for women who are a challenge and not easily trained. He enjoys breaking them himself. I bet this one would put up a fight."

One corner of Mercy's lip curled.

With one hand on his hip, Paranzino took a breath, then dropped his head. "I'll agree. She'll agree. I swear to that. I want to meet out in the open, though, to pick her up."

"We're not meeting, Michael. We're just going to drop her somewhere and text you the location after we do so."

Paranzino lifted his head to meet Mercy's gaze. Mercy couldn't tell if it was anger or frustration on the asshole's face. Or just plain fear. Mercy gave him a sharp nod, indicating what Nicco said was acceptable. The other man barked into the phone, "You have your damn agreement. Let's just get this done quickly."

The room went dead quiet for a few seconds after the call disconnected.

Paranzino needed the cold, hard truth, so Mercy gave it to him. "They're going to take both you and her out. Along with anyone you bring with you."

"Do you think so?"

Mercy kept his fists pinned to his thighs so he didn't pop the stupid fuck in the mouth for asking such a stupid fucking question. "Been doing this shit a long time. Dealing with terrorism, with hostages, all that fucking sticky bullshit. You think they're gonna just let her go because you agree to stop putting a hurting on their sex trafficking business? Or because Rissa agrees to keep her trap shut? Fuck no. They could kill her easily. Sure. They have her. But they want you, too. She's the bait. You're the target. She, and anyone who shows up with you, are expendable."

Paranzino dragged a hand through his hair. "So now what?"

"Now the good news is, we don't have to search for Rissa," Brick said. "We'll wait for the drop location and set up a perimeter wherever that is."

"He means outside of the perimeter Nicco's men set up," Walker clarified.

"Why wouldn't they just tell us now where they're going to leave her?"

Jesus fucking Christ. "Because they're trying to avoid us ambushing them. They're going to put her in a spot, set up perimeter and wait. Same shit we'd be doing if we had the location. The only good thing is, I'm sure his men aren't as skilled as Brick when it comes to picking motherfuckers off at a distance. Our perimeter can be broader than theirs."

"Nobody's as good as me," Brick chimed in with a cocky grin.

Mercy almost strained his eyes when he fought rolling them. "Right. They're gonna have a weapon trained on Rissa. They're gonna have one on you. I'm not worried about your ass. I'm worried about hers. So, we need to find and take out whoever is covering her. As for you," Mercy shrugged, "something happens to you, we'll consider it collateral damage."

"D hasn't been paid yet," Hunter reminded him.

Mercy shrugged again, ignoring Paranzino's gaping mouth. "I'll take the financial hit if D gets stiffed."

"K-Keep me alive and you'll get paid. Keep Parris alive and you get that bonus."

At this point he couldn't give a fuck about the bonus. And he really didn't care if Paranzino lived or died.

He cared only about Rissa. That was it.

Paranzino was expendable to both Nicco and Mercy. He'd be shitting his pants if he knew that.

Mercy stepped forward and shoved a finger into Paranzino's face. "When this bullshit is over and if you're still standing, you're cutting all ties with Rissa. You got me? She doesn't need to have your shit splattered all over her."

"She's not going to want that."

"Not up to her. That's going to be your decision, not hers. And you're going to be very fucking clear about it with her. Got me?" The last he said inches from Paranzino's face.

So close, that Mercy knew exactly when the man held his breath.

He didn't breathe again until he answered a few seconds later, "I understand."

Mercy stepped back and let his gaze slice through the room to the rest of the Shadows. "Gonna need to be ready for close quarters combat. Gotta go in quiet, take them out without tipping off the rest. Brick will set up far enough out to get the complete picture. The rest of us are going to start with a wide perimeter and work our way in, taking out whoever we come across. Don't think they'll be a lot of them. At most, the five that Paranzino's hired help couldn't locate. Thinking Nicco's keeping them close. Would like to snag one for questioning to find out Nicco's location since I doubt he'll be on scene. But maybe we can *convince* one of them to talk. Get Nicco located and dispatch him."

"No mercy," Walker murmured.

"No fuckin' mercy," Mercy agreed.

"'Justice is for those who deserve it; Mercy is for those who don't,'" Ryder quoted.

"'It is Mercy, not justice or courage or even heroism, that alone can defeat evil,'" Hunter also quoted but a lot louder.

"But you're not alone, brother," Brick reassured him.

No, he wasn't. He had good men at his back. Right now, even with a head injury, he had laser-sharp focus on his mission. Which was to get Rissa safely back. And to deal with any of the motherfuckers who touched her or put her at risk.

No fucking mercy.

Fuck.

Them.

All.

Parris couldn't stop trembling. Being used as bait for what she could only assume was a deadly trap, she never felt so helpless in her life.

She wanted to scream her head off to warn whoever was coming for her. Michael, most likely. But Mercy, too?

She'd been moved from her former location and now was outside in the open somewhere. The cut on her forehead was throbbing. She was sweating and could hardly breathe because of the gag. Her throat was raw from making noise, but all that effort had been useless since it was muffled.

They had dumped her on the ground somewhere unknown and all she could hear were birds chirping and leaves rustling in the warm, light breeze.

She was not only thirsty and light-headed, they never gave her a chance to relieve herself. She held it until she couldn't anymore. Now she had sat in her own urine-soaked yoga pants for the last couple hours and her skin burned from it.

She wanted to cry with humiliation, but not only did she have no tears left, mortification over doing something she couldn't control was the least of her worries.

She hadn't been tortured or raped. Peeing her pants was nothing compared to that. So, if that and her numb extremities were her only issues, she needed to suck it up and be thankful it wasn't worse.

However, the sun beating down on her wasn't helping her dehydration or the headache from her injury and she had no idea how much longer she'd have to sit there until something happened.

Was someone coming to rescue her? Were her captors just waiting for word from their boss to put a gun to the back of her head, too? At least being outside it wouldn't matter if they made a mess. Was that their plan? They could kill her and leave her there for the animals and birds to pick her bones clean.

Ryan, where are you? Are you alive? Please be alive. Please find me. Please be the hero I so desperately need right now.

Please.

But stay safe. I won't be able to bear it if anything happens to you.

When did this happen? When did she become attached to a man who kept himself so emotionally unavailable? A man she hadn't even known for a week?

Light, but rapid footsteps were heading in her direction. She turned her head until she could focus on the sound. Yes, definitely footsteps. They sped up the closer they got.

"Parris," Michael whispered.

She should be relieved he was there, but instead her anxiety ratcheted up a notch. No, ten notches. Whatever she was waiting for, whatever her captors were waiting for, was about to happen.

She was the trap. Michael the prey.

"I'm going to untie you as quickly as I can, but you're not to move from this spot until we get the 'all clear.'"

All clear? That sounded like a term that Mercy and his team would use, not Michael, which meant they were involved. She should feel relieved that they were, but instead it just made her skin crawl with unease.

He worked at the knot on her gag and once it fell free, she sucked in a breath. Seconds later her blindfold was ripped off her head. Overly sensitive to the sudden sunlight, she blinked her eyes until she could focus somewhat on her surroundings. She had lost one contact when those men had knocked her down at the cabin and she had banged her head. Michael was now on his knees behind her sawing jerkily with a knife at the bindings at her wrists.

She tried to speak, but it was almost like she had laryngitis. She struggled to push the words past her desert-dry throat. "What's happening?"

She jerked forward and gasped in relief when her bound hands became free.

Michael spoke low and fast as he sawed at the rope on her ankles. "They put you in a spot where I couldn't bring a vehicle. I had to walk in. We're surrounded. Diesel's men are out there supposedly taking out any threats."

Parris glanced around again now that she could see things more clearly. At least with her eye that still had its contact lens. She was in some sort of small clearing in the woods. She wasn't hearing anything that sounded like "taking out threats." She heard nothing. She had no idea if that was good or bad.

Either way... "This was a set-up," she croaked.

"Yes. Mercy said their target was me, not you, of course. This was to get me out in the open and to kill us both, unfortunately. Those men know what they're doing."

"Which men?"

"Diesel's men. I think whoever Nicco hired are killers, but Diesel assured me that his men were the best. Which was why I used his service in the first place to protect you." He hesitated. From behind her, his next words sounded bitter and angry. "Though they didn't."

"That was my fault, not Ryan's."

"None of this is your fault, Parris. It's mine. I'm sorry I put you in this position. You're the closest friend I have next to Joshua. And besides him, you're the only one I trust completely. Regretfully, I've messed up our friendship. I'm so sorry this has happened."

"You didn't trust me enough to tell me the truth," Parris tried to hiss with annoyance but instead it came out raspy.

Michael moved around on his knees to face her. He grabbed both of her numb hands and began to massage them to help the blood flow. "I'm sorry. We'll discuss this later… when we're safe."

"I just want to get out of here, Michael. We're sitting ducks."

"I know, but I was instructed to keep you right here until we're told otherwise."

"And what if all of the Shadows get killed? Are we still supposed to sit here and just wait for someone to kill us, too? We're exposed here, Michael." Parris bit back a sob at the thought of Mercy or any of his fellow Shadows getting injured or killed, all because of Michael's bullshit.

The more she thought about it, the angrier she got.

"Why didn't they at least give you a bullet-proof vest or something?"

"Because a vest doesn't save you from a head shot. And they also don't care if I live or die. They're only doing this to save you."

"Why would they care about me more than you? You're the one paying them."

"I can only guess it has to do with the bonus."

Oh, that's right. That fucking bonus. Of course.

MERCY STOOD after wiping the blood off his knife on the downed man's clothes to clean it off. He tucked his blade back in its sheath on his hip and pulled out his phone. One down. He was just waiting on word from the rest of his crew.

His phone was set to silent, so he hit the power button and checked his texts.

Ryder had sent out a group text to all of them, as well as to Diesel, with a photo of the guy he also took out with his knife.

Steel had sent a picture of another guy on the ground with what looked like an unnatural twist to his neck. Steel had the strength to snap a man's neck efficiently and quietly.

He had trained the rest of them to do so, but no one did it as well as him. And it wasn't like they got a lot of practice with it.

Brick sent a selfie which included a grin and a thumbs up as he cradled his MK-11 like it was a baby. He probably read his rifle bedtime stories and kissed it goodnight.

The good news was, four threats were now disabled.

If Nicco wasn't among them, they needed to keep one alive to find out where that fucker was.

He texted back, *Target?*

Paranzino had showed them a picture of the trafficker. But Hunter had dug up the fucker's mugshot, too, so they'd have a better idea of what the man looked like.

All answering texts returned with a negative.

Unfortunately, the dead guy at Mercy's feet wasn't Nicco, either.

However, he hadn't heard from Walker yet, so there was hope that he was either dealing with the head honcho himself or getting one of Nicco's heavies to talk.

Mercy had given his target two chances to tell him Nicco's location. When he didn't, Mercy took the appropriate action.

Of course, Brick hadn't gotten close enough to question any target in his sight.

Fuck. Mercy wanted Nicco so badly he could taste it. He needed to remove the head of that organization, otherwise, he'd continue to be a threat to Rissa. The man would just hire more muscle to get the job done. And hired guns were a dime a dozen.

Apparently Nicco didn't pay much for his labor since, so far, they'd been easy to take out. Not one of them had proved to be a challenge by the looks of the photos he'd seen.

As long as they heard from Walker. Since they haven't, he was getting concerned.

Mercy sent out another group text: *W's 20?*

No eyes, came in from Brick. *Gonna move south n look.*

Headn North til X paths w/ B, came from Hunter.

He needed to check on Rissa and let the rest of the guys search for Walker and whoever Walker had come across. He texted the order: *R & S spread out. Report back ASAP. Headn in.*

He still wanted to know where Nicco was. But even if the fucker got on a plane back to Vegas while he let his hired help stay behind to get rid of the two thorns in his side, Mercy had no problem catching a ride back on Paranzino's private jet to finish him off.

Rissa was not safe until Nicco was no longer breathing. She probably wasn't safe until she severed her friendship with Paranzino. Because there was no way in hell the casino mogul was cleaning up his act.

Nicco was only one battle in a struggle over power and wealth in that city full of greed and sin. And the taste of money was too addicting for a man like Paranzino to change his ways.

He took one last glance down at the gaping wound across the dead man's neck. They needed to decide what to do with the bodies. They couldn't leave trash behind.

Give a hoot, don't fucking pollute.

And Nicco's men were nothing but trash that needed to be properly disposed of.

Chapter Sixteen

Mercy had set his phone from silent to vibrate and it was doing just that in his palm as he picked his way through the thick brush to get to where Rissa was. He paused to read the text.

It was from Ryder. *W got answer. Nicco w8n 4 word A-hole's dead. Sittn n a rental 3 klicks North ready 2 head 2 airport. Keepn last 1 alive as insurance. If no witnesses, B's takn out Nicco from a distance. 10-4?*

Finally fucking good news. He texted *10-4* back.

They'd all have to circle back around and clean up the mess they made in the woods. But not until Brick drilled a hole through Nicco's melon first.

It would be better if the rental didn't get messy because if it did, they'd have to get rid of that, too, without a trace. One more headache to deal with. But he'd leave it to the rest of his team to decide how to handle Nicco.

Mess. No Mess. He didn't give a fuck.

One thing was for sure, this was all going to cost Paranzino. More than that fucking bonus.

He continued carefully trudging through the underbrush

until he saw the clearing. Paranzino was sitting on the ground, his arms wrapped around Rissa. And that right there made Mercy's trigger finger twitch.

He needed to keep his patience. He needed to get Rissa somewhere safe and make sure she was okay. Then he needed to get back to help clean up as soon as he could. This section of woods was remote, but last thing any of them needed was a Boy Scout troop out on some damn hike to trip over a few dead bodies.

Mercy wondered what badge they'd earn for that.

As he strode through the clearing, his gaze was locked on Rissa. Her face was streaked with dry tears and blood, her clothes were dirty, and she sat in a strange position on the ground. There was also a cut on her forehead above her eye. Had they violated her?

His heart began to race as he got closer. He wanted to ask her fifty questions but knew she might be in a fragile state, so he didn't want to push it. He'd get his answers. Again, he just needed to keep his patience.

Paranzino rose to his feet. "She can't stand. Her circulation was cut off for too long."

Mercy's head twisted toward the other man. The reason Rissa was on the ground at that very moment. "Shut the fuck up," he growled. Then before he could stop his knee-jerk reaction, his right fist shot out and landed square in the center of Paranzino's face. The man's nose blossomed under his fist, and blood splattered, causing blowback on both him and Rissa, but it was either punch the asshole or slice his throat in front of her.

The last would have to wait. Rissa had been through enough.

Paranzino had dropped to the ground with the impact and had both hands covering his nose as he whimpered and writhed around. Mercy was a cunt-hair close to spitting on the other man for good measure.

Mercy jabbed a finger at him and snarled, "Got shit to say and you're just gonna fucking listen. Only answer when I ask a fucking question." He didn't wait for Paranzino's response because he wasn't going to waste time. He needed to get Rissa out of there, but he wanted some assurances first. "You want Nicco out of the game? If so, you're paying Rissa a fucking million for pain and suffering, and you're not only paying my bonus, but a bonus to each of my guys for this bullshit. Otherwise, we're letting him walk and we'll let the best man win. With Rissa safe, I couldn't give a fuck if your whole business implodes."

Nicco was being disposed of no matter how Paranzino answered, but the man didn't need to know that. Right now, Nicco's life was a bargaining chip for Rissa to be compensated for the shit she'd been through. Which he didn't even know the extent of yet. However, besides the slice above her eye, she wasn't bloody or bruised anywhere else from what he could see. Her clothes, though dirty and disheveled, were in place and not torn. And for the most part she looked like she was keeping her shit together.

He was proud of her.

"Will it come back to me?" came the question through bloodied fingers.

Mercy's gaze slid back to the asshole. Only if they set it up to come back to Paranzino, which wouldn't be a bad idea. But if the authorities took him into custody for murder, the man would probably spill everything. Then Mercy would regret not killing him immediately by severing his windpipe. "No. But you know the deal."

Paranzino's eyes landed on Rissa for a split second before meeting his again. Asshole nodded, then winced. "Okay."

Mercy was sure his face hurt. Good. At least he was still breathing, even if it was only from his mouth.

For now, he was done with the asshole. He squatted next

to Rissa and cupped her cheek while searching her face. "You doing all right?"

"I'm ready to get out of here."

Her voice sounded scratchy. Half-moons of faint purple colored the skin under her eyes, her lips looked dry and cracked. She was probably dehydrated. She'd been held by Nicco's men for over eight hours. Which was eight fucking hours too long.

As she rubbed her wrists, he noticed the marks left behind from the rope that now laid on the ground next to her. He struggled to beat back the fury that bubbled up.

Patience.

Fucking patience.

Nicco was getting his.

Her captors got theirs.

Paranzino would pay.

Her legs were curled underneath her, making it easy to wrap his arms around her to pick her up.

Lift with the knees.

She was not a woman who, in any way, could be described "as light as a feather." But for fuck's sake, he was carrying her the fuck out of those woods even if it crippled him.

"Hang on," he grunted.

"You can put me down. I think I can walk."

The exhaustion in her voice made his gut twist. He wasn't going to argue with her. "Arms around my neck."

"Ryan," she whispered. "My pants. I—"

He quickly cut her off. "Don't give a shit about that." She didn't need to say it, he knew what she was talking about. "Arms around my neck."

"I'm too heavy."

"Arms around my fucking neck, woman." His control was beginning to fray and he needed to rein it back in. But he couldn't ignore the tightness in his chest, the scrambled thoughts invading his brain. The woman in his arms. Her situation. The possibility that she could have been killed, or worse, kept alive and been abused so badly she'd have a difficult time recovering.

All of that ate at his insides like acid, settled like cement in his bones. The fury burned so deeply that he was struggling to contain the storm that was building by the second.

He needed to concentrate on her. He needed to get her somewhere safe. He needed to finish this mission before letting the darkness overtake him. Before seeking relief of the tension he was feeling that went beyond a simple fuck or a session with a punching bag. Before the only thing that would right his tilted world was doing something very ugly.

"I was scared you were dead." Her words made his chest tighten.

Ditto. "Hard to kill me. No matter how many times anyone tries."

A sob caused her body to hiccup in his arms and he finally glanced down at her. He'd been avoiding that, meeting her gaze. Really looking at her. Seeing her. Who she was. What she meant to him.

Because the thought of losing her...

He'd never been afraid of much. But that thought...

That fucking fear...

Was the strongest he'd ever felt in his life. And he'd been in some precarious hair-raising, ball-shriveling situations.

The lone tear forging a path down her streaked cheek tugged at something deep inside him. It pulled at that frayed thread which threatened to send him spinning like a top.

"Damn these tears!" she exploded, swiping frantically at them.

"Rissa, you're allowed to be upset. Arms around my neck," he reminded her more softly this time.

When her arms squeezed him tighter and she buried her damp face in his neck, he almost fell to his knees right there in the thick of the woods, ripped his heart out of his chest and handed it to her. Even though it was black and withered, it was something he could give her, if nothing else.

For a long time, it had only beat to keep him alive.

Now, after barely a week, it beat for her.

He didn't know how that fucking happened.

But it did.

Apparently, the barriers he had put up for good reason had been breached.

Now, he needed to decide whether he should keep up the good fight. Or acknowledge defeat.

His face had been painted with greens and browns to match the camo-patterned military-style clothing he wore. He had a holstered handgun on one hip and a large sheathed knife on the other, making him look savage when he had made his way to her. She had wanted to rise and run to him with relief that he was alive. But her arms and legs wouldn't cooperate due to cramping and the severe pain as the circulation slowly returned.

Instead, she was resigned to wait for him to come to her.

Even though she could only see clearly out of one eye due to her lost contact lens, the air around them had been full of Mercy's barely contained rage.

She could see it in his eyes, his face, his body language.

And as much as she loved Michael, she had cheered a little inside when Mercy had broken his nose. He deserved it for everything that had happened.

If she hadn't been there, she figured Michael would have more than a crushed, bleeding nose. He'd be dead. Mercy left him in that clearing and, as he carried her away, yelled over his shoulder that someone would be back to get him.

She was pretty sure it wouldn't be Mercy.

She felt terrible that he had to carry her for what seemed like a mile. Finally, the narrow path had ended at another clearing where his vehicle was waiting. He had gently placed her on the passenger seat and dug out a first aid kit. After carefully cleaning her cut and closing it with two small butterfly bandages, he buckled her in as if she was helpless and without a word drove her to a place other than the previous two she'd been at since arriving in Shadow Valley.

This time it was an unassuming older Cape Cod-style house in the country. What was weird was an old minivan was parked in the driveway, children's toys scattered in the front yard and a swing set sat empty behind the house.

After parking his vehicle next to his Harley in the unattached garage, he came around to carry her but she had insisted she could now walk on her own. Ignoring her protests, he still assisted her out of the vehicle and into the house.

The inside was a total juxtapose of the outside. The interior was sparse and there were no signs of a family living there, especially children.

When she had stated, "This is your place," she only received a grunt in answer.

It only made sense that he'd pick a home that looked deceiving. To anyone driving by, it looked like a young family lived there, not a man like Mercy.

She spied her bags sitting by the front door and wanted to cry with relief. She needed to shower and not only wash off the dried blood, but peel off her soiled pants. She could hardly stand the smell of herself and poor Mercy had been subjected to that stink from the moment he had lifted her into his arms all the way until now.

When she turned her head to look at him over her

shoulder, she noticed he stood in the curved, open entryway between the small kitchen and the living room, staring at her. He quickly shuttered his expression.

His chest expanded as he took a deep breath and said in a tight, low voice, "Diesel dropped your shit off. Sure you're anxious to get cleaned up. There's some food in the kitchen. Not a great selection, but you need to eat something. Drink lots of fluids. Got some sports drink in the fridge. Besides water, want you to drink at least two of them before I get back."

Emotionless orders. Rules. Nothing more.

She turned to face him. "Where are you going?"

"Gotta finish what we started. Need to meet up with the rest of the team. Also deal with Paranzino."

Every muscle in her body tensed. "Don't kill him." She was pissed at him, yes, but she still loved Michael. No matter what, he was her friend and she didn't want him dead. Joshua would be devastated and lost without him.

And though she hated to admit it, she might be, too. Besides Londyn, he was her only family.

Mercy's eyes got more intense than normal. "He did you wrong, Rissa."

He did. But that didn't mean he deserved a death sentence.

"I know. He was only shielding me from the ugly side of his success. But even from what you said, he was trying to help men and women living and working on the streets who'd been abused. While his solution wasn't much better, it improved their lives in some ways. He also gave them a choice to get out of the life after giving them a hand-up."

"Don't go soft on what he got you involved in."

She wasn't. She had a lot to think about. Even so, she had some responsibility on how certain things went down. "I did it, Ryan. I created the problem when I stumbled across what I did by accident. He didn't put me in that situation.

Even worse, I did it again when I went against your orders and texted my sister. Some of the blame belongs on my shoulders."

"You wouldn't have stumbled across anything if he hadn't been involved in the shit he was. By keeping the truth from you, he put you in that position against your knowledge. If it wasn't for that, you never would have been in Shadow Valley in the first place to go against my orders. Think on that, Rissa. It all stems back from Paranzino keeping secrets."

She studied the tall man who, at the same time, stood so close but yet so far. The distance between them seemed daunting.

"We all have secrets," she whispered.

Mercy's jaw jutted out as he closed his eyes and curled his fingers into fists at his side.

When he finally opened them, they were once again cold, lifeless. He was Mercy, not the Ryan she had discovered in the past few days.

She nodded at the change within him. Understood it. He had put up his wall. Shut her out.

He had no right to judge anyone for keeping secrets.

"Diesel's sending two of his club brothers over here to keep an eye on things while I'm gone." All business. Steeled emotions.

Disappointment swept through her. "By things you mean me."

"Yeah, you. Wanna make sure there's no more threat before sending you home."

Home.

"Dawg's knowledgeable with weapons. Slade's a former Marine and a skilled fighter. They're two men I would trust at my back on any given day. You'll be safe here with them until I know things will be safe for you elsewhere."

Elsewhere. Meaning Vegas. Thousands of miles from

Shadow Valley and the man who stood stiffly before her, not letting anything that burned deep within him be visible.

She knew it was there, buried. He didn't want to recognize or reveal it. He mistakenly thought that would make him weak.

"How long do you think that will take?"

"Depends on the answers we get from Paranzino and one of Nicco's men that we have in our custody."

"When can I speak to my sister?"

"When we know you both are safe."

Of course. That made perfect sense. Parris nodded and turned away.

"That means you don't contact her until I tell you, Rissa. You need to listen this time."

More rules. More orders. Things he needed to help him function.

"I know. I will." She let her gaze bounce around the room, anything to avoid looking at him, because if she did, she was afraid she'd break down. She bit her bottom lip to keep it from quivering. At this moment, she needed to keep her emotions in check. Like him. "When will you be back?"

The hesitation before he answered was telling. He wouldn't. "When I know you and your sister are safe."

"But you'll be back before I head home?"

There was that word again. Home.

It gave her both comfort and anxiety. She needed to go back to everything she knew, everything she'd built, but she also didn't want to leave behind the one thing she'd recently discovered.

And while she had come to care for him in the short amount of time she'd known him, she also knew once she was safe and he had his bonus padding his bank account, he'd forget all about her. He'd move on to his next "job." His next paycheck.

Because, she needed to remind herself, that was all she was. His job.

That was cemented when he didn't answer her.

Jobs were clean, neat, easy to handle. They had a start and a finish.

Relationships were messy.

With disappointment coloring her thoughts, she grabbed one of her bags by the door and headed up the stairway that rose through the center of the house to where she assumed the bedrooms and the main bathroom were.

As the water pelted her in the shower, she sat at the bottom of the tub with her arms wrapped around her knees as she cried until the hot water ran cold. Until she felt hollow and numb.

When she was done feeling sorry for herself, she forced herself to towel off, blow dry her hair, and get dressed in clean clothes before heading back downstairs to do what Mercy ordered. He was right. She needed to get something to eat, something to drink. Maybe after she did so, she'd feel better. Maybe it would fill the pit in her stomach.

But when she had finally pulled herself together enough to go downstairs, she discovered what she already expected. He was gone. In his place were two large men, tattooed bikers, standing in the kitchen talking. One had a thick beard, the other had short military-short hair like Mercy's. Both wore black leather vests that declared them a part of the Dirty Angels MC. After introductions, they both watched her quietly as she numbly moved around the kitchen that felt even tinier with them in it to make a sandwich she didn't taste and sip on a sports drink that made her want to vomit, all in order to replenish her body.

While they were friendly enough, the two men keeping her company, keeping her safe, weren't who she wanted to spend her evening with.

They were still there when she finally went back upstairs

to curl up in Mercy's bed and eventually fall into a fitful sleep.

In the morning, when she woke up, he still hadn't returned. Instead, she was told to gather her things.

It was time for her to head home.

Chapter Seventeen

MERCY WATCHED as Diesel drove his classic GTO away from the house with Rissa and her luggage inside. His boss was taking her to the airport to send her home.

Where she belonged.

Once he could no longer see the old muscle car, he put his RPV in drive and pulled out of the spot where he had parked to stay out of sight.

He didn't want to say goodbye. He didn't want to see her before she left.

It might make things harder when he tried to eradicate her from his thoughts. His life. Somehow in the short amount of time he'd known her, she had found that crack in his armor and had wiggled her way inside.

She was about to hitch a ride back on the asshole's jet. He'd reminded Paranzino that once they returned to Vegas, he was to sever all ties with Rissa. He was also to wire money into her account immediately and send Mercy the proof once he did so.

Paranzino's dirty dealings were going to cost the man a fuckload of cash between D's fee, Mercy's hefty bonus, the rest of his team's bonuses and Rissa's "pain and suffering" compensation.

However, Mercy was pretty sure it wouldn't be much of a financial hit for the man. Maybe he should have insisted Rissa get ten million. Make the asshole feel it a little more. But she'd probably balk with the one mil she was slated to get, even though she deserved every red cent and more.

After parking his vehicle in the garage, he made his way into the house and threw his keys on the counter. It was weird to see dishes drying in the drain pan and items in the trash and recycle bins. He tried to imagine coming home to that sight every day.

Like someone actually lived there.

When he'd checked in with Dawg last night, the DAMC member had stated when Rissa came back downstairs after taking a longer than normal shower, her eyes had been red and swollen.

Which meant the day had finally caught up with her.

Even so, he was still proud of her. She had remained strong when she needed to be. She had every right to break down once the threat had passed.

However, the threat was now officially dealt with. He and the rest of the Shadows had gone back out into the woods once darkness hit so they could remove bodies and cover their tracks. Once he told his team about the bonuses they'd be getting for their assistance, Mercy swore they were kicking up their heels and whistling while they worked like Disney dwarves.

Now, he was alone. His house quiet. Rissa gone.

When they first met, he couldn't wait for her to shut the fuck up. So it surprised him to find he actually missed her voice, her constant chattering, even when he didn't respond.

Her conversations, though most times one-sided, had filled his brain matter with something other than the darkness that usually sat on the outer edge of his mind. He kept telling himself that fucking her had been a mistake. A step into that unescapable quicksand he'd been carefully avoiding. But in reality, every time he had laid between her sweet, soft thighs, every time he'd been inside her wet heat, he'd let her inside of him, too. It was dangerous and at first he fought it, but then she became an addiction he didn't want to quit.

Going cold turkey was best for her, best for him. She needed to return to her life where she belonged. Only, she needed to find a new bestie. If it was up to him, a woman this time. One that met her for a martini in the evening, went with her to see a chick flick, was her sounding board when the latest guy Rissa had been dating turned out to be a real dick.

She didn't need to be friends with a man who made insane amounts of money with illegal brothels, as well as legal casinos used for money laundering.

He set his house alarm, kicked off his boots and hoofed it upstairs, stripping off his camo gear as he went, not caring where it landed. Exhaustion pulled at him. For once he might be able to sleep a full night.

He needed to shower, get the face paint off, wash the sweat from his balls. Forget the beautiful face with the striking sky-blue eyes he saw every time he closed his own.

As he stepped into the upstairs bathroom, he hit the light and moved in front of the sink.

After a few seconds, a few breaths...

In. Out. In. Out.

In...

Out...

He lifted his eyes and some of the shit he'd fought so hard to keep at bay unexpectedly pulled him back.

Back...

Way back to a day he was sweating his ass off in civvies. His team had to blend in with the environment, with the culture, so they never wore anything that identified who they were, why they were there. Because they weren't. They didn't exist. They had no recorded location. Very few people even knew what their mission was.

They were ghosts moving through a foreign land pretending to be natives.

He was in Afghanistan to retrieve a hostage. Supposedly a political figure who had been taken by force for information. Their mission was to overtake the captors and get the hostage out in one piece. Of course, all done quietly, without drawing attention to themselves.

He had a Sig holstered at his waist and a knife tucked into his boot. The *dishdasha* he wore over his clothes kept his weapons concealed, but he hated wearing the long garment. The robe-like cover was supposed to keep men cooler in the desert heat, but it didn't help when he wore his normal clothes underneath. And worse, he hated that it restricted access to his weapons.

As they cautiously moved single file through the mud home, the interior was dark. He heard nothing, saw nothing. It was too quiet. Too easy.

The whole operation didn't feel right. His gut was in knots because something was off. He felt it. His fellow SO, Rendell, was tense as well. They had done this type of maneuver many times. Gone in, disabled the captors, rescued the hostage.

For the most part, routine.

That day would be different due to bad intel.

The captors knew they were coming. The "hostage" was part of the ambush, not who they were told he would be. However, Mercy didn't know that until afterward.

The fake hostage attacked them from the front. Two others attacked them from behind.

Even with Rendell having his back, they were quickly overpowered and went into hand-to-hand combat. Before he could free his weapons, his face had been slashed open by an unseen knife.

He'd been blinded by the blood running into his eyes and was knocked forward to the ground, and as he scrambled to draw his gun, was stabbed multiple times in the back. During the struggle to stop the man from killing him, his Sig dropped onto the dirt.

His partner shot Mercy's attacker, but only ended up wounding him. Luckily, the shot made the enemy drop his knife. Mercy crawled through the dirt searching for either his weapon or the knife. He came across the knife first. After wiping some of the blood from his face, he could only see out of his left eye but found his attacker writhing on the ground with a single gunshot wound to his gut.

After quickly dispatching him, Mercy crawled along the dirt passageway to find the so-called "hostage" who had shot Rendell, killing him instantly. Once he did, Mercy dug deep to take him down and out. Whether Mercy lived or died that day, he was going to make sure none of their attackers survived.

Once all threats were disabled, he had crawled to a hiding spot, keeping a wall at his back. He somehow staunched some of his bleeding back wounds with cloth torn from his attacker's shirt. Then he'd dug out the tiny sewing kit he kept in the pack on his belt so he could sew his own face closed. But without being able to actually see the damage, he could only do his best to close the skin flaps temporarily.

The time between making the last stitch through his own flesh and waking up in the hospital at Bagram Airfield was nothing but a blur.

Finally, the blur cleared, and he saw his own face in that mirror. Still covered with camo face paint. Still scarred.

He should have trusted his gut that day. He thought he

learned a lesson from an encounter that changed the rest of his life.

Now he normally trusted his gut instinct. Except he'd slipped again. He didn't listen when it was screaming at him.

He never should've touched Rissa. He knew better. He fucked up and now he was paying the price.

He had rules in place for a reason. And he'd broken not just one...

But one that made him feel something. Something he didn't want to recognize and had avoided for a very long time. A couple decades, at least.

It was the fault of the man behind the face paint, staring at himself in a bathroom mirror outside of Shadow Valley. A man who should've known better.

He learned a long time ago to follow his gut. It had kept him alive on more than one occasion. He ignored it that day in Afghanistan. And once again when he fucked Rissa on the counter in Nash's kitchen. Continually ignoring it put him in a position he currently didn't want to be in.

One where he might have to fight for his life all over again...

"You stupid motherfucker," he snarled at the man in the mirror.

And just like when he couldn't stop his reaction when he punched that asshole yesterday, he couldn't stop his fist as it shot forward and met the mirror. His nostrils flared as he pulled his hand back and studied the blood welling on his knuckles. Looking up again, he noticed the glass had spidered out from the point of impact. He studied his splintered reflection.

Now he couldn't tell what was real and what wasn't when it came to the lines across his face.

What a motherfucking mess he made.

Parris pounded on the door again. He had to be home. She saw a glow from the kitchen through the narrow pane of glass that ran alongside the front door. She hadn't left any lights on when Diesel escorted her out of the house with her bags earlier.

Mercy had to have returned after she'd left.

Did he do it on purpose? Time it just right so he could avoid her? If so, it wouldn't surprise her.

He was not the kind of man to say goodbyes. He probably liked clean breaks. Quick. Painless. Emotionless.

Because that was the kind of man he was. A simple handshake (if you're lucky) and a hand on your shoulder, not to squeeze it reassuringly, but so he can shove you out the door.

She shook her head and blew out a breath. What kind of fool was she to insist Diesel turn the car around and drop her back off?

Surprisingly, the big man had listened. In fact, besides a low grunt, he had barked out a single laugh. Or what sounded sort of like a laugh. She couldn't be sure.

He might have even called her a "crazy bitch" under his breath.

Well, fuck him. Maybe she was.

No matter what, she was not leaving things the way they were. She didn't care what Mercy's boss thought. Hell, she didn't care what Mercy thought. He was going to listen to her for once.

Yes, he was, damn it.

She pounded on the door one more time with the heel of her hand and was about to start shouting his name when, through that dirty window, she saw feet, then bare calves, knees, a towel, a bare chest, then a face wearing a stony expression.

Great.

The door flung open and, yep, he was only wearing a

towel that clung to things that she'd seen without one. His hair and skin were damp, so it didn't take a genius to figure out what he'd just finished doing.

After letting her gaze rake him head to toe, she realized now was not the time to appreciate the delicious package standing before her almost naked. *Stay focused!* She went to push past him, but he stepped between the door and the frame, blocking her entry with his broad, impenetrable body. His silver eyes rose above her head as his gaze swept the driveway.

If he was looking for his boss, the man was long gone. She made sure of it before she started knocking.

"You gotta go to the airport." No emotion colored those words. No anger. No surprise. No relief. Nothing.

Parris waved a hand over her shoulder, indicating the obvious. "My ride left."

His frosty eyes narrowed as they met hers. "I'll take you back."

"I needed to see you once more before I left." The "once more" was a bit of a fib but she was taking baby steps. She didn't want him shutting down and shutting her out before she even had a chance to talk to him.

"Why?"

That was a perfectly good question. Why indeed? Any woman in her right mind would have raced as if her heels had been on fire to board that private jet to go home. Back to her life. Back to normalcy.

Any woman in her right mind wouldn't want to deal with the type of man that stood blocking her way into his home.

Blocking her way into his heart.

But maybe she wasn't in her right mind. Maybe the certified sex therapist needed a therapist of her own, because what freaking woman would *want* to spend time with a man like Mercy? A man who locked people out for fear they may get in.

"Because I—"

Because I care wasn't going to cut it with him.

Because I need to figure out what's going on between the two of us wasn't going to work, either.

Because I can't walk away from you, you big asshole.

Because while you were fighting to shut me out, I foolishly didn't do the same with you.

Because everyone deserves to be loved. You deserve it, too, whether you realize it or not.

Because...

Because there are too many complex reasons why I ended back up on your doorstep. And every single one of them will freak you out.

Every single one of them will remind you how human you really are.

Every single one of them has the potential to make you vulnerable to feeling hurt, anger, fear and maybe even...

Love.

"What you want, Rissa, I don't have it to fucking give to you. It's better for this to end with you only being disappointed rather than being hurt and hating me in the end."

"I could never hate you."

"You can't guarantee that."

"No," she answered softly. "There's no guarantee of anything in life. You could end up hating me, instead."

He repeated her words back to her. "I could never hate you."

"You can't guarantee that," she echoed back.

Something moved behind his gray eyes. She saw it. She was sure of it. A flicker. Something. It gave her some hope.

"This isn't meant to be, Rissa."

"You don't know that if you aren't even willing to try." She tried desperately to keep the whine from her voice. She really wanted to stomp her foot, too, in frustration.

"You're right, I'm not. Because of that, I need to take you to the airport and you need to go home."

She wasn't giving up that easily. She wasn't. Everything she'd reached for in life, she'd achieved. It might have taken hard work, determination, a few knockdowns and a whole bunch of tears, but those struggles only made reaching those achievements even more worthwhile.

She stepped forward and let her fingers trace the chain that held his dog tags from the curve of his neck down. When she reached the metal tags, she lifted them and read, "Mercer, Ryan C.," before gripping them tightly in her palm. "While these identify you, they do not define you." She gently placed them back on his chest, which was rising and falling a little quicker now, though his face still showed nothing. She lifted her hand to his forehead and starting at the top, traced his scar slowly, while whispering, "While this identifies your journey, it does not define your future."

She started when he snagged her wrist tightly and jerked her inside the door, slamming it shut behind her and pinning her against it.

Before she could catch her breath, his mouth was over hers, stealing her gasp from her. He kissed her like it was the last time.

Because for him, it probably was.

His fingers dug painfully into her hair, holding her head still as he plundered her mouth and pressed himself against her, trapping her against the door.

She encouraged him to continue taking what he wanted by pressing her palms against his bare chest. His heartbeat thumped strong and rapidly under her hand.

He wanted to show the world nothing affected him. But it was a false front.

She affected him.

He ripped his lips from hers. "You came back here to fuck one more time? Then you're going to get fucked."

He wanted to believe the reason she returned was only about sex. It was more than that. So much more.

But if he needed to tell himself that was the only reason she returned, then fine, she'd let him believe it. At least it got her in the door.

She caught his gaze as she reached for the knot on his towel, but he stopped her again with strong fingers circling her wrist. He tugged her away from the door and pointed up the steps. "Upstairs. Now."

She reached for his hand when she noticed his knuckles had shallow slices and some deeper cuts on them. He'd been injured somehow dealing with Nicco? "Ryan..."

He jerked his hand away and repeated, "Upstairs. Now. You're going to get what you came here for."

No, she probably wasn't. But if he wanted to play that game? Fine.

As she started up the steps, she threw over her shoulder, "By the time you reach the top, that towel better be gone," then she jogged (okay, that might've been a bit of an exaggeration) up the rest of the way.

He wasn't his normal stealth self as he followed her up. She started to move faster as she heard his heavy steps quicken.

By the time she hit his bedroom door, he was on her, pushing her inside, pulling off her glasses and tossing them onto the nearby dresser, yanking her blouse over her head, unclipping her bra and letting it fall to the floor between them.

His mouth found her aching nipple and he sucked it roughly as he wrapped his arms around her to unbutton and slide down the zipper at the back of her skirt. He switched nipples, scraping his teeth over the hard tip as the skirt dropped to her feet.

She mourned his mouth when he released her to shove her panties down to her ankles. He dropped to his knees and lifted one foot, then the other out of the pile of clothing at her feet as he nuzzled her mound with his nose. His hot breath against her sensitive skin there made her shudder.

His long fingers curled around her ankles and then moved lower to slip her heels from her. When he pushed to his feet, she once again mourned his mouth.

Now she was as naked as him. Though, honestly, he was much more magnificent with his broad shoulders, his veiny, bulging muscles, his narrow hips, his thick cock jutting out from between even thicker thighs.

She had experienced the power behind those impressive thighs. She couldn't wait to feel it again.

"On the bed. Back against the headboard. Knees cocked and open. Want to see how wet you are."

Those rough demands made her even wetter, so it wasn't going to be difficult for him to see how he affected her.

She didn't hesitate to do what he instructed. Heat swirled through her and landed in her core in anticipation of what was about to come.

Which was her.

And him.

But she would be first, she thought, as she watched him prowl toward the bed, his expressions, his emotions still restrained as he pinned her to the headboard with his silver-gray eyes.

No matter how much he hid his thoughts, he still made her always feel beautiful when she was naked and exposed to him. She had no desire to hide herself from him as she had with some other men she'd been with. He accepted her just the way she was.

He was the most physically fit man she'd ever been with, but not once had he ever told her how she should eat, or exercise. Or tell her she had a pretty face, but if she lost a few pounds she'd be beautiful.

He never once made her feel self-conscious of the way

her belly rolled when she sat or the way her thighs jiggled, or how her breasts hung heavily. Because even though he hid a lot of things, he never hid the fact that he appreciated every curve of her body.

So, when he climbed on the bed and moved between her legs, she didn't hesitate to widen her thighs to make room for him, to open herself up like he demanded so he could see how eager he made her.

His dark head dipped, and he settled into place, pushing her fingers out of the way so he could take charge. Right now, her pussy didn't belong to her. It belonged to him. His actions proved that.

His mouth on her was incredible. It amazed her that a man like him, who could be so shut off emotionally, could be so in tune with her body. He knew how to make her float, to make her fly, to make her want him so much it was almost painful.

She wanted him.

And she wanted more.

He said he had nothing to give her.

He was so wrong.

He had plenty to give her. He just needed to see that, to open himself up to the possibilities. But again, he would never willingly do so because that would put him at risk.

His tongue, his lips, his fingers touched her in ways that made her thoughts swirl away and warmth rush through her. This man was so intense with everything he did, including what he was doing to her at that very moment.

That intensity also made her orgasms explosive. She'd never been with such a selfless lover, where her needs came first. Like everything else in his life, he considered sex as a mission to complete. And it would only be successful if she turned into a quivering pile of flesh and bones when it was over.

She was okay with that. More than okay. Because that

usually meant not one orgasm, but multiple. A few times it had gotten to the point where she thought about crying for mercy, and not his nickname, either.

She tilted her head back against the headboard, closed her eyes and just let the sensations wash through her. She blindly reached for him, her fingers brushing against his bristly, military-style hair, then curling around the back of his head, finding purchase. Until her fingertips brushed against his stitches.

She had almost forgotten about that wound. The one that could have killed him.

The one he got protecting her.

She pushed the thought of her being only a job to him out of her head. The job was over. He would be paid his fee and get his bonus. What was happening between the two of them right now needed to be about them, nothing else.

He sucked on one of her plump lips, then the other before going back to flick her clit with the tip of his tongue. He slipped two fingers inside her with ease because she was so ready for him.

She wanted to feel his weight on her again. Feel him inside her. A part of her. Two pieces, while so different, fitting together perfectly.

How could he not see that?

Maybe he could and simply ignored it.

Curving his fingers deep inside her, he found the exact spot that would cause her hips to dance. They began to do just that this time, too. He never let up, followed every lift of her body as she dug her heels into the bed. With every grind of her pussy against his mouth, his tongue continued to tease her, lure her closer to that edge.

Then she was falling, calling his name, unable to catch her breath for a moment as her muscles clenched and released around him.

Before she could recover, he was gone, nothing but

emptiness left behind where his heat had been. But it wasn't even a couple seconds before he tugged her ankles until she was splayed out flat on her back before him as he sat on his knees, his gray eyes traveling over every inch of her body.

Once again, she had no reason to hide her faults from him. If he could accept hers, she could accept his. Both of them were far from perfect. But being perfect was overrated and boring. Their faults, their pasts, made each of them who they were.

She lifted a hand, wondering why he wasn't moving. Why he only stared at her. "Ryan, what's wrong?"

Chapter Eighteen

Nothing was wrong.

Nothing was right.

His mind was a sea of confusion as he studied Rissa, naked, ready and waiting on his bed.

His bed. His house. Things that were his. But she wasn't one of them, as much as he could see it in her face that she wanted to be.

He couldn't allow that. It would turn out badly for both of them. He'd never survive her looking at him with horror or censure, shock or shame.

And that was bound to happen eventually.

Her being in his bed wasn't a "happily ever after" like the end of the romance books she submerged herself in. He wasn't suddenly going to open his heart to her, declare that he couldn't live without her. That he loved her more than life itself.

He would never be that man who would beg her to stay, to ask her to deal with everything that made him who he was.

It wouldn't be fair to ask that of her.

She needed to get on that plane and get as far away from him as possible.

For her sanity.

And for what remained of his.

Her excuse to return was that she wanted to see him one more time. However, she couldn't—or wouldn't—answer him when he asked why. Most likely because if she had been truthful, he probably would've slammed the door in her face.

He could never be what she wanted, what she needed. Someone who could love her deeply, worship every inch of her body, cherish every word she uttered, appreciate every thought in her intelligent mind.

His own haunted memories and twisted thoughts would eat him alive if he dropped his barriers. If he allowed himself to feel.

Out of all the hostages he'd rescued, she had been the most important to him. The most valuable. With a few exceptions, most had been just names and faces.

A mission, a job, an assignment. Nothing more.

She was much more than that. For that reason, she deserved so much more. More than anything he could ever give her.

He lost track of how long he sat on his knees, staring at her. It wasn't until her eyes became shiny with tears and she reached out her hand, whispering his name...

Ryan.

...that he could shake his thoughts free.

Falling forward, he covered her, snagging one of her peaked nipples into his mouth. He surged forward and up, taking her completely with one stroke. A single thrust of his hips.

He regretted things couldn't be different. That, because of how he was, he couldn't love this woman as she was meant to be loved. Because if he could, Rissa would be his.

He wouldn't just be claiming her in his bed, he would be claiming her as his permanently.

But for now, for this last time in his bed, he could pretend that it would work, and they could be a normal couple. That there was no risk of him hurting her in any way.

He dug his knees into the mattress ready to give it to her as hard as he had almost every other time he'd been deep inside her. But surprisingly, this time he wasn't experiencing that frantic pull, he didn't crave total control. Instead, he wanted to savor this last time. While she never minded how rough he'd been with her in the past—in fact, she'd encouraged it, digging her nails in and riding him hard—he didn't want this time to be like that.

This time needed to be different.

She needed to know how much she meant to him. Since he was unable to say it with words, he would show her instead.

He wouldn't—*couldn't*—say it out loud because he didn't want to give her hope.

Her thighs squeezed his hips and she met him stroke for stroke, lifting her hips, squeezing him tight. Hot velvet encased him, drawing him deeper. So deep he wondered if he'd ever escape.

Just like that fucking quicksand. If you weren't looking for it, and you stepped in it, you could become trapped.

He switched nipples and sucked the other one hard enough she gasped and clawed at his back, encouraging him to get rougher, move faster.

Once again, he resisted doing just that.

He needed to remain focused on her. Her body's reactions, the little cries and gasps, the moans. All of which drove him forward.

He wanted to remember all of that. How incredible it felt to be inside her, enveloped in her slick heat. How, when she came, her thighs would quiver, her breath would catch, her eyes would meet his.

She rarely closed them. Instead she watched him, more closely than he liked. And while they would lose focus, they always remained on him. It was as if she was trying to stare into the depths of his soul. To catch a glimpse past the darkness that hovered on the edge.

She mistakenly believed somewhere beneath the surface, there was light. And he didn't want to prove her wrong. Unfortunately, that's what would happen if she stayed.

Even so, she couldn't stay here. With him. In Shadow Valley. She had an established life elsewhere, in a city where she was successful. Where she owned her own business and was her own woman.

And no matter what she thought, he wasn't worth the sacrifice of giving any of that up. Again, she'd find out the truth, that he wasn't worth it, and she'd come to hate him. Despise him. Regret her decisions.

If that happened, it could result in a final break which he could ultimately never recover from.

He released her nipple, shiny and swollen from his mouth and shifted until his face was directly above hers. Her eyes had followed him and now with her head on his pillow and her long, light brown hair spread out, she almost looked like an angel. Untouchable, unreal.

A dream.

In the end, he could be her nightmare.

He rolled his hips gently, slowly and he dipped his head until his lips were right above hers.

He wanted to whisper her name, but he couldn't get it past his lips. Instead, it swirled like smoke inside his head until it vaporized.

Jesus fucking Christ, he didn't want her to leave.

But he couldn't rid himself of the truth. He'd destroy her if she didn't.

Yes, she was strong, but was she strong enough? Could she handle everything that he'd kept buried? Because as a therapist, she would try to dig all that shit up. Maybe not in the beginning, but eventually she wouldn't be able to resist.

Eventually she'd want to know what made him tick. Not like a clock, but a time bomb.

His thoughts swirled again, now like a tornado. Picking up speed. Becoming dangerous to anyone in its path. He needed to shut that shit down.

He took her mouth, tangled their tongues, capturing the groan she released.

He wanted to speed up, fuck her hard, fuck her fast. Instead, he forced himself to keep at his slow rhythm, to draw this out, to make this last.

Because soon he'd only have another memory. Remembering Rissa would be a good one to add to his mental bank, which already included too many bad.

He needed to hold onto this memory of her. Ignore the rest.

He deepened the kiss and even though he thrust slowly, he took long, full strokes. All the way in and almost all the way out. Just to the point where he didn't quite leave her, but the chance was there.

He needed to keep that connection between them. For once he needed someone other than himself. Someone other than his team at his back.

Someone to show him the softer side of life. Someone who could bring him some happiness.

He broke off the kiss when he realized the direction his thoughts were headed. Again, he felt the drag of the quicksand. The closing of his throat. The restriction of air.

He couldn't breathe.

He needed to breathe.

He needed Rissa, so he could breathe.

He was afraid he couldn't breathe without her.

How did this happen? When did she become a necessary part of his very existence? When did she become someone he couldn't live without?

This was all wrong. He didn't need anyone.

No one.

Not one soul.

He pressed his forehead against hers when her second orgasm began to build. He now recognized the signs, the reactions of her body.

He wasn't wrong. He paused when her muscles rippled around him, so he could concentrate on remembering that sensation, too. And when she was done, her warm breath beat rapidly along his cheek.

The longer this time with her lasted, the more his thoughts began to spin. So maybe it wasn't a good idea to extend their pleasure. He quickened his pace a little more, making her mouth part, her breath escape in a rush with each forceful thrust.

Once again, her name was on the verge of leaving his lips, but he wouldn't let it go. Instead, he swallowed it and kept it for himself. He would tuck this moment, that unfamiliar feeling away. He might need to revisit it sometime in the future. Use it to ground him.

She was still matching his movements, keeping with his slightly quicker pace, digging her nails into his back, like he craved so much.

He needed that reminder he lived. That he wasn't just a shell, that once he'd been someone who had empathy for others. At one point in his life, he hadn't been so cold and calculating, shutting everyone else out.

She whimpered when he plucked her tightly beaded nipple and rolled it between his thumb and forefinger. The harder he twisted, the louder her cries became. Her back arched and her head tilted back, but he stuck with her, keeping their foreheads pinned together. Feeling those warm puffs of breath along his own heated skin.

Rissa whispered through his head. *Rissa.*

Fuck!

He released her nipple, dug his fingers into the hair on both sides of her head and began to pound her like he needed. Like she wanted.

He crushed his lips to hers and took her mouth fiercely. Completely.

With a hand now wrapped around the back of his neck, she squeezed, and twisted her head to break the kiss.

Was he hurting her?

"Ryan," she cried out.

No, there wasn't an ounce of pain in the name she cried out. The name no one used but her.

He demanded against her ear, "Tell me how good this feels," before catching her earlobe between his teeth.

"You tell me how good this feels," she countered on a groan.

Like nothing I've ever experienced in my fucking life.

"Tell me how much you like this," she demanded.

I don't like this. I live for this. Being inside you. Being a part of you. I can't get enough of you.

The word *addiction* blew through his scrambled brain like a wild wind before a violent storm.

He released her earlobe and asked, "What do you want from me to make you come again?"

He needed for her to come one more time before he did. His balls were getting tight and his heart was pounding uncontrollably. He was approaching that ledge and scrambling to hang on before he fell.

"Come for me once more, Rissa. Once more. Let me feel it one more time."

She went completely pliant, almost melting into the

mattress at his words. She probably was surprised he uttered them. But not as surprised as he was at her next plea.

"Stop fucking me. Make love to me instead."

His pace stuttered at her request.

She wasn't done with her demands. "Slow down. Look at me. *See* me."

I do. "I see you."

"No, Ryan. *See* me."

When he asked that simple question, he was not expecting that complicated answer. He lifted his head, staring down into her eyes, once again shiny with unshed tears.

Fuck!

"Rissa," he whispered roughly. "I see you."

He caught a flicker of disappointment, even a bit of frustration, behind her blue eyes. She didn't believe him. The last thing he wanted was to be the source of her disappointment.

"Then let me see you," she insisted.

Impossible. He struggled to get his response past the closing of his throat. "You won't like what you see."

"Let me decide that."

I only want to save you from a world of hurt. Shock and disappointment when you discover who you've been sleeping with.

When he didn't answer, one of the unshed tears slipped down her cheek, disappearing into her hair.

He closed his eyes, warring with himself. And when he opened them again, a few more tears were escaping unchecked.

This cemented what he believed. She needed someone to make her happy, not someone who made her cry.

Somehow he needed to turn this around, to keep this memory a good one, instead of one full of tears and regret. He just didn't know how to do that without ripping himself open and serving up his past to her on a plate.

He had wanted to give her one more orgasm, but unfortunately, he feared they were past that point, so he needed to end this before things got worse and became darker.

With his thumb, he wiped the one lone tear that remained hovering at the corner of her eye, then leaned in to kiss her gently.

The kiss he intended to be more soothing than sexual became frantic when she clutched his cheeks and held him there, sweeping her tongue through his mouth, exploring every corner, taking it deeper, encouraging him to continue.

She gave control over the kiss back to him and he began to move again, rocking against her, capturing her sexy little mews.

When he broke the kiss, he shoved his face into her neck and murmured, "Come for me one more time, baby," against her heated skin. Her head tilted back again, exposing her delicate throat, and he traced the tip of his tongue over her pounding pulse, sucked her flesh into his mouth, then ran his lips across her jawline.

He shoved one arm beneath her hips, tilting them to a sharper angle and he began to piston his own at an almost desperate pace. Her cries, no longer contained within his mouth, rose into the space around him, filled his head, making it difficult for him to wait for her to come.

But he was determined her next orgasm would wash away any sadness that remained, to make this time together something worth remembering.

Whether for later today. For tomorrow. Or for forever.

As her face went slack, as did her mouth, his name once again escaped her on a breath. She clenched around him tightly, dragging him along with her. Thank fuck for that, because he couldn't hold back any longer.

His whole body heaved forcefully when he came deep inside her. He hoped she thought it was from him coming and not from something so foreign ripping through him at that moment it almost tore him completely apart inside.

He ground against her as he kept his face buried against her neck because he was afraid she'd be able to see how exposed he was. She'd be able to see it on his face, in his eyes. How desperately he wanted to hold on to her. To keep her for himself. To do his fucking damnedest to be the man she wanted. To be everything she needed.

But the truth was, he'd fail.

He'd fail.

He knew when a mission was impossible. And he wasn't going to set himself up for that failure.

He'd never survive it.

Chapter Nineteen

HOURS.

They laid there for a couple hours. Their limbs tangled. The sheets a tousled, damp mess.

Silent.

Nothing said. Not one thing discussed.

Just complete... utter... silence.

It had taken him longer than normal to disengage himself from her after he came. Even after his breathing had returned to normal, he had kept his face planted firmly in her neck. It wasn't until his cock softened and slipped from her that he finally moved.

He only shifted enough to slide to her side, a heavy arm draped over her waist, pinning her in place, while he tucked his other arm under her head. But through all that, his face remained pressed under her chin.

Hidden.

She beat back the disappointment creeping through her, because she had asked him to show himself to her. The real Ryan Mercer. Not the Mercy he showed everyone else.

But he hadn't. He either outright refused to or was incapable of it.

The reality was, he wouldn't rip himself open for her. And while she understood why, it still made her chest tight and her heart squeeze that he'd let no one, not even her, in.

She had hoped by showing back up on his doorstep, he would see how much she cared for him. How hard she had fallen in the short amount of time they'd spent together. But all that was nothing but an illusion. Some stupid pipe dream she got from all the romance novels she read, making her believe it was possible for them to beat the odds and have their "happily ever after" despite his issues.

Now she knew it was impossible.

He wasn't willing to bend.

He simply couldn't. He just wasn't wired like that.

She needed to accept it and move on. Return home.

He'd been right. He couldn't be what she wanted or needed.

Again, it had only been a messed-up fantasy created in her head. As a therapist, she should know better. It was healthier to face reality head-on than ignore it.

Even so, she didn't push him away. She allowed him to remain where he was, his breath warm and steady as it swept over her throat. The fingers of the hand tucked behind her head entangled in her hair. The thumb of the other, mindlessly brushing back and forth over her ribs.

But it was getting late and she needed to go. Remaining where she was only prolonged the final goodbye.

Her bladder had also begun to complain a half hour ago. Unfortunately, it was now screaming for relief and she could no longer ignore it.

She needed to move, clean up, get dressed and head home.

The sooner she did that, the quicker she could put the man named Mercy behind her and get on with her life. Slap a Band-Aid over her bruised heart until it healed.

One day she would find a nice man with a normal name who lived a normal life capable of loving her.

It was not Mercy.

It would never be Ryan, either.

"I—" She cleared her throat of the thickness and tried again, "I need to clean up." She pressed a hand to his massive bicep, indicating he needed to let her up.

He only moved enough so she could slip from beneath the weight of his arm and roll from the bed. Without a glance behind her, she snagged her panties and bra from the floor as she headed out of the room and down the hallway to the bathroom.

She stepped inside, flipped on the light and froze, her brain taking a second to process what she saw. The mirror had taken a direct impact at its center and shards of glass along with dark drops of dried blood lined the bottom of the sink.

After shutting the door behind her, she quickly cleaned herself up before pulling on her underwear. The whole time she couldn't take her eyes from the damage.

Those scratches and cuts on his hand weren't from dealing with Nicco and his men. Something had driven him to the point of punching the mirror.

Why?

Did he not like the person whose reflection looked back at him? Did he feel as if he deserved to be punished for some reason, which caused him to react like he'd done with Michael when he'd broken the man's nose? Or did he do it simply out of frustration? And if so, why was he frustrated?

His mission had been successful. Parris was still breathing. The threat had been neutralized. He was getting paid, and he'd earned his hefty bonus.

How could any of that have driven him to the point of striking out?

She fought the urge to clean up the evidence of his tipping point. But as much as she knew she shouldn't ask him about it, she had to see if, just maybe, he wanted to discuss it.

She was unable to just let it go.

Though, anyone else in their right mind would. But, oh no, not her. She was a glutton for punishment.

However, she worried about his mental state. She was concerned about what he might do once she was gone, and he was once again alone.

She shouldn't be. He survived for decades without her.

Even so, she cared too much for him not to try. If it worked and it helped him... great. Even if he hated her for it, then fine, she could live with that, because she was heading home soon anyway.

Honestly, she had nothing to lose except maybe pushing him to the point of lashing out once more.

She turned off the light and headed barefoot back down the hallway to his bedroom. She paused in the doorway, surprised he hadn't moved.

He remained lying on his stomach, his bare back exposed, his powerful build impressive. Breathtaking, in fact. Unlike the breath-robbing half dozen thick scars along his broad back or the long, raised scar that marred his handsome face. Those reminded her once again, he'd been through so much. Things he didn't want to share.

Not only that day he almost lost his life, but years of war, combat and killing. Whatever affected him was deep-rooted. PTSD impacted everyone differently. For some it became so overwhelming that they decided to end the internal torture by ending themselves. That night she'd seen him with the gun sitting between his feet, she had wondered if he'd ever contemplated taking that final step.

Sometimes physical or mental agony made people do

desperate things just to get it to stop. And other times, people dealing with that kind of pain lashed out instead. Like a normally faithful, but injured family dog unexpectedly snapping at its owner.

Like a man driving his fist into a mirror.

He had to have known she'd see it since there was only one bathroom upstairs.

Maybe he hadn't had time to clean up the mess because she showed up on his doorstep without prior notice. Or maybe he wanted her to see it, to scare her away. To prove his point that he could never be what she needed.

Well, he could be. He just didn't want to be.

She moved deeper into the bedroom, picking his T-shirt up off the floor and tugging it over her head. As she perched on the edge of the mattress she wasn't sure how to approach what she saw and the reasoning behind it. He turned his head on the pillow to the other cheek, so he could see her, but other than that, he still didn't move.

He tensed as she lifted his right hand off the sheet and brushed her fingers lightly over the cuts on his knuckles. Then, even though he slightly resisted, she raised his fist up and gently kissed each knuckle before lowering it to her lap, gripping his fingers tightly in both of her hands.

His voice was low, flat and gruff when he said, "If you think we're going to talk about it, I'll stop you before you start. We're not." He rolled to his side and sat up, surprising her by not jerking his hand free. "I can see what you're gearing up to do. You can't help but keep fuckin' with my head. Worse, you don't come from the front. I can see that now. You come from the side. Cold-cocking me even though I'm aware you're about to do it."

His tone held no anger, but instead a touch of desolation, which made this even more difficult.

"I'm worried that you could eventually break through

and you'll see the real me, Rissa. And I swear to fuck you won't like what you see. You'll be fuckin' horrified. But you'll try your best to drag me deep, to crack me open, and if you achieve that you'll end up running as fast as you can to escape what you find. And if that happens, it'll break me. Not because you've figured me out, but because you couldn't deal with what you discovered. The day I see that on your face, it will destroy me."

She remained quiet, not wanting to interrupt him because he had dropped his guard. He was allowing her to see something he normally kept hidden. He wanted her to see he *could* care, it just took too much of an effort that could cost him dearly.

"You want to believe that a man named Ryan Mercer exists. But he no longer does. He hasn't for a long time. Only Mercy has survived. He's the man who busted Paranzino's nose. The man who smashed that mirror. I swear to you Mercy's not who's right for you. And you will regret making any effort to find Ryan. That effort will not only destroy you, but it will destroy me, as well."

She couldn't stay silent any longer. He needed to know she was willing to do whatever was needed. "I think I can handle whatever haunts you, Ryan."

With one hand still in her lap cupped between hers, he lifted his other, curling his fingers along her jawline, and his gray eyes, holding a deep-seated hurt that made her want to cry, met hers. "But I can't. I can't live like that. I can't watch every move, every word I say simply because I'll think you're analyzing it. I'm sorry, Rissa, but I can't be what you need me to be. It's not fair to you for me to pretend that I can." He shook his head and his fingers twitched within hers. "I can't. That's the hard, cold facts." He sucked in a slow, audible breath, almost as if bracing himself for what he said next. "You never should've told Diesel to drop you back off.

So now you need to get dressed and I'm taking you to the airport."

With quiet reservation, she had done what he said. She had gotten dressed and without anything left to say between them, followed him downstairs where he gathered her luggage off the front stoop and loaded it into his massive vehicle.

Armored. Bullet-proof. Just like him.

The drive to the airport was also too silent. It was difficult to believe that it had only been about a week ago when she'd arrived in Pittsburgh, in Shadow Valley, in Mercy's life.

Now everything was being rewound. She was leaving Ryan's life, Shadow Valley, and soon Pittsburgh.

This time it wouldn't be on a fancy jet with one mysterious, handsome stranger. This time she would board a commercial flight with a plane full of strangers, going back to a life she wasn't sure she wanted to go back to.

Yes, she loved her career. She did look forward to getting back into that groove. But she wasn't sure how things would be with Michael from this point on and without her best friend and without the man next to her in the driver's seat, she already felt lost. Alone.

She'd go back to an empty house. And then she would bury herself in what she did best. Work.

It was better than nothing, she supposed. At least she had something to keep herself busy and her mind off the sullen man beside her.

She had wanted to argue everything he said when they were in his bed. But she couldn't. His expression, which was normally neutral, had said it all. For once, for a very short period of time, he dropped his barriers, allowing her to see his fears. If only to drive home the meaning behind his words.

For most people, that wouldn't have taken much of an effort. For Mercy, it was huge and probably took a lot out of him. While she appreciated the effort, none of it was what she wanted to hear.

She had to recognize that some things weren't worth fighting for, because in the end, it could be a situation where if you won, you truly lost.

He was right, she'd never stop trying to dig deeper with him, expose his inner thoughts, his past, his pain in an effort to help him. However, she knew to force it wouldn't do him any good. He would continue to resist and eventually it might only make him hate her.

And just like he thought she wouldn't be able to handle seeing the real Mercy, she wouldn't be able to live with him hating her, blaming her for shattering everything he held onto so tightly.

He just didn't understand that she'd be there to help pick up the pieces. But, again, he needed to be willing.

He wasn't.

So, there was nothing left for her to do but throw in the towel and go home. She'd only known the man for a week, so it shouldn't be so hard to walk away, to put him behind her.

But as he pulled up to the curb in front of the Pittsburgh airport, her stomach clenched and twisted. She clamped her jaws together so she wouldn't beg him to rethink everything he said.

She was resigned to the fact that Mercy was not a flexible man, he wasn't going to be swayed, nor would he change his mind. He was a man set in his ways and would stick with what worked in the past because that's what he knew. He was not a man who would sit in a therapist's chair and slice himself open and allow himself to bleed just for a woman.

He was also not a man who normally said goodbyes, but he was getting one from her whether he liked it or not.

She climbed out of the RPV as he went around to the back and handed her luggage to a skycap with a cart. After he slipped the man some cash and the airport employee rolled the cart inside, Mercy slowly turned to her where she had remained on the sidewalk, her feet feeling as if stuck in concrete.

While his gray eyes were not cold, they revealed nothing.

"Ryan..." she whispered.

He lifted his hand to stop her and shook his head. "Rissa, take care of yourself."

No move for a kiss or a hug. Nothing. Not even an impersonal handshake.

"Yes, you, too," she murmured, forcing herself to keep eye contact. "And..."

His lips flattened, and his shoulders tightened as if he was bracing himself.

Her voice sounded thick as she continued, "Thank you for keeping me alive."

As his mouth opened, she held her breath and waited. After a slight hesitation, he finally closed it and said, "I was just doing my job."

She finally dropped her gaze to the concrete at her feet, fighting back the burn in her eyes as she nodded and whispered, "Goodbye, Mercy."

Without waiting for an answer, because she knew none would be coming, she turned and pushed through the revolving glass doors into the cooler interior of the airport.

As she wound her way through the cordoned-off lines leading up to the airline's ticket counter, she glanced over her shoulder to see him still standing at the curb. He was watching her, his face unreadable, his fists pinned to his thighs. Maybe he wanted to make sure she was safe before he left.

Fifteen minutes later, after obtaining a plane ticket for the next flight to Vegas and heading toward the security line, when she checked again, he was still out at the curb, but this time sitting in his vehicle that was hard to miss. Airport security had pulled up behind him and one of the officers was standing by the driver's door, most likely ordering him to move. But he was clearly ignoring the uniformed man, instead still staring in her direction.

She lifted her hand slightly in a half-hearted wave, but as she expected, he didn't return it.

It was a good reminder that she needed to continue forward, not keep looking behind. Swallowing hard, she steeled herself and headed toward the security lines. But with each step she took, she kept her ears peeled carefully for him calling out her name.

Admitting he made a mistake.

Ordering her to get out of the security line and go home with him.

Until finally...

Finally, when she heard her name being called, her heart skipped a beat then began to race as she turned, a smile on her face and fresh tears in her eyes. Right then and there, she realized she was willing to accept him however he came to her. Whole or broken. Even shattered into a million tiny pieces.

She would accept him as he was.

What she found was only an older gentleman holding up her driver's license. "Miss, you dropped this."

Miss. Not the "Rissa" she so desperately wanted to hear.

With trembling fingers and a crooked, pasted-on smile, she accepted the license from him, forcing out a "thank you."

She was a fool. Because Mercy wasn't the *run-through-the-airport, drop-to-his-knees-and-declare-his-undying-love* type of guy.

No, he was the *punch-a-man-who-lied-to-his-friend-and-put-her-in-danger-then-make-the-asshole-apologize-and-swear-to-never-do-that-again* type of guy.

That's who he was, that's who he'd always be.

Her gaze scanned the crowd behind her one last time, just in case she was mistaken. But after a few seconds, with a nod to no one but herself, she turned around and got in line.

She refused to glance back over her shoulder again.

Chapter Twenty

"FIND HER!" Mercy heard his boss roar in his typical Diesel-self they all came to know and love.

Well, maybe not quite that last part.

Who the hell was D demanding his crew to find? Was it Rissa?

His heart began to thump wildly at that prospect—especially since the last he knew, she'd been safely back in Vegas for a couple of weeks now—until he heard Ryder's pissed-off answering growl coming from D's office. "Fuckin' send somebody else! Had more than my share of that fuckin'..."

Mercy held his breath and waited for Ryder to fuck up. After a second, he breathed again. *Good choice, Ryder. Don't let it slip in front of D.* Otherwise, they'd be cleaning up Ryder's remains.

The argument had to be about Kelsea. Once again.

Mercy stepped into the shadows just outside of his boss's office. Last thing he wanted was to be spotted and sent to clean up D's cousin's latest fucking mess.

"Find her. You now know all her typical landin' spots. Brooke said she hasn't fuckin' shown up for work in a goddamn week. Brooke's done. Jag's done. I'm fuckin' *done*," D yelled like it was Ryder's fault.

Poor sucker.

"I'm fuckin' done, too," Ryder shouted back.

"Ain't fuckin' done 'til you get her ass the fuck home in one piece. Then I'm gonna deal with 'er an' she ain't gonna like it. Probably hangin' with that Slit guy."

Hanging. Kels wasn't *hanging*. The only hanging to be had was probably her pants around her ankles as she bent over for a bunch of strange dick.

"Slash," Ryder growled.

D grunted. "What-fuckin-ever. That whole fuckin' MC needs wiped the fuck out."

Mercy's ears perked up. Now *that* job sounded more up his alley. Taking out members of an outlaw MC versus retrieving an out-of-control c— *Kelsea*.

Maybe he could sneak out of the warehouse before either of them knew he was there. He only stopped in to talk to D about finding him a new assignment as soon as possible. One that would take his mind off other shit.

But no matter how antsy he was, he was not willing to handle Kelsea. Ryder had become an expert at wrangling her ass, so that's why D always reached out to him. But eventually Ryder would threaten to quit because he couldn't take any more of the woman's bullshit, then someone else would become the next sucker.

Hopefully someone other than him, as long as he kept out of sight and out of mind. He was an expert at extracting hostages from volatile situations. He had no patience to babysit a messed-up woman who acted as if she was a spoiled teenager having a temper tantrum because life had thrown her a curve ball.

Fuck that.

He quickly and quietly moved down the hallway and...

Fuck me.

Came face-to-face with Jewel. And of course, he couldn't push past her, pretending he had somewhere important to go because she was blocking the hallway with a double stroller.

Both baby girls spotted him at the same time Diesel's ol' lady did.

He was fucked.

Indie waved her arms at him and gurgled happily, wanting him to pick her up. He winced when Violet called out his name.

"Fuck," he muttered under his breath.

"Hey, handsome," Jewelee said with a wide smile.

He bit back a sigh at being discovered. "Hey, sexy momma."

"Don't worry, I won't tell him you're lurking out here trying to avoid getting pulled into that Kelsea bullshit."

"Thank f—" He bit off the last part and glanced down at the girls.

"You know they hear it constantly, so don't stress it. Emma might have convinced Dawg to use 'fudge' instead of 'fuck,' but I knew it would be a wasted effort with D. Or hell, any of the brothers. I'm sure we'll be getting calls from their teachers about their offensive language when they're old enough for kindergarten."

Mercy cocked a brow. "You're saying D's gonna let them go to kindergarten?"

Jewel laughed, then released a loud, exaggerated sigh. "I'm sure I'll be homeschooling them." She frowned. "Why did I ever have two kids with that man?"

Mercy's lips twitched. "One, because you guys can't stop banging. And two, because you love him."

"Oh, yeah, that's why. I almost forgot." She smiled again, her blue eyes that reminded him of Rissa's lighting up.

"Sure you did."

Jewel had long hair like Rissa, too, but her brown was a lot darker. And, even after popping out two Diesel-sired babies, Jewel was still petite. Total opposite of her beast of a man and also unlike Rissa, who was not petite or vertically challenged at all.

He needed to stop thinking of her. She was gone. A finished job. Another reason why he needed to move on to the next one.

Which brought him back to how he was here to talk to Diesel. But, again, that would have to wait until it was safe, and Ryder was on the road to retrieve Kelsea.

"Mercy!" Vi yelled again, lifting her little, pudgy arms and making grabby hands.

With a sigh, he reached down, unbuckled the belt that secured her in the stroller and lifted the toddler until she looped her arms around his neck, giving him a sloppy kiss on the cheek.

"Indie's going to be jealous," Jewel said softly, her expression as she watched them just as soft. "Is it wrong to say that seeing you holding a baby makes my ovaries explode?"

His eyebrows rose in surprise. "You want more?"

"Fuck no!" she quickly answered. "It's just very... *hot* to think of you *making* babies. Not the actual babies themselves."

"For fuck's sake, you're going to get me shot if you say that kind of shit."

Jewel laughed. "He didn't hear it. He's too busy arguing with Ryder."

Mercy tilted his head and listened. She was right. But still...

"You never wanted kids of your own?" Jewel asked carefully.

Mercy gripped Vi a little tighter and had to fight to keep his body loose. It was one thing to hold D's girls when their father wasn't around, but it was another to consider having babies of his own.

It had never even crossed his mind. He wasn't made to be a father.

Or a husband.

Or even a boyfriend.

Or, hell, even a repeat visitor in a woman's bed.

"You miss her?"

That question drew his attention back to Jewel. "Who?"

But he knew who she was fucking talking about. *Goddamn it.*

Jewel plugged her hands on her hips and lifted her brows.

He mentally cringed. The woman was a compact powerhouse. One who could stand up to any of them, since she had a lot of practice with her beast of an ol' man. She could look the devil straight in the eye and spit in his fucking face while laughing.

"One day I went up to Diesel's room at church—which was gross by the way—found him in bed with one of the sweet butts. Skanky Tequila to be exact, if you need to know."

He didn't.

"But the reason I'd gone there was to let him know I was giving up. I had enough and was tired of beating my head against the wall trying to get him to see *us*. Us. Me and him. He fought *us* so hard that I was exhausted. I couldn't fight anymore. He refused to see what was right in front of his eyes. I wanted to let him find the right woman for him. Someone who made him happy. At that point, I was convinced it wasn't me. I couldn't give him what he needed. Guess what, Mercy?"

Oh fuck. He wasn't falling for that trap by answering.

"It *was* me. He was just so motherfucking stubborn he was blind. Sorry, girls," she said quickly. "You know, Diesel's kind of like you. He doesn't usually show his feelings. He doesn't do PDA. He doesn't even tell us he loves us, even though he shows it. The way he is with me when no one is looking.... The way he is with the girls and doesn't give a shit that anyone is watching. That's how he shows us."

The man definitely showed it. His actions spoke much louder than any words he could ever grunt out.

"He would die for you, Jewelee." That man would sacrifice everything for his woman, for his daughters.

"I know."

"For the girls, too."

"That I definitely know. I never expected a man like him to be such a great father. But what scares me the most, handsome, is that I almost gave up and walked away. I could've ended up with someone who wasn't a part of my very soul. Or I could still be alone." She shrugged. "I don't know Parris. I didn't get to meet her or talk to her. But, even so, after the time you spent with her, you're different."

No, he wasn't.

"I see it in your face. You deny it to yourself, but it's true. You think you're incapable of love, just like D did. You believe you don't deserve it. You worry that someone might love you back and that person will be dealing with things no one should ever deal with. But, handsome, Diesel is no cake walk. But you know what? To me, he's worth every difficult step." Her words caught. "I accept him as he is. I don't try to change him. Why deny yourself a piece of that? Do you think she wouldn't accept you as you are? D said she's a therapist. Wouldn't someone like her be the perfect person to understand and accept you and all your real and imagined faults?"

"A *sex* therapist," Mercy clarified in a mutter.

"Oh, that's right. The guys did say that. But still..." Her head tilted. "Wait, you're not having any problem in that department, are you?"

Jesus fucking Christ.

Jewel waved a hand around in the air. "Never mind. I don't want to know if you are. I want to keep my fantasy alive." She grinned, then sobered quickly. "But seriously, you deserve someone, just like the rest of us."

"Why are you suddenly playing matchmaker? There are five other men you work with that are single."

"I'm not playing matchmaker. I'm just trying to get you to see the light. You deserve to be happy. We all do. Why deny that? Like I said, I've seen the change in you since that job ended. To be truthful, D's noticed it, too."

Mercy's narrowed his eyes on her. "Did he tell you to talk to me?"

Jewel barked out a laugh. "He's D. He told me to leave you," she lowered her voice two octaves and grunted, "'the fuck alone,'" her voice went back to normal, "when I expressed my worry."

"Nothing to be worried about. Nothing's fucking changed, Jewel. You're just imagining what you're seeing."

Jewel tilted her head and studied him for a long minute.

Oh fuck. To avoid her gaze, he bounced Vi in his arms and glanced down at the gorgeous little girl who it was hard to believe came from D's loins.

Jewel jerked the wide stroller to the side, so she could climb around it and go toe to toe with him.

Oh shit.

She reached up, her fingertips lightly brushing over Vi's dark, soft hair, then cupped his cheek before he could pull out of reach. *Son of a bitch*, she was sneaky.

"Handsome... If anyone can handle the muck I know you have swirling deep down inside you, it's a woman who's trained and has the experience to do so. D also told me how on the way to the airport, she made him turn around and go back to your place. So, not only does that prove she's stubborn, she wouldn't have done that if she wasn't willing to be with you. *You*, Mercy. And all the baggage that comes along with you."

"She doesn't know everything."

Jewel lifted one shoulder in a half-shrug. "And she probably never will. There's shit that you and the rest of the Shadows have done just in the time that you've worked for D that *no one* should ever know. And I can't imagine the shit that you've dealt with when you all were active military doing your Special Forces G.I. Joe shit. I know your backgrounds to a certain extent, I can figure out the rest all on my own. I watched you guys deal with the Warriors. I *know* you guys have done some questionable and heavy shit. Do you think she needs to know all of that?"

"Do you?"

Jewel pursed her lips and, after a second, shook her head. "You're a good man, Mercy. I can't imagine you've done things to people who are innocent and didn't deserve what was done. I know how protective you are with women. I saw it with Kiki and Jazz. I saw it when the Warriors grabbed me. I saw it with Jayde. What's normal for you might be considered horrendous to someone who doesn't know the truth or reasons behind the actions. But maybe you just need to show her that you only do what's necessary to help others. Because in the end, no matter what you've done, there's always been a good reason." She raised a hand to stop him when he opened his mouth to argue. "And you can't tell me otherwise. You, handsome, are a true fucking hero."

She gave him a small smile, dropped her hand from his cheek and stepped back, taking Violet from him. She gave the toddler a kiss on her forehead before lifting her gaze back to Mercy.

"Everything I just said is true, Mercy. And if you can only believe that, then I promise you that you can be content with the choices and actions you've made, no matter how brutal they were. But one mistake you *have* made is letting Parris go back to Vegas when that was the last thing you wanted her to do. Am I right?"

He wasn't going to answer that. "You don't know her."

"No, but I know you. Or at least the parts that you've allowed me to see. Weirdly enough, I love you like family. Nothing you could tell me would ever make me change my mind about that. Because, again, you've made choices no one else could make, and by making those correct but difficult decisions those actions that have affected you. No one should ever judge you for that. If she does, then she's not the right woman for you. If she understands, then she is. But in the end, it's up to you to tell her your secrets or not. She might not want to know. She might just accept that you did everything you did for a just cause. Because, Mercy, that's what it was. No matter what you think."

As she was putting Violet back into the double stroller, she said, "One more thing..."

Mercy bit back a groan.

She finished strapping Vi in and straightened. "I'm proud to know you and the rest of the crew. I'm so grateful you have my ol' man's back. I'm so glad you have helped out my family, whether club or blood. You've never balked once at anything D has asked from you. None of you have. Not counting Kelsea." Her lips twisted. "You have put your life on the line, you have risked being caught and arrested. You guys have truly become family, not only to each other and to D and me, but to the DAMC as well. I know D has tried to keep you guys on the outside for good reason, but you all have become an integral part of the brotherhood. I just want you to know that."

"While I appreciate—"

Jewel wasn't done yet. "Now, don't be a fool. Go bring your woman home. There's always room for one more seat at the DAMC sisterhood table. We'd be glad to have her because, for fuck's sake, we sure need a therapist amongst our midst with us having to deal with a bunch of pig-headed, stubborn fucks."

"Woman!" D bellowed from the direction of his office.

"Fuck," Jewel whispered and rolled her eyes.

"Your beast is paging you." *Thank fuck.* The woman had run her mouth way too much at one time for him.

He certainly wasn't ready for all the truths she had laid on him.

She lifted her hand. "See? There you go. Who couldn't use a good couch session when dealing with someone like that?" She sighed. "He must be going through withdrawals since I've had his girls all morning."

Mercy smirked.

She climbed back behind the stroller and shoved it forward, running over Mercy's toes, even though he had flattened himself against the wall. He was glad he had steel-tipped boots on.

Jewel paused. *Goddamn, this woman was relentless!*

"She might be the one, Mercy. Don't miss out on what you could have. She might be good for your soul. Think about it. Then think about whether you can handle her being with someone else. Loving someone else. Especially if she truly belongs to you."

Fucking motherfucker. The woman knew how to drive the final nail into his coffin, that was for damn sure.

As Jewel steered the stroller into D's office, Ryder was squeezing his way out, his face twisted with fury.

As he stomped down the hallway, he spotted Mercy and pointed a finger at him. "You! It's your fuckin' turn. I'm so done with that goddamn bitch. You've got nothin' else going on. Time for you to step up."

Mercy lifted his palms. "Sounded like D wants you to deal with it. Not going against the boss's orders. And I got something to do anyway."

"What? What cake job did you fuckin' get?"

If Ryder thought what Mercy had to do next was cake, he was so fucking wrong.

For fuck's sake, he'd prefer to go back to the Middle East, swallow a mouthful of sand, dodge .50 caliber bullets and tip-toe through a desert full of land-mines than do what he was thinking about doing.

Which would be the hardest thing he ever did in his life.

Epilogue

It had become habit. The first thing she'd do after waking up is slip into her bathing suit and dive into her in-ground pool to do laps. Since coming home about three weeks ago, Parris found it a good way to clear her thoughts. She'd always loved swimming, but now it was more like a type of therapy.

And she needed it to get *him* out of her head. Especially since he was stuck in her noggin like nicotine gum on the bottom of her Manolo Blahnik shoes.

She stood at the tiled edge of the swimming pool, then, pushing off with her toes, sliced cleanly through the air and into the crystal clear water.

Okay, at least it felt like she cleanly sliced through it. She was going to hold onto that imagery as if she was some sort of self-proclaimed Olympic diver. She swam underwater for a distance like a sexy, lithe mermaid before popping up at the center of the pool.

Boy, she was on a roll this morning with her out-of-control fantasies.

"I hate this city."

She coughed as she swallowed some awful-tasting pool water when she gasped.

Holy shit. Her thoughts were *really* out of control! Now she was having delusions. Maybe she was developing some sort of personality disorder.

She really should see a therapist about that.

She jerked her head from one side to the other to shake the water out of her ears.

"I hate that you live here. You shouldn't."

Okay, yes, a one-sided conversation was filling her head. That was not a sign of a sane person. Her obsession with a man who had what was equivalent to an emotional black hole was apparently driving her over the edge. And not the good kind of edge, like right before having an orgasm.

She watched in stunned silence as that very obsession walked around the side of the pool to stand in her range of vision. Her blood began to pulse in her veins like an early 80's NYC discotheque.

Holy shit.

So, she wasn't crazy after all. Okay, she could still be crazy. But she wasn't imagining the handsome dark-haired, expressionless eye candy in sinfully soft jeans that clung to legs the length of the Stratosphere Tower, was she?

She swam closer to the edge where he was standing. Then it hit her she probably looked like a drowned rat with her hair plastered to her head instead of a sexy siren beckoning passing sailors with perky tits and a beauty pageant wave.

She gripped the curved tile tightly so she wouldn't drop like a sand bag to the bottom as she blinked up at the uber masculine mirage before her. "What?"

"I hate this city. You shouldn't live here. You need to move."

She truly was losing it. Maybe she should reach out and poke at him to see if he was real. But then, she'd end up disappointed if she discovered she was only dreaming this all up.

"Just like that, huh? Tell me... where should I live?"

"Not here."

Well, in her fantasy her perfect man would communicate with complete sentences and paragraphs full of valid and logical information. "Do you have a better suggestion?"

"I'll come up with some."

She raised her brows. "Some?"

"One."

"One in particular?"

He ignored that question, instead asking one of his own, "Are you coming out or am I coming in?"

Damn, her imagination was pretty damn impressive. She should write one of those romance books she lost herself in. She could make millions. "Do you have a bathing suit?"

He arched an eyebrow at her.

She shot him an inviting smile. Because why not? Why not play into the delusions she was having? "Then you are definitely coming in."

Well, that decided it. This *had* to be an illusion because the man who never smiled just gave her a wicked grin!

She closed her dropped jaw and struggled to swallow (sans pool water this time) as he began to strip off his clothes. First, that stupid jacket he wore in this insane summer desert heat. Then the leather shoulder holster.

Her heart began to thump wildly and her pussy clenched involuntarily as he tossed his T-shirt to the side, exposing his broad, hairless chest and his *so-ripped-you-can-bounce-a-penny-(*No, a Susan B. Anthony dollar coin!)*-off-of-it* stomach.

For goodness' sake, she just might drown. They'd find her days later floating face-down and bloated with a stupid smile frozen on her face.

When his long fingers went to the top of his jeans, she

squeezed her thighs together and held onto the side of the pool more securely because if she did drown she would miss this show which might very well be the best male revue on the whole Vegas strip.

He left those worn blue jeans gaping open with just a few dark hairs peeking out as he bent over to remove his boots and socks. Yes, his feet were still sexy as all get out. His were the first toes she'd actually considered doing very obscene things with.

Her breath caught as he straightened and, keeping his gray eyes locked to hers, slowly stripped off those jeans. He shoved them down his long muscular thighs, then his calves, before stepping out of them completely.

While his cotton boxer briefs weren't silky Ranger panties, they still clung to everything that was Mercy. And, *oh good lord,* she hadn't had breakfast yet so she was beginning to salivate.

Within seconds after dropping those briefs, he dove cleanly into the pool with hardly a splash and she remained frozen where she was. Her breath fled her lungs when he surfaced behind her and pressed his *hard... wet... hot...* (let's not forget *naked)* body against hers, sandwiching her between him and the side of the swimming pool.

While she was not a big fan of sandwiches, she could appreciate this one. Especially since an anaconda must have slipped into the water because it was poking her ass. She suddenly discovered a fondness for large snakes, too...

Her heart did flips as he pressed his mouth to her ear and, in a low voice that caused tingles in the very places she wanted him to touch, murmured, "Didn't recognize it for what it was."

His words (among other things) weren't helping her heart palpitations and the *other* palpitations occurring between her thighs. Her voice was unnaturally husky when she finally managed to ask, "What was it?"

"Not was. Is," he corrected as his arms circled her waist and one hand splayed over her stomach while he spread the fingers of the other directly above her throbbing mound.

Would it be wrong to push his hand lower? Yes, because he was trying to communicate something very important here.

"I thought an addiction. I was wrong."

"I'm not addicting?" she teased a little breathlessly, her lips curling slightly at the corners as she leaned her head back on his shoulder and turned her face until her cheek pressed against his damp neck. "So, what is it that had you get on a plane, which you admittedly dislike, and come to a city you despise to face something you're feeling, which I *really* know you hate being forced to do."

"That's simple."

"Then it should be a simple answer."

"And just to be clear, I'm not being forced to do shit."

"You're not, huh? You want to be in Vegas with me in my pool admitting to something which most likely feels more torturous than pulling off your fingernails one by one?"

"You got one thing right."

"Which part?"

"The part where I want to be with you."

I WANT *to be with you.*

For good. Forever. Completely.

If you'll have me.

"Do you?" Rissa lifted her head off his shoulder and twisted in his arms until her back was pressed against the side of the pool and she was blinking her sky-blue eyes surrounded with damp lashes in disbelief at him.

I might not be able to say out loud everything I'm feeling right now, but I hope you'll be patient and the day will come that I can do just that.

Jesus fuck, he'd missed her. That was a strange, unfamiliar feeling, but admittedly it existed. He could no longer ignore it. Not after he thought long and hard about Jewel's unwanted lecture.

"You pushed me away, Ryan."

Because this whole thing is a struggle. But it's a fight I'm willing to fight.

He hated the disappointment coloring her accusation but he couldn't deny what she said. "Yeah."

"Yeah?" she echoed in a squeak, becoming stiff in his arms.

Fuck. He needed to be upfront with her as much as he could if there was any chance of this working between them. "Yeah. To be honest, it might happen again. It might happen too many fucking times. Can't promise it won't. Just asking that you hang tight during those times until I get my head straightened out."

She softened against him, curling one hand around the back of his neck as she brushed her fingers over his jaw, then settled her palm against his chest.

She could probably feel how wildly his heart was thumping. He was struggling to tamp down the rising panic. He needed to concentrate on how much he wanted the woman in his arms. What he needed to do to keep her. Nothing else.

Nothing was more important.

"So, you're admitting you might try to drive me away?"

"Possibly. But for fuck's sake, Rissa," his words caught in his throat so he cleared it, "when that happens don't give up on me. You're stubborn and strong. You'll just have to dig in your heels and ride it out."

Her eyebrows pinned together as she frowned. "Why should I? Why would I want to make my life difficult like that?"

"Because..." *Fuck.* He once again thought about Jewel's words of wisdom. "Because I think *we* are worth it. *We* are worth fighting for."

I believe it. Do you?

Can you?

He waited. Eventually, he thought she wasn't going to say anything but, *Jesus fuck*, was he wrong. He should've known better since this was Rissa he was dealing with.

"I have an easy life here, Ryan. Well, until I was hunted down and almost killed. But besides that... I have an established practice. I can't just close up shop just like that." She snapped her fingers before planting her hand back on his chest. "Simply abandon my patients. Because I'm assuming you aren't moving out here, right? You expect me to just pick up and move to Shadow Valley? You're not proposing some sort of long-distance relationship, are you? Oh shit, are you? Is that what you're proposing? A long distance thing where you call me every once in a while and say nothing on the other end of the phone? Where I'm supposed to carry the whole conversation and I only hear your heavy breathing? Then once a year you fly out here to scratch an itch but I'm not allowed to see any other men? And then—"

He shut her the hell up by crushing his lips to hers and tangling their tongues together. After a few moments, once the tension left her body and she melted against him once more, he lifted his head. "Jesus fuck, woman, don't make me rethink all of this," he grumbled against her lips.

"I can't just up and leave, Ryan. Relocate my practice, my house, my life! Hell, my sister is coming to visit next month!"

I'm asking a lot of you, I know. Just have some faith in me.

"Instead of having to get on a plane to Vegas, Londyn can drive to Shadow Valley and visit," he said. A simple solution to a simple problem she wanted to make too fucking complex.

"Oh, can she now?"

"Yeah, she can."

"And what about my business? My home here?" She put a hand to her mouth. "My friends?"

He frowned. "Friends like Paranzino?"

"Well, yes! I know you don't like him—"

Mercy grunted.

She waved a hand around between them. "Even so..." She paused and her brows furrowed. "Speaking of Michael... He deposited a million dollars into my account. I thought I had imagined it that day in my delirium. Am I wrong? Did you actually demand he pay me a million dollars?"

Since that was a question she most likely knew the answer to, he wasn't responding to that one. He wasn't stupid.

"I decided to give it to a charity which helps sex workers."

She did what? He couldn't stop the growl in his voice when he stated, "You gave the money away."

She stared at him. "Uh, yes, since it wasn't mine and I didn't ask for it. I had assumed it was money he gave me out of guilt. But I couldn't ask him because he refuses to return my phone calls or texts."

Good. As it should be. Otherwise, Paranzino was going to disappear like his former competition Nicco. Mercy wouldn't hesitate for a second to take that motherfucker out if he needed to.

"I don't need it. I'm fine."

"You could've used it to pay for your move across the country."

"No, *you're* going to pay for it with that outrageous bonus you extorted from him."

Was she agreeing to eventually move to Shadow Valley? She might be agreeing, even if it wasn't right away. They'd have to work out the details but right now he wasn't going to question it because he didn't want her changing her mind. Instead he used a distraction tactic. "Earned every fucking cent of that bonus having to listen to your mouth."

Her head snapped back and her eyes narrowed. "Really."

That "really" sounded deadlier than an M67 grenade.

And, *Jesus Christ*, did she just wind herself up and chicken neck?

"If you expect me to be some sort of quiet mouse who does what she's told, you're in the wrong woman's pool."

No fucking shit. "I expect you to use that mouth for something other than talking."

"Oh really?"

Fuck me. She was lobbing grenades left and right. He had no choice but to slap on a flak jacket and tactical helmet and go in with guns blazing...

"Yeah, really. If you need to flap your gums, do it with your new fucking patients in your new fucking practice in your new fucking town." So much for working out the details.

"Says you!"

"Fucking-A right!"

She pinned her lips together and her eyes crinkled at the corners. "That's the only good use for my mouth?"

"No."

"What else?"

He reached down, grabbed her waist and lifted her out of the pool until she was sitting on the side with her feet dangling into the water.

"Gonna show you."

"How about you show me what *your* mouth will be busy doing first?"

"How fast can you get that bathing suit bottom off?"

She glanced down at herself and when she lifted her head back up, she was smiling. "It's a one piece."

He stopped fighting it and returned the smile. "Even better."

"That means if I take it off, I'm going to be out here totally naked."

"That's exactly what it fucking means."

"You might have to cover my naughty bits with your hands and your face for my modesty."

"I can try."

"Oorah!" she shouted to the sky.

He fought the roll of his eyes. "That's Marines, not Army."

She lifted a shoulder. "You'll have plenty of time to teach me the ins and outs of the Army."

"This soldier is an expert at the ins and outs."

"You'll have to prove that to me, Sergeant Major. You can start now."

Mercy leaned over her, staring down directly into eyes that struck a chord deep in his very soul. Those blue rings had become his lifesaver, tossed to save him from drowning in that quicksand.

Even so, life wasn't going to be easy for her. For him. For either of them. But he was going to do his fucking best to make it worth her while.

He might not be able to give her everything, but he would give her everything he could. Hopefully that would be enough.

He would also do his fucking best to make her never regret being with him, even on his bad days. And on his good days, he would do his best to show her what she meant to him.

"Hooah," he finally whispered against her lips.

Then proceeded to prove his claim of expertise by making her his.

Forever and completely.

Hooah.

Guts & Glory: Ryder

Turn the page for a sneak peek of
Guts & Glory: Ryder
(In the Shadows Security, Book 2)

Sneak peak of Guts & Glory: Ryder (Unedited)

Chapter One

Out of all the places his ass could be, this county was not a place he wanted to be in. While he was sure some parts of West Virginia were just fucking lovely, this area was known for hillbillies, white supremacists and rednecks who thought bullets were more important than teeth.

If that wasn't bad enough, it was infested with members of the motherfucking outlaw MC, the Deadly Demons.

How he got pulled into this detail, he'll never know. No, fuck him, he knew. He drew the short straw this time. Just like he drew the short straw last time. And every other time when it came to this particular "job."

Ryder jerked the wheel of his '78 International Scout into a dark, rutted dirt driveway surrounded by high weeds. After a few seconds his headlights bounced off an old farmhouse that was lit up from the inside.

At least the shit hole had electricity.

He pulled his Scout up to a line of Harleys parked across the uncut grass and sat staring at the run-down hovel for a few seconds as he braced himself for what was to come. Letting a searing curse rip, he shut his treasured vehicle off, yanked the keys from the ignition, and shoved open the driver's side door. After climbing his tense body out, he jammed his keys deep into his jeans' pocket, locked the door, and slammed it shut.

The weight of his Glock .45 in its holster under his jacket, along with his tactical knife hanging on his hip at least gave him a little reassurance since he was walking alone into this den of vipers. Worse, he wasn't even sneaking in. He was walking right through the fucking front door.

He stalked to the rickety porch steps, carefully picking his way up the rotting boards. Ignoring the handful of drunk Demons hanging out on the slanted front porch drinking beer and smoking dope, he pushed his way past them through the wide-open door of the house to shouts of:

"Who the fuck are you?"

"Who's that motherfucker?"

"What the fuck?"

If he cared, he'd be asking them the same questions. But, yeah, he didn't give a fuck who those wasted, washed-out, beer-bellied bikers were.

Once he stepped inside, he paused to inventory his surroundings and get his bearings.

To say this house was bad was an understatement. It wasn't only a complete fucking shit hole, it smelled like one, too.

A tweaked-out, half-naked chick sat on the filthy floor of the hallway, the wall barely holding her ass upright. He nudged her with his boot to get her attention, since she was totally spaced. She might have been pretty once. But her bloodshot eyes, long stringy, unwashed hair and hollowed out cheekbones did nothing for her now.

"Lookin' for a woman," he grumbled.

She managed to straighten herself up some more, raking her glazed eyes down his body and running her fingers through her hair as if that would improve the nest that rats build on her head. "Found her."

Yeah, no. He'd prefer eternal celibacy than to stick his dick in anything like her. He lifted his hand to about mid-chest. "'Bout yay-high, long dark blonde hair, pretty blue eyes. Ain't all bones like you, though. Got some meat on her." Did she ever, the bitch had it all in the right places, too. "A bit of a stupid fuck, though." Because that was the goddamn truth.

She had been making way stupid decisions lately, and tonight was another one in a long list of them.

"Slash's slit?"

Slash.

His jaw got tight. That wasn't the first time he heard that name. But it was sure as shit going to be the last.

"Where's he at?"

She lifted a finger that had one spot of black nail polish left in the center—the rest looked like it had been picked or chewed off—and pointed to the ceiling. "Probably up in his room. Said I couldn't join 'im when they walked past."

Thank fuck for that.

Ryder lifted his chin in thanks and pushed past her, even though she reached out to grab his leg and gave a disappointed, "Hey, I could be your woman tonight."

"Next time," he threw over his shoulder, as his balls shriveled up into his body to hide.

At the end of the hall full of peeling wallpaper and water stains, he bounded up the stairs Hitting the top landing, he tilted his head and listened carefully. It was difficult to hear shit, since what sounded like a stereo blasted somewhere outside as well as another stereo blasted inside but with a different song. Even so, he held his breath, stilled every muscle, and listened anyway.

Above the din, a female giggle came from two doors

down. One that was closed with light spilling out from underneath it.

In a couple long strides, he was in front of it. With a lift of his boot, he kicked the door with all the power he could muster causing it to splinter and crash against the wall as it swung hard.

His eyes landed on the mattress that sat in the middle of the floor. Looked like Slash had been a busy boy.

A naked man with shitty tattoos and long black hair sat up in surprise and the two other women in bed with him didn't even notice the interruption.

No, they didn't. They were still going at it with each other, one on top of the other, kissing, fingering each other's pussies and pinching each other's nipples.

What. The. Fuck.

The one he was searching for was on the bottom, her normally pretty blue eyes closed, moans and groans coming from her as the fingers being plunged into her pussy sped up.

Jesus fuck. Normally, this shit would get him rock hard. Right now, he wanted to fucking puke.

"Who the fuck are you?"

"A figment of your imagination. Just pretend I'm not here." Taking two steps into the room, he wrapped his arm around the waist of the redhead and yanked her from the woman on the bottom, tossing her onto Slash.

The biker grunted, and the redhead squealed as she landed on him.

Before the blonde-haired one could react, he had her up and thrown over his shoulder. He didn't give a shit if she was naked or not.

He didn't even care if she just got robbed of a fucking orgasm. She wasn't laying in that bed or staying in that house one more second.

"Hey!" came the very intoxicated complaint.

"Shut the fuck up," he barked. Making sure he had a good grip on her, he turned on his heels and strode toward the door.

"Hey! Where... where... you takin' me?"

He tightened his jaw so he wouldn't snap the fuck out on her and headed down the dark hallway.

"My clothes!"

He didn't give a shit about her clothes. She should have thought about them before she took them off.

"Hey! Can't do this!"

The fuck he couldn't.

He was only following orders. Because he certainly wasn't there because he wanted to be.

Fuck no.

And this was the last fucking time he was doing one of these details for Diesel. The very last fucking time.

As soon as he could find a safe place to pull off, he did so. He checked the rearview mirror one more time to make sure none of those Demons were following them. Though that wasn't much of a worry, since apparently Kelsea was Slash's "slit" and no MC he knew of took care of their women like the Dirty Angels.

He was also sure the Deadly Demons wouldn't give their right nut for Kelsea.

Which was once again why he had a naked woman passed out in his passenger seat. He wanted to pull her out and take a fire hose to her to clean off all the filth from that house, Slash and whoever that other skank was who was fingering her and shoving a tongue down her throat. That shit had turned his stomach.

Not because he didn't like a little girl-on-girl action, what heterosexual man didn't? He just hadn't wanted to witness it with the pain-in-the-ass sitting next to him.

Princess Pain-in-the-Ass was pressed against the passenger side window, her long hair covering her face, and the only thing holding her upright was seatbelt which was cutting in between her naked tits. Luckily, he'd had the aftermarket 3-point seatbelt installed when Jag Jamison restored his Scout, otherwise she'd be lying in a pile on the floorboard.

His nostrils flared with annoyance. "You awake?"

He didn't miss the slight movement. She was fucking awake.

"No," came the slurred answer.

A muscle popped in his jaw as he shoved his shifter into neutral and set the e-brake. They were on a quiet, dark back road somewhere between West Virginia and Kentucky. Since they had about a four-hour drive to their destination, her remaining naked the whole way just wasn't going to work for him.

So, he needed to do something about that little problem. Plus, he wasn't sure if Slash's DNA was leaking all over his seat.

If so, that shit would put him over the edge.

While his boss sent him to "save" his cousin, if she was taking Slash's dick without a condom, Diesel might have to save Kelsea from Ryder. And worse, he'd have to burn his passenger seat, which would be a sin since he'd paid a pretty penny to have it reupholstered.

With a curse, he pulled the keys from the ignition. Shame he didn't trust her not to take off with his vehicle and leave him stranded on the side of the road by a lonely stretch of woods. Then he shoved open his door and slammed it shut once more after unfolding his ass from his Scout.

He hated taking his anger out on his baby, but he either

did that or on the woman he wanted to strangle. Though calling Kelsea a "woman" was a stretch since she'd been acting like a petulant child for the past year or so.

He knew why, but right now he didn't give a shit. It was getting old and she was pushing away the people who loved her.

He dug around in the back of his truck until he found his survival kit and located aspirin and a silver emergency blanket. He also grabbed a large bottle of water from his supply he kept in the back.

Once he had everything he needed, he went around to the passenger side door, yanked it open and unhooked her seatbelt, letting her tumble out of the truck into the grass of the pull-off.

"Hey!" she yelped as she landed in a naked heap.

He tossed the blanket at her. "Wrap this around you and make sure you keep it so that your cunt isn't in direct contact with my seat."

She slowly rolled herself over and *sort of* sat up. "Why you worried about that old thing?"

That old thing?

"That old thing is worth a lot more than you right now, darlin'. No fuckin' joke. Wrap that blanket around you before a tick bites your snatch and get your ass back in my truck. Or I'll leave you here for a coyote's breakfast."

He wasn't sure if it was the threat of a tick or a coyote that got her moving, but she finally did.

When she struggled to get the thin mylar blanket around her, he lost his patience and helped her, doing his best not to touch her. He was done touching her. It was bad enough when he had to carry her naked ass out of that hell hole and toss her into his truck.

Until she showered in Lysol or bleach, he wasn't taking any further risks. He wasn't getting hazard pay for this job.

In fact, his ass might get fired with what he had planned.

Once they got to the cabin, he'd call Diesel and tell him the details. Until then, he was putting a few hundred miles between him and D's massive fists.

"Get in the truck," he muttered once she got to her feet.

Watching her wobble back and forth a couple times made him realize she wouldn't be able to get her ass in his truck under her own power.

Fuck.

Holding his breath so he didn't have to inhale her stink, he bent at the knees and picked her up before planting her now covered ass back in the passenger seat. He latched the seatbelt back around her, then tossed the bottle of water in her lap and held out his hand with three aspirins.

"Take these, drink that and shut the fuck up for the next few hours."

Before she could respond, he slammed the door shut and jogged around the front of his Scout and climbed back in.

He waited until she downed the aspirins and chugged a good amount of water before turning the key and coaxing his baby into first gear.

Within five minutes, her head was back resting against the passenger-side window and she was asleep.

With a sigh, he found a country station and turned that shit up until he could no longer hear her godawful snoring. He might as well be in an underground den with a hibernating Grizzly as loud as she was.

For fuck's sake, he wished he was back dodging IEDs and taking out suicide bombers in Afghanistan instead of dealing with Kelsea Dougherty.

Fuck my life.

Learn more about Ryder's story here:
https://www.jeannestjames.com/guts-glory-ryder

Acknowledgments

Thanks to Alexandra Swab for coming up with Parris's occupation of sex therapist. ALSO, I have to thank her for her assistance with Mercy's blurb. Most authors hate writing short descriptions of their books and I'm no exception!

Thanks to all the support from my readers in my FB readers group: Jeanne St. James' Down & Dirty Book Crew. You always give me great ideas.

As always, thanks to my alpha reader, fellow author Whitley Cox, and my beta readers Andi Babcock, Sharon Abrams and Krisztina Hollo.

If You Enjoyed This Book

Thank you for reading Guts & Glory: Mercy. If you enjoyed Mercy and Rissa's story, please consider leaving a review at your favorite retailer and/or Goodreads to let other readers know. Reviews are always appreciated and just a few words can help an independent author like me tremendously!

Want to read a sample of my work? Download a sampler book here: BookHip.com/MTQQKK

Also by Jeanne St. James

Made Maleen: A Modern Twist on a Fairy Tale

Damaged

Rip Cord: The Complete Trilogy

Brothers in Blue Series:

Brothers in Blue: Max

Brothers in Blue: Marc

Brothers in Blue: Matt

Teddy: A Brothers in Blue Novelette

The Dare Ménage Series:

(Can be read as standalones)

Double Dare

Daring Proposal

Dare to Be Three

A Daring Desire

Dare to Surrender

A Daring Journey

The Obsessed Novellas:

(All the novellas in this series are standalones)

Forever Him

Only Him

Needing Him

Loving Her

Temping Him

Down & Dirty: Dirty Angels MC Series:

Down & Dirty: Zak

Down & Dirty: Jag

Down & Dirty: Hawk

Down & Dirty: Diesel

Down & Dirty: Axel

Down & Dirty: Slade

Down & Dirty: Dawg

Down & Dirty: Dex

Down & Dirty: Linc

Down & Dirty: Crow

Guts & Glory Series

(In the Shadows Security)

Guts & Glory: Mercy

Guts & Glory: Ryder

Guts & Glory: Hunter

Guts & Glory: Walker

Guts & Glory: Steel

Guts & Glory: Brick

Audio Books by Jeanne St. James

The following books are available in audio!

Down & Dirty: Zak (Dirty Angels MC, bk 1)

Down & Dirty: Jag (Dirty Angels MC, bk 2)

Down & Dirty: Hawk (Dirty Angels MC, bk 3)

Down & Dirty: Diesel (Dirty Angels MC, bk 4)

Down & Dirty: Axel (Dirty Angels MC, bk 5)

Down & Dirty: Slade (Dirty Angels MC, bk 6)

Down & Dirty: Dawg (Dirty Angels MC, Bk 7)

Forever Him (An Obsessed Novella)

Rip Cord: The Complete Trilogy

Damaged

Double Dare (The Dare Menage Series, bk 1)

Daring Proposal (The Dare Menage Series, bk 2)

Brothers in Blue: Max (Brothers in Blue, bk 1)

Brothers in Blue: Marc (Brothers in Blue, bk 2)

Brothers in Blue: Matt (Brothers in Blue, bk 3)

Coming soon:

The Dare Menage Series (Books 3-5)

About the Author

JEANNE ST. JAMES is a USA Today bestselling romance author who loves an alpha male (or two). She was only thirteen when she started writing and her first paid published piece was an erotic story in Playgirl magazine. Her first erotic romance novel, Banged Up, was published in 2009. She is happily owned by farting French bulldogs. She writes M/F, M/M, and M/M/F ménages.

Want to read a sample of her work? Download a sampler book here: BookHip.com/MTQQKK

To keep up with her busy release schedule check her website at www.jeannestjames.com or sign up for her newsletter: http://www.jeannestjames.com/newslettersignup

www.jeannestjames.com
jeanne@jeannestjames.com

Blog: http://jeannestjames.blogspot.com
Newsletter: http://www.jeannestjames.com/newslettersignup
Jeanne's Down & Dirty Book Crew: https://www.facebook.com/groups/JeannesReviewCrew/

facebook.com/JeanneStJamesAuthor
twitter.com/JeanneStJames
amazon.com/author/jeannestjames
instagram.com/JeanneStJames
bookbub.com/authors/jeanne-st-james
goodreads.com/JeanneStJames
pinterest.com/JeanneStJames

Get a FREE Erotic Romance Sampler Book

This book contains the first chapter of a variety of my books. This will give you a taste of the type of books I write and if you enjoy the first chapter, I hope you'll be interested in reading the rest of the book.

Each book I list in the sampler will include the description of the book, the genre, and the first chapter, along with links to find out more. I hope you find a book you will enjoy curling up with!

Get it here: BookHip.com/MTQQKK